BOUNDARY WALL

Tristan Hughes was born in Atikokan in northern Ontario, and brought up on the Welsh island of Ynys Môn. He is the author of four novels, *Send My Cold Bones Home*, *Revenant*, *Eye Lake* and *Hummingbird* (the latter of which won the Edward Stanford Award for Fiction with a Sense of Place and the Wales Book of the Year People's Choice Award) – as well as the collections of interlinked short stories, *The Tower* and *Shattercone*. His short fiction has appeared in various journals, including *Ploughshares*, the *Southern Review*, and *New Welsh Review*. He is a winner of the Rhys Davies short story prize and an O Henry Award.

Also by Tristan Hughes
The Tower
Send My Cold Bones Home
Revenant
Eye Lake
Hummingbird
Shattercone

BOUNDARY WATERS

Tristan Hughes

Parthian, Cardigan SA43 1ED
www.parthianbooks.com
© Tristan Hughes 2025
Print ISBN: 978-1-914595-84-4
Ebook ISBN: 978-1-917140-59-1
Editor: Gwen Davies
Proofreader: Sarah Harvey, https://sarahharvey.me
Cover Design: Matt Needle
Typesetter: Elaine Sharples
Printer: 4Edge Ltd, England
Published with the financial support of the Books Council of Wales
British Library Cataloguing in Publication Data
A cataloguing record for this book is available from the British Library.
Printed on FSC accredited paper

For Abby

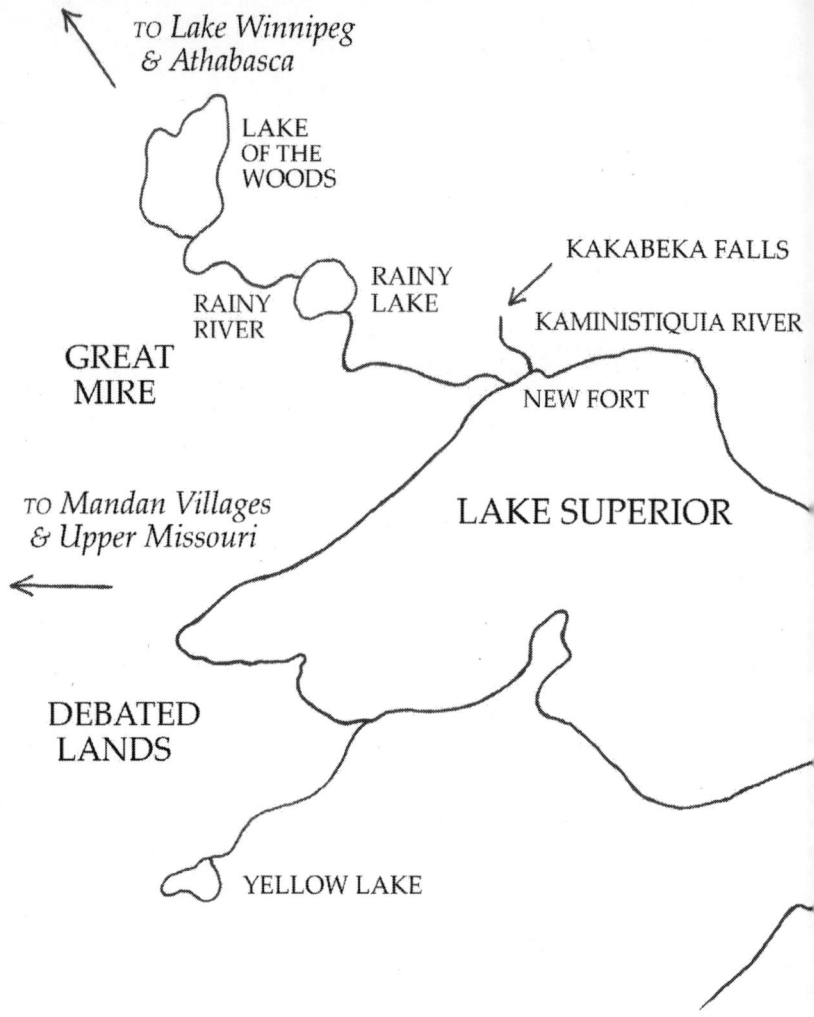

A Map of the North West Countries Exhibiting Arthur's Track

PROLOGUE

Your uncle once asked me, Esther, why we white men came into this country, if we thought the Cow Country we left behind so wonderful. It was a long journey to starve like helpless children, he said.

It was the beginning of Winter. I'd not eaten for almost two days and was begging your uncle for a single fish. There it lay between us, on the ice at the edge of Yellow River: a pike of no remarkable size, writhing as I was in its freezing predicament. Who knew where my trade goods were cached? I was asking for this fish on credit.

I told him he knew very well why we came here. For the furs.

It was a long way to travel for something to make a hat, he said.

It was, I agreed.

He said I could have this fish for a keg of rum. An outrageous barter.

The pike glistened greenly upon the ice. I said when I found my goods, I'd give him two.

He said perhaps it would be better if he found them himself, considering this was not Cow Country and none of us could find anything here. Or anyone, for that matter.

And I think it was because I made such a wretched bargain that he began to consider me the better prospect for you. Up there in the North West countries the ways of looking were ever one and then another. To be poor at trade in the eyes of the Companies was to have a more open and generous hand in the eyes of your uncle. McLeod would have offered him half a keg and starved. Herse would have made a joke of it and taken the fish. As for me, Esther, I would have offered all my worldly goods and the moccasins from my icy feet, and crawled back to the trading post on my hands and knees, for you to have agreed with him.

But all that is by the by. I'm writing this because I hope ink travels faster than hands and knees. And besides, I'll meet you soon enough in the writing of it. So, let me begin before that meeting and answer your uncle's question more entirely and truthfully. It wasn't the fur I came for, and I didn't consider the place I departed so very wonderful. And since much of this account will hang in some way upon your father, I'll start with mine.

It was on a Sunday morning, during the second week of May, that I entered his study in our home in Sorel, a little town outside of Montreal, to tell him I'd decided to join the fur trade. He shifted slightly on his high-backed wooden chair, moving his weight from his left buttock to his right, and this was the full extent and expression of his surprise.

He asked if I'd signed a contract.

I said I had. I'd been in Montreal the day before and gone to the offices of Parker, Gerrard & Ogilvy and signed for the XY Company.

'Then it is done, I suppose,' he said, looking down at a piece of bread left over from his breakfast. He considered this for some time, as though dissatisfied with its marmalade. Through the windows, the grass in the garden was throwing off its Winter browns and mouldy greys, and turning green. Not long ago it had been heaped with snow, and he'd been asking me if it was not time I considered a profession. The room was cold, as if remembering that snow, and the end of my father's nose was pink. A drip fell from it onto his waistcoat. 'And this is what you have chosen?'

I said it was. I'd have to leave before the end of the day.

And where would I be going?

To the North West countries.

'That's a long way,' he said.

In that moment, I confess I'd wished for nothing more than for him to jump from his chair and berate me for my foolishness, my blockheadedness, my slowness, as he'd often done when I'd once toiled in this same study over Dictionaries and Grammars. But those days were long gone. He looked at the world in a different way now. When, eventually, he did rise from his chair – whose high, hard back had never stopped his spine from stooping – it was only to walk over to the consoling bookshelves which lined the walls.

'Take this,' he said, drawing out a volume. It was a copy of Xenophon's *Anabasis*. One glance was enough to transport me back into a tangled, bewildering thicket of Greek, an Alpha and Omega of mazes and thorns. 'It's about getting home from distant places,' he said somewhat wearily, seeing my panic and perplexity, and doubtless recalling those earlier days when his hopes for me had been blunted on my obdurate inability to conjugate a single verb. 'About finding your way to the sea.' A pause. 'I told you the story when you were a boy.' Finally, 'The sea that will bring you home.'

I thanked him for it, and we shook hands.

Another drip fell from his nose, and he contemplated the stain as though it had come from the sky. 'A moment,' he said, returning to the same corner of his study and taking up his old hat. I thought he might walk with me then, and we might talk along the way. 'You should take this,' he said. 'You'll need a good one, I think.'

I thanked him again and turned to go, and my hope persisted that he rush up behind me, grab hold of my shoulders, and say, 'You should not do this.' This hope accompanied me each step until at last I was out in the hall, holding my hat and my book.

I'd like to think he at least watched me close the door. Perhaps he did, perhaps he didn't. The single thing I know for certain is that he would have considered each step I took away from him just one more further down the ladder for the house of Stanton, one Age declining into the next.

In his later years, my father had become a country schoolteacher and thought much – from his reading of ancient writers – of Ages. They were gold and silver and bronze and iron, and the one was always looking back askance at the other, jealous of its perfections. It seemed to me then that those Ancients were a gloomy bunch, who spent half their time searching the sky for rainclouds and thinking of the different ways the world was getting worse – which must have been one reason my father was so enamoured of them. For by then he was sure in his own sense of life's trajectories and how they tended. He looked at the world and his fortunes as though they were a round boulder pushed by the Fates from the top of a hill.

It was an inauspicious time and place to live with such a philosophy, surrounded as he was by men who thought they were pushing the boulder up the hill, ever nearer the sun. Our neighbour in Sorel, Mr Bennington, for instance, needed only to see a few meagre spruces in a swamp for him to envision it all meadows and haystacks and red-cheeked daughters milking cows and burly sons ploughing fields. He'd allow that some of those might unfortunately be French daughters and sons; but would also comfort himself with the notion that the Indians would have all conveniently taken themselves away into the sunset. For in the eyes of men like Mr Bennington (as you know well enough) the sun that was rising for some must also be setting for others. It's the way of civilisation, he'd say to my father, ticking along like a clock towards a finer hour. And my father would look gloomily down at his shoes. These men and their visions of futurity wearied him. His own favoured civilisations had all fallen. He was a great admirer of Mr Gibbon.

I know I bothered your ears enough about my father up there in the fur country, Esther, but I'll beg your patience a minute to add a brief word here about his history, because it's partially my own. He was born the middle son of a gentleman in Sussex. Since, you see, the oldest son would inherit the English estate, my father was sent to one of the Universities to get an education, and then on to the family's second estate in Massachusetts, where he might play at being a gentleman farmer, a kind of new world Cicero. Those were the Golden Ages for him. It was during them he married my mother, a Welsh woman of no family or fortune (he had no concern then about this lack, imagining he already possessed both). He had two sons, who he named Edgar and Alfred after Saxon kings, thinking of his family's estate and the long, unbreakable roots of Nations.

And then came his first great lesson in Mutability.

When the rebellion came, my father remained a Loyalist and was eventually chased from his estate in a hail of insults and dried cow dung. Subjects, he learnt, could quickly become Citizens. Englishmen could become Americans. Countries could become other countries.

I was born under a three-penny planet on the long and bitter journey he made with his wife and sons to Lower Canada. Having seen their fragility, my father wasn't so impressed now by Saxon roots, and let my mother name me. She called me Arthur.

The land near the town of Sorel, that he was given by the King in recompense for his Loyalty, was little more than a few swampy fields, where all the Latin and Greek in the world would not turn mosquitoes into Dryads and Nymphs; and since my father had made a better gentleman than farmer, he made no improvements to them, instead falling back on the education he'd once considered an ornament of his station in life and becoming a schoolteacher. My brothers did well enough in this new world. He'd prepared them for professions from an early age. Edgar would be a lawyer, Alfred a surveyor. Both far less, in his eyes, than a landed Gentleman, yet something. But as for me, I'd arrived in another Age, as the boulder began to roll down, and came to personify it. I showed no aptitude for scholarship and would ever see his disappointment as I struggled over the simplest Latin and stood dumbfounded in front of Greek. I was the child of his decline and fall.

And just when he felt there were no further for that boulder to roll, my mother died. He had loved her very much, and the blow was hard and bitter. You could not trust in the permanence of Nations, of Empires, of Kings; you could not trust in the permanence of Love.

But all this is his story and, if he wrote it, I don't know in which dusty drawer it's hidden. He's departed this sorrowful realm of hills and boulders, and I hope most dearly he's in a nice flat valley somewhere, in whatever eternity he's gone to. For though we had our differences while he lived, of late I cannot help agreeing with him. It seems to me I've had my Ages too, these last years – an Age of farming, an Age of losing logs on rivers and chasing pigs in their pens, and most lately an Age of lancing boils and plucking leeches – but the one I return to most often is the one I shared with you in the North West countries. Call it the Fur Age.

PART ONE

L'Enfant Perdu

1

It was already late in the afternoon when I saw them come around a bend of the river, in sight of the Lake of the Two Mountains. Two of them, though from a distance it was difficult to be certain. The willows and alders along the bank weren't fully in leaf, and against the almost bare branches their limbs and torsos appeared a tangle of moving shadows, not quite entirely anything yet – part bark, part paddle, part men.

I listened, in case they might be singing – as our men had done all the way from Lachine that morning – but the only sounds came from behind me: faint snatches of liturgy, bits and pieces of Latin, the sorrowful groans and whimpers of McLeod. The taste of last night's shrub was still on my own tongue; nothing I'd eaten or drunk since had managed to dispel it; my vomits seemed only to season it. It was best to concentrate on looking. On they came, as mercifully silent as apparitions, these emissaries – as I imagined them – of the country we were about to enter. Their canoe was small and light and cut quickly through the water. An experienced man would've been able to calculate the weight of its cargo.

But there was only McLeod and I on the bank. The rest of the men were inside the church, paying for masses (or at least promising to pay for masses) and beseeching the Saint and Good Lady to bless their journey.

'Oh Lord,' said McLeod. It wasn't the beginning of a

prayer. He was sitting on the damp grass, clasping his head in his big freckled hands as though he were holding it up for an offering. He hadn't noticed the approach of the canoe.

As it got nearer, I could make out the dirty white linen of the men's shirts, the handkerchiefs tied around their heads, and lifted my hand in greeting, thinking this was probably what you should do: treat others on the same road as comrades, of whatever Company they might be; whether North West men or Hudson's Bay men or with the XY Company like ourselves. I wasn't sure what the custom was. We'd travelled this road for less than a day. Until that morning, I hadn't even known roads could be on water.

But they didn't lift their hands in return, keeping to the same stroke, as steady in its rhythm as the songs they didn't sing, skimming the canoe closer and closer to the shore. A few hundred yards out they startled a tired-looking goose from its hiding place in a patch of reeds. It lumbered skyward in a reluctant commotion of wings and webbed feet and honking.

'Oh Lord,' said McLeod, who at last looked up. 'Show me mercy and shoot that fucking bird.' His skin shared the dull pallor of the clouds. The light of the day, which had never been more than a greyish haze, was ebbing.

The men alighted just before the bow touched the bank. Submerged to the knee in the freezing water, they untenderly unladed their cargo and carried it ashore, wrapped in a blue-and-red blanket, which came slightly loose as they placed it on the grass. It was the fourteenth of May, and although it'd been cold these last days, the season no longer Winter but not yet fully Spring, the reek was powerful enough to begin McLeod on his puking again. Whatever the weather where they'd started their journey, these men had been paddling steadily into a thaw. When the blanket came further askew, I began on my puking again, too. I'd never smelt that scent before.

Seraphin and Hyacinthe were the first out of the church. A hawk and a turtle. The one all sharp points and perilous edges, the other all creases and flat surfaces. Our steersman and bowman, in the same order on land as on water. Behind them came Old Crebassa, creaking down the path, happy to have made his bargain once again with the Saints and Virgins. And last: the younger men, Young Godin and Narcisse, stepping more slowly, savouring the earth beneath their feet.

They were much transformed since the night before in the Lachine tavern, my first in the fur trade. Whatever preliminaries there'd been, I couldn't properly recall them. Only that at some point I'd learnt the name of the man opposite me was Hyacinthe and he was a bowman and he wouldn't let me pass on my cup of shrub; though I'd already drunk several cups by then and the effects of another were foretold in the sorry condition of one of the younger men, who was crawling like a gut-shot dog between the tables, his knuckles worn red by the rough boards, a dark patch on his trousers marking where the spirits had made an untimely egress.

'Drink,' roared Hyacinthe, and fists had begun to thump on wood. The man sitting beside me had no ear. In its place, the skin had healed in livid whorls around a small pouting hole, like a gasping minnow's mouth. Hyacinthe was missing his nose. The North is a devourer of men, I'd thought, and I'm sitting with the gristle.

'Drink.'

This shrub was an abomination. Good things had gone into it to die and be inverted: rum, a piece of orange peel, the climes of warm countries, a sprinkling of sugar. It burnt my throat and performed terrible alchemies in my stomach. What has happened to my bones, I'd thought. My head was suddenly too heavy for the willow bough of my neck. My legs had become eels. The hole that was once an ear puckered in the light of the candles, as though poised to force a lipless kiss upon me. Hyacinthe had tired of administering his torments by then and begun a song about the road to Rochelle City. *It is the paddle that brings us, that brings us....* Nobody noticed me slide from the bench. The tobacco smoke was so thick above, it was like another sky.

Down below there was only the younger man, a line of puke across his shirt, at the mercy of the beef boots and moccasins that stamped the rhythm of the song. I considered dragging him out from under the table, but there was nothing to be done. A man with no bones can't carry anyone.

A draught snuck in from beneath the door, a river breeze, a lick of the St Lawrence's tongue. Follow it. This was the only thought the shrub had left me.

Lying outside in the mud of the street, I pictured the warm and softly blackened stones of the kitchen hearth, and the bundles of herbs and flowers my mother had once collected – and my father wouldn't throw away – made dry and brittle by several Winters' worth of smoke. Inside my pocket the paper rustled, the one I'd signed in Montreal. I, Arthur Stanton... will undertake, will do, will promise, will serve.... Five years. I, Arthur Stanton.... Five years. And at the bottom, the inky spider's dance of my signature. The blubbering had come on quickly then. And why hide it. Everything else was coming out of me, the shrub erupting in its second and third incarnations.

When I looked up, a pipe was glowing opposite me across the street, its light illuminating the whites of a man's eyes, streaked red by the shrub that sat beside him on the ground in its little keg like a poisonous mushroom. All around us were the stone warehouses of Lachine: dark hulks and shadows, filled at this time with the goods of the trade – blankets and kettles, guns and shot and powder, brooches and beads, oceans of rum – but which I imagined already full of the cargo of furs that was being paddled down the rivers of the North and West towards them. The warehouses would become a charnel house of animal skins, and in their stead a whole country of skinned beasts.

After a few seconds, the sitting man stumbled awkwardly up onto his feet, swaying left and right, his pipe a tiny lantern on the deck of a listing ship. Following it with my eyes had my stomach churning and roiling, as though it were filled with bilge. Then it came above deck, rushing out of my mouth in a vile torrent.

When I looked up again, the pipe was extinguished, and its smoker had fallen into the middle of the road. He lay there for some while, face down and silent in the mud. The singing of the men sounded impossibly far away. In the delirium of the shrub, it seemed the skins of animals were shuffling against each other within the warehouses.

Eventually, the man regained his feet, retrieved his keg, and staggered over. Slumping down against the wall of the tavern, he stared at me as if I were some ghoul or apparition, though it was I who might have suspected this of him. His shirt was torn, his jacket grimed with mud, his face smeared with it; long strands of hair clung to his face and neck, turned up here and there with the memory of curls. He might have stepped out of the staved hull of a ghost ship.

'You must be Arthur?' he said at last.

'I am,' I said, wishing I wasn't.

He looked at the pool of vomit before me. 'I think this is your first time in the trade?'

'It is.'

'And so, you've met the men.'

I nodded.

'Well, Arthur, I should say welcome,' he slurred. 'I should say good fucking luck.'

'And you are?' I asked, noting he'd done neither.

'McLeod.'

'And this is your first journey, too?'

'Oh no,' he said, lifting the keg mournfully to his lips. 'I'm that special type of fool who makes another.'

At the river's edge, I didn't know which way to look. On one side of me, the water looped and coiled, a grey-brown serpent waking, my old fears come back to life. *Do not think of it, I told myself. Do not think of it.* On the other, Hyacinthe rubbed the fleshy stub of his face. Young Godin and Narcisse hung back and kicked at river stones. Old Crebassa and Seraphin were speaking to the two men from the canoe, who it turned out were brothers. McLeod hadn't taken his eyes from the blanket. And in truth, they were all a solemn lot now, and – as the brothers spoke – became more solemn still. If this was an Augury, it wasn't a good one. They'd asked Saint Anne for blessings and protection and been delivered a corpse.

This is what the brothers told us.

That they were with the North West Company and had brought this body with them from the New Fort. They were part of the 'Express' – carrying letters between the northern posts of the Athabasca country and Montreal – and had travelled a good part of their way by dog and sled, and then by canoe as the waters became navigable. They'd started out from Athabasca towards the middle of January, reached New Fort a month ago, and then been fortunate with the ice (or the lack thereof) on Lake Superior. Being at once grateful for this early thaw and not grateful, they said, gesturing to the blanket and holding their noses.

Who was it in the blanket? What misfortune had come upon them, Crebassa asked. It was a while before the brothers answered, and I noted a certain loftiness in the way they addressed us – in the way they stood amongst us too – which I'd learn was sometimes the way of those who manned the very northern posts, as though distance of one sort bred distance of another. They knew almost nothing, they said at last, least of all who this was – as if the identity and fate of men below a certain line of Latitude were a puny type of thing to consider – only that he'd been delivered, as dead as he was now, to the New Fort in the Winter, where they'd stored him, buried beneath a stack of frozen whitefish. The head of the fort, a doctor named Munro, said he'd been given a small sum to pay for this body to be returned to Montreal.

Given by who? asked Crebassa.

By the man who'd delivered him to the fort, said one of the brothers.

And who was that?

Who knew, said the other brother with a shrug. They'd had five Spanish dollars for the transport of him.

And they'd put him in the ground here?

No. They'd only stopped here for prayers. They hadn't seen a church for three years and had been sitting with a dead man for a month. The body was to go to Montreal when they were done.

They trooped up to the church then, leaving their cargo with us, as I gulped at the immensity of where I was going; that men could start off from the far North West in January, and only now be reaching us.

And gulped in something else too.

Where the blanket had come away, a lock of black hair and a big toe were visible, horridly waxy and moist. By instinct, we'd gathered around like mourners at a graveside. McLeod went and knelt beside the blanket. He smoked one pipe, then refilled the bowl and smoked another. At last, he leaned over, and pulled it further open. 'My God,' he said. 'It's Labrie.'

The name rippled across the men's lips, a breeze through poplar leaves. Hyacinthe spat on the ground. Old Crebassa scratched where his ear would have been. Meanwhile, all the remaining blood had flooded out of McLeod. His face was as white as a Winter's moon. His hands were shaking as he lit a third pipe.

The men's eyes kept moving from the blanket to McLeod and then back again. And this movement appeared to spread to their feet. For I noticed they'd begun to edge backwards, in small, shuffling steps, and supposed it was to distance themselves from that awful smell, which in truth there was no escaping. McLeod, though sunk in his pale shock, must have recovered himself sufficiently to take note of this. 'We leave,' he said in a low, cracked voice, as if concerned those steps would lengthen backwards, and take them all the way back to Lachine. 'We leave now.'

And so it was we embarked from the church of St Anne, moving slowly up the cold, grey waters of the Ottawa river – heading North and West to where we would join the Mattawa river, and thence towards the great lakes, Huron and Superior – with the scent of a corpse in our nostrils, and the country up there all before us.

2

But before getting my feet well and truly wet, I must add a brief word here concerning what we thought was the fleece of our little Argosy.

We weren't a full outfit, barely the rags and bones of one. That much, even in the first flush of my greenness, was clear to me. During my single day on the wharves of Lachine, I'd watched the brigades of the XY and North West Companies as they'd embarked in their great Montreal canoes – so long and wide they must have left some birch forest naked and shivering – piled with bales of goods until their gunwales almost touched the water. Off they'd gone, by three or four or more, like ships to Troy, with sweethearts weeping and hollering from the banks and lusty fellows hollering lustily back, promising to be forever true. But though we carried goods to trade, our solitary canoe was half their size, lusty a word too far to describe any of us fellows, and nobody wept at our departure except Young Godin's mother.

So let me shuffle backwards from that river a moment, back from my farewell with my father too, and all the way onto the cobbled streets of Montreal. Where, one afternoon three days before, seeking to escape Sorel a while – and having recently made an armchair tour of the globe through various Tales and Travels from the bookseller, filling my head with vague ambitions of adventure and journeying, and images, wool-gathered, of magic carpets and distant isles and unknown lands (intermingled with oppressive thoughts of the doleful meadow outside our house, my lack of talents and prospects, and the drip, drip, drip of my father's perpetually disappointed nose) – I'd looked up to find a sign above me: Parker, Gerrard, Ogilvy & Co.

Now what more foolish notion is there than that the Heavens might peek inside our skulls and, seeing the thoughts and daydreams there, decide to send us a Miraculous Solution. But it seemed to me then that this sign was indeed Heaven-sent, a nudge in the ribs from the Fates. (Of course, if I'd looked up a hundred paces further on, another sign would have said Gerald, Finch & Co, Haberdashers and I might have considered the Miraculous Solution to be the manufacture of gloves and hats.) And since the three Weird Sisters, rather than my own footsteps, appeared to have decided all this, I'd walked directly through the door.

Within, a cavernous room stretched back towards two high dusty windows. On each side it was filled with desks, at which men laboured with quills upon mountains of leather-bound accounts, nibs scraping and scampering over paper like squirrels' toes on Autumn leaves. And in some measure the figures they were scraping were indeed animals, or at least that portion of them that had been converted from swimming, stalking, walking things into pounds and shillings to be herded obediently into columns.

In the centre of the room was the very largest desk and the very smallest man, sitting on a chair so high he might have been a monarch in miniature, a visiting king from Lilliput carried up there by attendants and minions. It was Mr Ogilvy himself, chief partner of the Company, which in turn was a partner in that joint Company, the XY.

'Step forward,' he said brusquely, looking up from some papers. I obeyed. 'What's your business here?'

I explained to him – as though it was a long-held ambition, and not a thought two minutes old – that I wished to join his Company as a clerk.

'A clerk, you say. In this office?'

'A trading clerk, sir,' I replied. 'In the North West countries.'

'Well, well,' he said, brightening, as though I was his own Miraculous Solution. 'Then step a little closer.'

The table was piled high with ledgers and papers, some of which were weighted down with the fragment of an enormous and ancient-looking bone.

'Your name?'

'Stanton, sir. Arthur Stanton.'

'Stanton, you say. Is that a Scottish name?'

'No. An English one.'

'Ah,' he said in disappointment. Quite suddenly, he reached across the table and gave one of my lapels a vigorous tug. 'This is decent cloth.'

I thanked him. It was my best coat.

He asked what my father's profession was.

A schoolmaster, I told him.

'I see. So, not a poor man?'

'Not poor, sir, and not rich either. In a middling way.'

'Yes, yes. And may I ask if you have been in any troubles of late? Perhaps difficulties with the Law, or with matters of the heart and such?'

'No, sir.'

He appeared both perplexed and dismayed by this. 'So, you are not poor, or Scottish, or in difficulties?'

'No, sir.'

'Might I ask what attracts you to this trade then, Mr Stanton?'

'I'd like to see the country up there.'

'Oh dear,' he said. He considered me a while then. Scrape, scrape, scrape went the nibs of the quills, a wolf becoming a sixpence, an otter a pound. At last, he lifted the bone from his desk and held it up, as though he were a pygmy wielding a club. 'You see this bone here, Mr Stanton. Have you beheld one like it before?'

'No, sir.'

'They're intriguing objects, are they not? Curiosities, novelties. Wonders, even. I hear there are men from museums who venture hundreds of miles into the North West countries solely to discover and collect them. They say they're from gigantic beasts, who roamed the earth before the Flood.' We both contemplated the bone. 'But best to remember what a man in your position – if you should have that position – must consider first.' There was a long pause. 'Well?'

I told him I wasn't certain.

'Not certain,' he boomed, with a voice twice the size of the man. 'What covers it, of course! Our business is in fur, Mr Stanton. Bones are extraneous,' he said, thumping it on the desk. 'Bones are secondary. As is seeing the country. The XY wouldn't care a fig if you set eyes on a new continent, if it didn't have beavers swimming in its rivers.'

He asked what experience in the trade I had, and I had to admit none.

But could I read and write?

I could. But not in Latin, I added. Or in Greek.

'We wouldn't be sending you there to be a Priest or Professor, Mr Stanton. We are – how might I put it – rather short of men at present.' With this, he took hold of a piece of paper and scribbled on it for several minutes before passing it across to me. 'Sign this,' he said. 'If you're decided.'

It was a contract. I tried to read it, but the words swam away from me. There was a considerable gulf between Miraculous Solutions and Legal Documents. What would my duties be, I asked?

'Duties! Are they not there very plainly in your contract, Mr Stanton? You will trade for furs. You will obtain furs. You will procure furs. Now you may sign it or not sign it, as you wish. I don't have the livelong day.'

It was only on looking down at the shaky signature it had made that I realised my hand was trembling. Had the contract said five years? A quick and panicked reckoning: a quarter of my life so far. What a plummet in my belly! The room began to feel even more large and cavernous. When next he spoke, Mr Ogilvy's voice appeared to come from as far away as the land of the gigantic beasts. 'Very good, then. I hope you have no obligations. You'll leave the day after tomorrow, from Lachine.'

'The day after tomorrow. To trade for furs,' I said, for all I could do in this cavern was echo.

'Oh, and one other matter, Mr Stanton, in addition....'

Here followed Mr Ogilvy's 'in addition', which on reflection sounded much like the main purpose of our outfit.

It concerned the securing and transport of a considerable number of furs – *exceedingly valuable furs* – recently obtained by two XY traders in *certain new territories* (this uttered softly, softly, with a finger placed against his nose, as though his Kingdom might be full of spies). The first cargo of these should by now already be safely stored in the warehouse of the XY fort at the mouth of the Kaministiquia river on Lake Superior. We would rendezvous with the clerk in residence there and discover from him when exactly he was expecting MacDowell and Ross to return with the remainder. MacDowell and Ross, I echoed? The *two traders*, coming from *the certain territories*, repeated Ogilvy, less softly, softly, but nevertheless with a slight purr in his voice, no doubt caressed by the thought of all those excellent and easy furs. Oh, and I should know that in the way of the trade, one of its sillier customs, men were often given nicknames. So MacDowell I might hear called Long Arm, and the trader Ross, Copperhead. Why those... I began, but he waved this off. Once we were in possession of these furs, it would simply be a matter of our transporting them down the shore of Lake Superior to the main XY fort at the Grande Portage, from whence they'd go to Montreal. All this should be accomplished by the Summer's end, he said, making it sound as though my beginnings in the trade would be something of a jaunt, to be concluded with a Winter spent feet up in the fort.

Oh, and in addition to the addition. When these two traders arrived, I should glean as much as possible from them concerning the *certain territories* they had operated in. The trader MacDowell, especially, could be a... a rather independent fellow. Good at finding new beaver grounds, but occasionally forgetful of sharing such geographical details with his Company. A flicker of anxiousness now crossed Ogilvy's face. It was imperative that those furs were transported as quickly as possible. Did I know what Loose Fish and Fast Fish were, in the language of whalemen? No. A Loose Fish was a whale yet to be properly taken possession of. A Fast Fish was one with a harpoon in it, at which point it belonged to the whaler rather than the ocean. Those furs would be Fast Fish once they were under his own nose in Montreal.

The flicker now blossomed into a full-blown frown. I should pay especial attention to safeguarding the furs from our rivals in the North West Company, who were a parcel of scoundrels, etc. In particular, he had had intelligence of two NWC traders who would be travelling North to the Kaministiquia at the same time as us. An Englishman named Herse and a Scotsman named George Mackenzie, who I might hear referred to as the Sail. I should keep a sharp eye on them. Did I have any questions?

Questions! My head had begun to ache and swim with them. Meet with a man called MacDowell, who was also called Long Arm, who was coming from…? Be wary of a man called the Sail, or was that George? Be something or other of a man called Copperhead, whose actual name was… and a fellow called Herse, who I was to be careful of, or seek out, or…? There were several matters I wasn't quite certain of, I began to say.

Which he ignored, informing me the trader I'd be apprenticed to would elucidate such matters.

'Trader? Apprenticed to?'

'The Deuce take it, man! Is there wax in your ears? Yes,

apprenticed to,' said Mr Ogilvy, extremely slowly and loudly now, as though for a deaf man or dullard. 'And remember, Mr Stanton,' he said, waving me away with the mysterious bone. 'Furs.'

And then there I was, back on the street beneath that sign. I had walked in with daydreams and dissatisfactions and walked out with a legal obligation, a Company, and a master. As for the rest, it was no clearer to my scrambled brains than the origins of that bone.

3

And now to shuffle forwards again.

To where, three days out on the Ottawa river, I was beginning to realise that canoes are not magic carpets or armchairs, while watching the world familiar to me vanish: the fields dwindling, the Seigneuries becoming solitary clearings, becoming single columns of smoke above the trees. Until there were only the trees, and beyond them a distant line of unknown hills covered in more trees.

'What are you writing in your book, Mr Arthur?' Young Godin asked, turning in the canoe to face me. We'd stopped for the men to smoke their pipes and I'd taken the opportunity to read over my journal.

An account of my travels, I told him. He appeared greatly impressed by this. Over the gunwale, I watched as the current of the river curled itself around the point in the lee of which we were sheltered, lingered for a second, and then swirled onwards as though it were a disappointed dog sniffing for meat behind a kitchen door.

'Like the Knight's?' he said. For so the men styled Alexander Mackenzie, who'd lately become very famous and a Sir for his account of his travels and discoveries in the North West countries and the Pacific coast. He was the prime partner of our XY Company. He was also, so we assumed, not far behind us on the road.

It would be nothing quite as grand or accomplished, I told Godin. Simply a few observations to share eventually with my father and brothers. I harboured no thoughts of publishing. (For how could I have explained to him my recent and ridiculous ambition? That one day my name would also be on a book of Travels, and my father and Alfred and Edgar would open its handsomely bound covers in surprised admiration, astonishment even, and think how I'd made of my situation a finer thing, turned bronze into silver, and distilled my folly into Authorship.)

'I am sure it will be a fine book,' he said. 'Perhaps you will read it to me when it is done.'

That was kind of him, I said, moving my hand to conceal the first page – even though Godin couldn't have deciphered a single word, as it was both in letters and in English (and you'll see I've translated him, as I have the other Frenchmen, to help ease the confusion and predicament of tongues). If he had, he'd have discovered the following:

May 14th, 1804. Arrived at Lachine. Warehouses. Shrub – an abomination.

May 15th. Departed Church of St Anne. Dead Man.

May 16th. Rain. Trees. Try not to think of the water.

I wasn't confident this would make me a fêted author and a Sir.

Was this my first time in the North West countries? Godin asked. He was only two or three years younger than me, perhaps sixteen or seventeen, and had the plump and healthy cheeks my father's favourite poets often gave to shepherds, along with flutes and lyres and such. They looked more wholesome now than when they'd been besmeared with puke beneath that table in Lachine.

It was.

And his also, he said, with his shy and crooked smile.

Behind us, bent miserly in the stern like Father Time, Seraphin watched the coals burn down in the bowls of the men's pipes, waiting to call for us to embark once more. He was the one who called pipe stops and pauses, and as such was the measurer of duration and distance both. We moved from pipe to pipe as others might from hour to hour and mile to mile. In the lingo of the trade, we were ever four pipes from this place, or ten pipes from that one, and so on and so on.

All this was new to me then, our tiny floating world. Young Godin and Narcisse in front of me; Hyacinthe in the bow, peering over the water like a ship's figurehead chipped by a storm. I'd get to know the sight of their backs uncommonly well. Behind me, Old Crebassa, cursing his stiff joints, and then Seraphin in the stern, interpreting the river. Because it was never the same, he said, though he'd travelled it countless times. The other men said he must have travelled all those other times with his eyes closed, such was the zig-zagging course we took. Narcisse said it was remarkable how a man with a face like a hawk could have the eyes of a mole.

And there beside me was McLeod, a remnant of our departing day's vomit still clinging to his lip. He'd barely uttered a word since, and I was beginning to consider my first impression quite true: that I was apprenticed to a shipwreck, a broken mast, a Gilly-Gaupus in his cups. For he had at least a foot on every one of us, his knees sticking up above the gunwales as if he were a heron sitting in a bath, making an awkward and unusual cargo for these parts. Up here, the ideal shape of a man was a triangle: all shoulders and back, with short legs pegged on as an afterthought. My father's Greeks, had they washed ashore in these parts, would have had to re-chisel their statues. When we came to a portage, the men would rise from the canoe and make their way stooped beneath their packs like turtles who'd lost their forelegs, followed by a great long beetle made of bark.

At Seraphin's mark, the men emptied their pipe bowls and on we paddled, towards my first disgrace.

For our next pipe, the men were obliged to bring the canoe close to shore, to prevent it being swept backwards. The dog behind the kitchen door was getting hungrier and hungrier. 'Have you noticed the current is moving more swiftly, Godin?'

'It is, Mr Arthur,' he replied, turning to face me, half-choking on the smoke he was learning to inhale, these pipes not being those the shepherds trilled upon. Narcisse turned around, also. Although only a few years older than Godin, he had two Winters behind him in this business, and nobody would have made a poem of his cheeks.

'We're approaching the Long Sault,' Narcisse said.

'The Long Sault. What's that?'

'Where the river comes alive,' he said, grinning, showing that gap between his two front teeth that made him look mischievous and sly.

I glanced over at McLeod. McLeod said nothing.

Less than a pipe further on, we came upon the first of the crosses. It was a simple thing: two pieces of wood nailed together. 'La Pointe of Berthier,' Crebassa called out, doffing his red cap. The others followed. Several lifted their paddles in salute.

We came to a second. 'Jourdain of Sorel,' he called, louder this time, as the noise of the river had increased. Again, the doffing of caps and lifting of paddles.

'What happened to those men?' I asked McLeod. He looked stonily on while the men increased the tempo of their strokes. The sound of the moving water was now the sound of blood rushing through my ears. *Do not think of it*, I thought. *Do not think at all*.

'Bonhomme.'

'Lamarche.'

Birchbark is very thin, I thought.

'Those men,' I repeated frantically, although it was clear enough what had happened to them.

'Most of them on the way *down* the river,' McLeod said at last. 'Not up it.'

'Chenette, Brunet,' called out Crebassa, as if he'd known every unfortunate one of them. 'Young Roi of Terrebonne.' His cap was off his head more often than it was on it. This road that was on water was also a graveyard.

All things now seeming contrary, the men paddled at a furious pace and the canoe slowed. We hugged a narrow stretch of smoother water near the bank. Towards the other bank, and in its centre, the river bulged and rushed over stone, rose in ripples and hackles, frothed white. An entire tree bounced over a rocky island. And then there was no holding it back: I thought about breathing in water. How cold would it feel in my lungs? Would it fill them at once, or in increments? I pictured my own eyes, staring wide at me from below.

At a signal from Seraphin, the men put down their paddles and brought out long poles which they used to push the canoe forward inch by precious inch. It was better, I thought, in the way animals think, that I wade to the shore and meet them beyond what I knew now to be our first real rapids. The canoe, at least, would be lighter. I turned and shouted this to Seraphin.

We'd not reached the carrying place, he shouted back.

'For God's sake man,' cried McLeod. 'Sit down!'

'I am sitting,' I said. And then realised I wasn't sitting. My body was barely my own. 'It would be better....' I began. McLeod reached over and pinioned my thighs in his long arms. Hyacinthe leaned backwards and knocked me roughly into a sitting position with his pole, flattening the crown of my father's hat.

'Is he having a fit?' I heard Narcisse ask.

'I think,' shouted Hyacinthe, amazed, 'he is afraid of the water!'

'Afraid of the water,' repeated Crebassa, as though it were the name of another of his fallen comrades.

We reached the carrying place soon after, and my legs, released by McLeod, took me shakily to the shore. As the men unloaded the canoe, he asked in astonishment if I had a fear of water. And if so, had I thought about my choice of profession. I said it wasn't my fault. When the thoughts came, I could sometimes not control them. McLeod, the blood beginning to return to his cheeks, said if I had thoughts about standing adverbially up in a canoe, it was better to keep them away from my adjectival legs. I told him I'd not expected my fears to remain so strong. They were something from my childhood. 'My God,' remarked McLeod, 'what has Ogilvy given me?'

'Arthur,' he then added in the voice of a man who is constantly being dealt low clubs and a three of diamonds, 'we have a thousand fucking miles to travel, and not a hundred of them by land.'

'What would you advise?' I asked meekly.

'I'd advise you go home and lay your head upon your mother's lap. But since that's not possible, I'd advise you to keep your arse on its seat and your eyes shut.'

That night I lay on my cot, thinking the contract in my pocket was an anchor of lead, its five years a cliff I'd walked off.

As a child, I'd often spent idle afternoons with some of the boys who came to study with my father. Had he overheard us, he would have been dismayed to find we didn't discuss Cicero or Hesiod, but instead the stories we'd read about the adventures of Sinbad, Crusoe, and Gulliver. We played long games of What Would You Have Done, taking scenes from each book and putting ourselves in the place of the hero. What brave and doughty fellows we were in those games!

'What would you have done,' us boys might ask each other, 'as Crusoe watched the cannibal feast?'

Not one of us said, 'I would have wished myself at home and blubbered like a baby.'

At last, McLeod turned to me in the dark of the tent.

'Arthur,' he said, 'I don't mean to be unkind, but can you please stop your blubbering.'

'I'm sorry,' I said.

'The best kind of sorry out here is silence.'

As trader and apprentice, we shared a tent, while the others slept under oilcloths with their heads beneath the canoe. Up to this point, McLeod had put himself to sleep each night with an embrace of Mistress Shrub, and so I waited for the raggedness of breath that signalled she'd returned him there. Somewhere out on the river a loon moaned. Down by the shore, one of the men let out a long and trilling fart. A few lecherous frogs were beginning to wake in the ponds. And over their chirruping it had come again, as though beyond my control. Sniffle, sniffle, sniffle.

'You know,' McLeod said, 'it is a long fucking way before we reach the Kaministiquia. If I ask what the matter is, will you stop this?'

'I'm trying.'

'Arthur, what is the matter?' The frogs chirruped some more. Somewhere in the woods behind us, an unknown animal brushed through the branches.

'It's not how I thought it would be.'

'It's not how you thought it would be. Let me tell you a secret, it's never how anybody thinks it'll be.'

'I thought I'd get used to it, like Crusoe.'

'Crusoe?'

'Crusoe from the book.'

'Good frigging Lord. You thought it'd be like a book?'

'I don't know what I thought, now.'

'It's not like a book.'

'No, it's not.'

'Now go to sleep, Arthur.'

And I tried. But after a few minutes it seemed as though I could hear all the shuffling, whispering, ominous things that moved around us in the thousand-mile night. I counted up the crosses we'd seen. I thought of the waxy big toe of the dead man.

'McLeod?'

'Good Fucking Lord Almighty,' said McLeod, sitting up on his cot and taking a long swig from his keg. What the adjectival Deuce was it this time? Had I thought this would be like a play? A story from the scriptures, perhaps?

I asked him who that dead man had been, and how he'd known him.

McLeod was quiet for so long I might have suspected him fallen back to sleep, except that his breath remained steady, and he was unaccustomedly silent and still. For each night, Mistress Shrub seemed to conjure two figures in McLeod's dreams. The one he gently beseeched, muttering and mewling endearments and apologies; the other he cursed and called a Devil and such like, while thrashing on his cot.

At last, he spoke. He said Labrie was the resident clerk of the XY fort at Kaministiquia River.

The clerk Ogilvy said we were to rendezvous with?

The very one.

'Oh dear,' I said.

'Oh dear is right, Arthur. Oh fucking dear.'

But what had happened to him?

McLeod said he had no adjectival clue what had happened to him, beyond what those brothers had told us. All he knew for certain was he hoped to God Almighty that Long Arm and Copperhead arrived at the fort with the rest of the furs soon, otherwise everything would get much adjectivally harder for us.

Long Arm and Copperhead, who were also called MacDowell and Ross?

Yes.

And why were they called that?

It didn't need one of my books to work that out – MacDowell had one arm longer than the other, and Ross had red hair.

I said how Ogilvy had told me they were coming from *a certain place*.

McLeod said he wondered why Ogilvy was still trying to keep this under his hat. Word travelled as quickly through the fur trade as canoes. The fact was that they'd set off the previous year to explore the upper Missouri and its tributaries, somewhere beyond the Mandan villages. The rumour was they'd done well, extraordinarily well. That they'd stumbled upon a beaver El Dorado and these Missouri furs were some of the finest imaginable. The *specific place* where they'd obtained them would indeed be a very valuable secret, but the Missouri country itself was extremely large and mostly unexplored.

The Missouri, its tributaries, the Mandan villages. McLeod might as well have said Thule or Atlantis or Timbuktu, for beyond the shores of Lake Superior my knowledge of up there was as misty and unfilled as the inside of Mr Bennington's head.

And why were we being sent to fetch them?

In truth, we were being sent because there was nobody else available to send. And because Ogilvy didn't trust Long Arm.

Why was that?

Because Long Arm was a man with his own ideas and ways of doing things. And besides, when it came to furs, Ogilvy didn't trust anybody.

And what of our rival traders in the NWC? Ogilvy had mentioned a man named Herse, and one known as the Sail? Or was that George?

Verb the Sail, exclaimed McLeod. And adjectival Herse as well. And with that he took a mighty draught of Mistress Shrub, lay down his head, and began to snore.

And as he does, Esther, let me begin to answer the question your uncle asked, and McLeod more roughly, and my father not at all. Why did I listen to that Miraculous Solution and walk into the offices of Parker, Gerrard & Ogilvy? I had no connection to this trade, though many in the town of Sorel did, which at the end of each season would fill with voyageurs back to spend what little of their wages they had left. I had no love of hardship, or commerce, or water for that matter – that is, the true pillars of this profession. But if my own experience has taught me anything, it's that young men have very few thoughts in their heads at all, beyond whatever Fancy is immediately before them. They are mostly a cloud of moths in a room full of candles.

A little reading of Defoe and the Arabian Nights, some volumes of Travels that probably had even less truth in them, a few conversations with those Frenchmen swanking it up in town, a daydream on a cobbled street in Montreal – that was all the candle I needed. But there also is the thing you fly from, as much as the thing you fly towards. For it seemed to me that since my mother had left us, I'd lived in a sad house, with a sad and disappointed man, and prospects as grey and plain as a stone.

And then there is the thing you fly towards, only wishing for the hand on your shoulder that will stop you.

For in that way, we are not like moths at all.

4

May 19th, 1804. Les Chaudieres (rapids!) Rain. Men fix the canoe. Rapids.

May 21st. Les Chats (rapids!) Trees. Rain. Hyacinthe punches Narcisse. Hyacinthe burns toe in cooking fire. Rapids.

May 23^{rd,}. La Montagne (rapids!) Old Crebassa kills turtle. Trees. Men fix the canoe. Rapids.

May 25th, 1804. The Grand Calumet (rapids!) The Hill of Difficulty. Black Books. Long Arm and Copperhead.

It was not like a book. Or if it was, then it was one the printer had bungled and mackled, blurring all the letters. My memories of that first week are scant enough.

I took McLeod's advice, viz rapids and eyes, and it seemed to me when I properly opened them again we'd already travelled many pipes and were floating in a drowned forest. They called it a road, they called it a river, but sometimes it would turn into a lake so wide you could hardly see from one shore to another; or else a mazy channel through an archipelago; or else a cataract tumbling foamily over a precipice.

In that drowned forest, rain was falling onto the newly unfurled leaves of oaks and beeches, dripping into the grey-green gloom. The current was gentle, the water blessedly quiet. For days, the noise of the river had been like an enormous worm that'd burrowed into my ear. It was there at night when I tried to sleep, there when I woke, and there all the other hours of the day – its cold body shifting and slithering into the liquid roaring of rapids, the rush and press of narrows, the steady rumbling of a straight.

'You know,' remarked McLeod, almost cheerfully, 'we were better off if all our portages were flooded like this one. We could travel as easily as Noah.' It was as if one of the trees themselves had spoken. I could've counted upon a leper's hand the sentences McLeod had uttered to me thus far. The sunny ones, none. As for instruction, my master in the trade had had fewer words for me than a dunce of a parrot. Without any explanation, the most rudimentary customs of the trade were mysteries to me. On one occasion, I'd picked up a paddle and Seraphin had cried out, aghast, eyeing my clumsy grip. 'You do not paddle.' It appeared as though clerks, or apprentice ones at least, didn't do many things. They didn't hold back on rations of rum. They didn't carry the packs of trade goods at the portages. They didn't ask whether it was safe for the canoe to pass over rapids. On all these matters, McLeod had been as eloquent as an obelisk.

I'd assumed the prime cause of his continued gloom and taciturnity to be the discovery of Labrie's corpse, which in truth had cast a shadow over all the men – for they believed in omens as steadfastly as Apollo's priestesses and thus far had only been delivered the worst sort. And more than that.

Ogilvy must have given them an inkling at least of our main errand and presented it – as he had to me – as the easiest of assignments, a mere Porkeater's jaunt. A single season to collect and transport some furs and then back to Lachine with full pockets before the snow. But, if it was to take any longer, then they might be looking at a whole year up there or more.

This alone would have darkened their tempers. But there was another thing I'd noticed. Whether it was on a portage, or when we stopped to eat, or indeed any occasion when we weren't in the canoe, they quietly (who did few things quietly) shunned McLeod. Those shuffling, backward steps outside the Church of St Anne had become an extra foot or two away when eating, a few additional yards on the portage trail, an avoidance of his eyes when he spoke. Since Lachine, they'd treated him like some twitchy fellow they'd found lingering around the docks at Joppa. There were dark mutterings and rumours too, which I wasn't privy to, only catching snatches of interrupted confabs, conversations halted the moment my ear approached too closely. But several things were clear enough from these snatches: that they concerned McLeod; that they did not concern McLeod as a paragon and great leader of men. All of which is to say we were a generally down-hearted crew; a parcel of long faces, led by the longest – for when the shrub wasn't doing its oblivion work, McLeod looked like my father did while reading about the decline of Athens.

His words then were a spark to be kindled. 'Seraphin says we'll reach the Grand Calumet before midday,' I said brightly.

'Oh,' McLeod said, his voice returning to its customary moroseness. 'Then scratch Noah and substitute Cain. Or Moses. In the desert.'

'Will it be bad?'

'No doubt,' he said.

There in the forest, which was now the river, the rain began to fall more heavily. Most of the men had taken off their shirts, though it was cold enough almost for snow, preferring to come to shore with dry clothes in their equipment. Their long hair fell over their necks, to help ward off the mosquitoes this rain would soon hatch. The scars on Hyacinthe's back and shoulders flexed as he paddled, like albino snakes. His vertebrae were a craggy ridge, tufted with whorls of lichen-dark hair.

Hyacinthe began a song, singing a verse and waiting for the others to chant the melancholy refrain. It was a ballad about a young man pining for his love in a village in faraway Normandy. They stopped briefly, mid-verse, to push a squirrel from the branch of a tree. And then clubbed it to death with their paddles as it tried to swim away.

Then on we went, through the forest-river, towards the Grand Calumet, in time with that forlorn lover.

I was sure the men had heard my blubbing, to add to the shameful spectacle I'd made of myself at the first rapids, and so on reaching the Calumet portage I told McLeod I'd like to carry a pack, wishing to prove myself in some manner.

McLeod stared at me as if he was only a quarter wakened from a dream, and I was a man with a donkey's ears and tail. 'I'd advise you didn't, Arthur.'

It would be a good thing if I were seen to try.

He didn't think it would be. Not at all.

Better than doing nothing, I said.

So be it, he shrugged, turning onto the portage trail. He couldn't be responsible if I didn't listen.

Listen, I thought bitterly. To whom? I might as well put my ear to a barrel of shrub. I hoisted the pack on my back, placed the tump line over my forehead, and regretted it immediately.

The next I saw of McLeod was his knee.

Did I need a hand? he asked. I was a third of the way across. The trail had become a deep puddle, and I was up to my waist in it. 'The others won't stop, you know.' I knew. I'd had a good view of their knees as they'd gone by.

'What an odd fellow,' Narcisse had said in passing. 'Sitting there like a white frog.'

The tump clung to my forehead like a wrestler's arm. The bale of goods attached to it was wrapped tightly in white canvas with the letters XY painted on it, as though a numeral signifying its weight, or the date of my death on a tombstone. Beyond McLeod's knee lay another puddle, and then another. It was better I prove myself to the men, I said, through chattering teeth.

So be it, said McLeod, disappearing into the green murk of the trees. All shadows here soon enough became green.

Out of the puddle, I only proved my own misery to myself, staggering on like a feeble ant with a bloated kernel of rice until, after a small, painful distance, I discovered McLeod, pipe in hand, at the bottom of a rocky hill laced jaggedly with half a lightning bolt of white quartz. McLeod eyed where the trail led up over the steep ground. He eyed me and the muddy pack. 'Well then, Arthur,' he said. 'I suppose we have ourselves a Hill of Difficulty.'

'A Hill of Difficulty?'

'As the old Pilgrim would have it.'
'What old Pilgrim?'
'The Pilgrim from the book.'
'You mean Bunyan's book,' I said.

Later, I'd learn how a sternly spiritual aunt had flogged that Pilgrimage into him when he was a boy, and there it had stayed in bits and pieces of Pilgrim topography, which now and then he would affix to the landscape around him. It was McLeod's one habit of poetry.

'So, it *is* a little like one,' I said.
'A little like what?'
'Like a book.'

He considered this a moment, and then a rare and new thing: a rose blooming in a desert, a Unicorn's horn falling from the sky: a smile. 'I suppose it is,' he said.

And in that brief sunbeam, I thought I might ask what it was the men muttered about him, and hope to discover it nothing but the usual grumblings, about a lack of drams of rum, etc. Instead, I took another feeble step. McLeod continued to watch, in the lee of that Difficult Hill and its lightning bolt. 'Arthur,' he said at last, 'for the love of frigging God, give me that pack.'

At the head of the portage the men had set up camp. Seraphin was running his hand over the bottom of the canoe. Narcisse was trading with an elderly Iroquois woman and her daughter for the withered roots they called *wattap*, which we used to sew patches onto the canoe's damaged bark. Hyacinthe was scrutinising a kettle of bubbling pine gum, holding his absent nose above it as though he were making soup. The canoe was to be fixed. It was always being fixed. It often seemed a wonder it floated at all.

I took out my journal and sat shivering on a rock. Close by, Crebassa squatted in a cloud of pipe smoke, telling Godin a tale about how, in the Old French Time, the Good Lady had saved a voyageur from a scalping at this very spot. One voyageur, he said, not the others with him, for even Crebassa's miracles usually ended with somebody mutilated or dead. Ahead, the river curved around a rocky point and was swallowed up by the endless line of trees.

I'd intended to write brief sketches of my companions, as the writers of Travels customarily did, but my companions remained mostly mysteries to me. Take our own Nestor, Old Crebassa. What did I know of him? That he liked to tell stories; that he loved his pipe and tobacco pouch, and might justly have been called the Greatest Smoker in the North West countries. Yet what impelled him back into this country, I couldn't have said. My guess was it was something related to his missing ear, which I'd discovered was not missing at all: he kept it, salted and shrivelled, in a small leather bag hanging from a cord around his neck. On occasion, when he thought himself unseen, you might spy him in spirited debate with this bag.

Or take Hyacinthe and his nose. There wasn't any reason to believe he'd been a gentle soul before its violent abduction, but its loss appeared to have provoked a host of bruising Angels within him. I picture him even now, freshly woken in the morning and already angry, his sandy hair frizzled and cow licked, a furious owl in an ivy bush. There were times, when we struggled against a current in the canoe, I feared he might leap from the bow and punch the river like some pugilistic Canute. I saw him rail against tree trunks and contend with raindrops and hold up his fists to the mosquitoes like a hare in March.

Or Narcisse, who was quick to tease, and quick to complain, and was ever provoking and bickering with Hyacinthe. I can see his muddy brown mop, his sly grin, his head tilted slightly to one side to hide the cheek cribbaged by the pox. He was the artist amongst us, constantly whittling this and that. His paddle was intricately carved, though his art tended in the direction of those scandalous pictures over which the ash of Pompeii pulled its veil of modesty: if you looked closely, you might see the curve of hips on its blade and the top of its handle globed and cleft like buttocks.

Or Seraphin, who spent most of his time staring at the river as though it had cuckolded him. What I'd first taken as sharp and angular in his face was in fact a perpetual and squinting perplexity, as if all the rivers he'd contended with had corroded his features, leaving only the beaky bedrock behind.

And lastly Godin, as green as me, and in those early days, my one friend. He'd also been troubled by his father, though far more roughly than I ever was. In everything he told me about his life on his family's farm there was an anxiousness, the ghost of a violent boot or fist, which I supposed fed his habit of constant and fretful looking, like a deer which cannot place a hoof upon a field without the anticipation of wolves.

So there are the sketches I never wrote. For as the sun slipped behind a mass of grey-yellow clouds, I put down my journal despondently, without adding a word. I'd thought books opened men and countries, but here the country felt like a closing of covers. I might have torn off a scrap of paper and penned the whole journey there in a minute. We paddle, we stop, we carry, we fix the canoe, we smoke, we paddle, we fix the canoe, we sleep, we shit, we eat peas and pork and grease, we fix the canoe, we sing, we smoke, we fix the canoe, we paddle, we fix the canoe, we drag the canoe, we pull the canoe, we carry the canoe, we pole the canoe, we eat peas and grease. The rest, I feared, would only be my blubbering transferred into words, my wretched tears into ink. What would my father think? He admired a man called Diogenes for having lived in a barrel.

Soon enough the familiar stench of our porridge of peas and corn meal and pork grease wafted over to me. Our dinner. And our breakfast, too. And then again tomorrow. And the tomorrow after. And all the tomorrows until we reached Lake Superior. One by one, the men gathered around the tripod to stare hungrily into our Hecate's cauldron, their long hair dangling in the steam. It wouldn't have been wise to act as their Familiars. Any creature we encountered on the road not fortunate enough to run or swim or fly away found its way into the pot. Tail of porcupine. Embryo of seagull. Head of pike. They considered these our lucky days.

'How is your book, Mr Arthur?' asked Godin, who'd come to sit beside me with his bowl.

I told him it was coming along very nicely.

It was here, as the rest of the men sat wolfing at their bowls by the river, and above us a raven cawed from a tree, that Godin told me of McLeod's Disgrace, as he'd heard it from Crebassa.

It was barely a year old. The previous Spring, apparently, McLeod had made an expedition to the Athabasca country, along with another NWC man (McLeod being then employed by our rival Company). They'd taken an unusual route, so those who knew the country said. But somehow, the other man didn't arrive along with McLeod.

At the Athabasca posts?

Hadn't arrived anywhere, Godin said. It was assumed – and here he lowered his voice – that he'd been left behind to perish.

Left behind by McLeod?

Godin nodded. McLeod himself had been discovered in a pitiable condition by some of the northern Indians, who'd delivered him to the nearest trading post. The NWC had deemed his conduct lamentable and suspicious, inked his name in their Black Book, and sent him down to Montreal (which is what they called it – and what they did – when you were thrown out of a Company, said Godin).

It was what all the men said. They claimed McLeod had been mad and raving when he was found. And even more mad and raving afterwards, when they shipped him to Montreal, babbling in his delirium about how he must return to some river immediately. The NWC thought his Upper Storey quite gone. They'd had to tie him up to stop him jumping out of the canoe and swimming back.

My God, I said. Didn't the XY Company consider this before they engaged him?

Godin said he supposed the XY had their own Black Book, and McLeod wasn't in that one.

And this is why the men avoided him?

The raven above us blinked and moved his head fretfully this way and that. Godin did the same. He said it was, and because of the dead man, Labrie, also. 'They say McLeod's bad luck, Mr Arthur.' Taking the opportunity of Godin's confidences, I asked him if the other men had said anything of the traders we were supposed to meet with at the Kaministiquia. Oh yes, he replied. According to the others, Long Arm and Copperhead were greatly admired in the trade, both as excellent traders and excellent fellows. Long Arm being renowned as a sort of Columbus of the fur countries – a pathfinder and discoverer of new beaver grounds; while Copperhead had a reputation for being generous with drams, considerate of voyageurs, and possessed of a cheerful and genial temper. The strong feeling amongst the men being that they wished most dearly they were being led by these two men, rather than seeking them out under the guidance of a notorious, sotted, ill-starred booby. Godin also hinted that McLeod had some kind of prior connection with Long Arm, though as we were interrupted in our confab at this point, he didn't have a chance to enlarge upon it.

It was a lot to mull. And mull it I did, lying awake in our tent that night. There was a sinister edge now to the raggedness of McLeod's breathing. And I wondered whom it was exactly he wooed in his dreams, and whom he cursed.

I was to find out both soon enough.

5

May 26th, 1804. Deep River. I become something.

In Sorel, I'd known fur men were split into two stations: the Voyageurs or Engagés (who were almost all Frenchmen), and the Bourgeois – the Clerks and Partners or Big Wigs (who were mostly Scotsmen). And I knew vaguely how these Big Wigs were divided into those who stayed in the fur country and those who did the books in Montreal, and that they would come together for a few weeks each Summer for a Great Rendezvous (at a fort, halfway between the outermost reaches of the North West countries and Montreal, which previously had been the Grande Portage, but now – for the NWC at least – was the New Fort). But it wasn't until I entered a canoe that I began to understand the finer gradations and distinctions there, and that where you sat was in somewise who you were. As a voyageur, you could be a Steersman or a Bowman or a Middleman. And there was this additional distinction, that applied to every rank and station in the trade: for you might be a Partner or a Middleman, a Steersman or a Clerk, but if you wintered in the North West countries you were a Northman (or Hivernant); if you journeyed from Montreal to those countries and returned before the Winter, you were a Porkeater; and if you were stationed in the farthest North you were an Athabasca Man.

I wasn't sure yet what I was.

It was still dark the next morning when Seraphin woke us with the call to embark. These first hours, before the sun had risen, were the easiest for me. Not being able to see the river greatly eased my fears of drowning in it. In the darkness it was like floating in the air, and before the men found their voices there was only the rhythmic sound of their paddles kissing the water. There was no wind that morning and the dark leaked into blue, and then a milky light. Poplar leaves trembled into view before being swallowed up by a slow-rising river mist. It swallowed us up too. Out of our sight, geese fell swishing onto the water. Invisible creatures slipped into the river from the bank. At this hour they were safe from the men's paddles.

As the mist began to clear, I found the country had flattened. The river spread out and eased along sandy banks and marshy shores. We passed a dilapidated hovel that McLeod called a Fort (it being a peculiar part of the gammon and patter of the trade: to call every heap of logs a Fort or House or Post) which he claimed would be the last civilised habitation we'd see until we reached Sault Saint Marie. He was almost chatty. It seemed the mist had softened him, for it was often the way with McLeod – just after you'd imagined him in the worst kind of light, he showed himself in a better.

When we stopped for the day's first pipe, he passed me a cup of rum. 'Just drink it,' he said.

'More rapids?'

'The Allumettes.' And as he said this, I caught it: the faint, low rumble; the wisps of foam in the air. I drank the rum and closed my eyes.

When I opened them again we were approaching a long sandspit.

'Baptism Point,' announced McLeod.

'Another Pilgrim sort of landscape?'

'Not at all,' he said. 'And you'd better take this,' he added, passing me a small keg of rum.

On the sandspit, I knelt as Crebassa held the kettle over my head. The others were gathered around me in a semi-circle. The water flowed coldly down over my ears and eyes, blurring their faces. For a panicked instant, their lips moved but no sound came to me, only the rushing of water. Narcisse's grin was a bleary grimace; Hyacinthe's red cap a blotch of paint in a heavy rain.

And then I was back with them, spluttering and gasping, and Crebassa was asking me, as solemnly as a sermon, to swear never to kiss one of their women without asking. I swore. Glancing around, it seemed an easy promise to make. Hyacinthe asked for the rum.

I asked McLeod how much to give them and he suggested the whole lot.

For an hour they leapt around the fire, celebrating my baptism rite, performing jigs and reels, and dances I'd never seen before and wasn't sure had a name. And then Seraphin called a start and everything changed again.

The river narrowed and narrowed, so that if a strong man had thrown a stone it might have reached from one side to the other. The banks rose sheer into brown cliffs and high barren hills, topped here and there with lone firs, some lightning-blasted and burnt. In places, the faces of the cliffs were solid sheets, in others they were cracked and fissured, gnarled pines and miniature birches sprouting from them like the meagre tufts of a geriatric beard. It was as though the world had become suddenly older. I knew then we'd reached that stretch of the Ottawa they called Deep River. The crew's songs – louder and lustier than usual – echoed from bank to bank, as though choirs of stone men were singing them back to us.

Night fell quickly and we camped on a patch of rocky ground. The high cliffs blocked out the last rays of the sun, and soon there was only a thin strip of starry sky above us. The men retired early, worn out by their dancing and the keg of rum. They slept near the shore, their heads beneath the overturned canoe, their legs sticking out; the composite limbs of a great beetle in repose, and all about it a twittering and bellowing of pea and grease farts.

McLeod and I sat on the higher ground, outside our tent. We'd made a small fire.

'You might try smiling,' said McLeod. 'You've been baptised.'

'What does it make me?' I asked. 'Am I a Northman now?'

'Not yet.'

'Then a Porkeater, at least?'

'You've reached this far and you're still alive. I think that's what it makes you, Arthur.'

I asked if he'd undergone a similar rite. He said he had, at the very same sandy point, on his first journey into the country. There was that melancholy in his voice that men get sometimes, when recalling childhood gardens and faithful dogs and schooldays and such things. The sound of Golden Ages remembered. I waited for the scent of shrub or rum to waft my way, but it never did. This was a sober McLeod. I asked how long ago that had been. He said it seemed about a hundred years ago.

And what had led him into this profession?

He told me there'd been little enough leading and choosing to it. It was what McLeods did. His father had been a fur trader before his untimely end, as were his three uncles. His cousins shared their fathers' professions, all except one, who'd darkened the family name by becoming a sailor. His grandfather had come from Scotland to trade in furs. And if family lore were to be credited, his ancestors had been skinning beasts for so long they'd emptied Scotland of beavers back in the olden, olden days, when God's dog had been a puppy. All of which was to say, this trade had once seemed less a choice to him than a destiny. When he signed his apprentice papers, the ink might as well have dripped out from his birthing cord.

Emboldened by our unaccustomed conversation and my baptism, and McLeod's sobriety, I mentioned his being sent down to Montreal.

He said it might be best not to believe everything I heard.

I said I'd been surprised to hear he'd once been with the other Company.

I shouldn't be too surprised. NW and XY were letters in the alphabet, not branding irons.

I confessed how many aspects of the trade remained mysteries to me. I wasn't even certain what the country up there would be like, and that when he said things like Missouri tributaries and Mandan villages, he might as well be speaking of the Moon.

McLeod almost smiled. He went into our tent and returned with a book. Casting some sticks on the fire and waiting for the flames to cast their light, he said, 'If you need this journey to be like a book, perhaps this one might work.'

It was a copy of the Knight's *Travels*. McLeod opened it and out came a quarto page, much worn and thinned about its folds, which he passed to me. A Map of America announced its title in bold letters, while beneath, almost as bold again, Exhibiting Mackenzie's Track. This track was a meandering line of red and yellow, going out from Montreal towards the unknown western coast, forking somewhere near the Athabasca country, with the yellow line continuing to the Pacific Ocean, the red to the Arctic. It passed through names encountered and familiar – Les Chats, Les Allumettes, the Long Sault – and then names to come, anticipated and ominous – Vulture River, Cascade, the Great Discharge, the Great Mire. Around it spread the whole northern portion of the continent: Lower Canada, Upper Canada, the northern territories of the United States, with hardly a mark to show where one began and the other ended, but instead crisscrossed by rivers and lakes and bays, and stitched around them, in long ragged shadows, Heights of Land and mountains. I traced the route I'd taken, and then followed the red-yellow line to Lake Superior. From here on my knowledge almost ended, like a sailor of old, falling off the flat edge of the world. I knew the Athabasca country was that area far to the north and west, to the left of Hudson Bay, with Lake Winnipeg halfway, but beyond it the whole map appeared mostly blank in the flickering of the firelight. And so too if you moved an inch or two below and beyond the western shore of Superior. Which is where McLeod's finger was pointing.

'Somewhere around there,' he said.

'What?'

'The moon, Arthur. The upper Missouri.'

'But there's hardly anything there.'

'Not on the map, no. Which is why there are still furs there. Which is why Long Arm and Copperhead went there.'

'And we are going?'

'Here,' he said, pointing to the North shore of Superior.

My eye wandered left an inch. 'And what lake is that?'

'Rainy Lake.'

And then sauntered another inch, to a lake sat above the Great Mire. 'And that?'

'Lake of the Woods.'

Between these two lakes was a river, named Rainy River, marked by a smudged circle, the colour of a bruise, where a finger smeared with ash and grease had travelled around and around and around.

'And....'

Seeing where I was about to point, McLeod now snatched the map roughly back, his better humours vanishing instantly. This must be the scene of his disaster, I guessed, picturing a haunted man in a lonely garret in Montreal, reliving his misfortune with his fingertip. This map before him, Mistress Shrub at his side.

We sat in silence, then. A night breeze rose and gently fell, the stone men in the cliffs taking long sleeping breaths. I poked at the fire with a stick.

'Go on, then,' said McLeod at last.

'Go on, what?'

'Go on and ask me.'

'Ask you what?'

'About the expedition to the Athabasca country. About McLeod's Disgrace, as I think it's currently known. Ask me if I left that other man to perish. I know they must talk of it.'

I asked him.

'No,' he said. 'I did not.'

'Who was the man?'

'His name was Sugar.'

I said I was sorry he'd lost a companion in the trade, and perhaps a friend.

McLeod laughed bitterly, spat into the fire, and said I shouldn't put too much store in names. Sugar was a scoundrel, a weasel, and half an adjectival madman too. And if he was to walk out of the woods this very moment, he would be overjoyed to punch him in the face and throw him in the river.

I asked if I might have one question more. He looked up forlornly at the narrow sky and said it would have to be the last.

I asked him why people seemed to *think* he'd abandoned the man called Sugar up there?

He said that wasn't entirely adjectively accurate, as some people suspected he might have murdered him. Or eaten him. Or both.

Middlemen, Steersmen, Bowmen, Clerks. Northmen, Porkeaters, Athabasca Men. Where you sat and where you'd been. Our surface selves were simple enough in this business. But that night I imagined I'd peeked below and glimpsed the hidden measure of McLeod: that he was a man brought low in his profession and reputation, dogged by bad luck and misfortune, who was attempting to salvage his name in the eyes of the trade.

As for my baptism, I cannot tell a lie: I felt much the same man after as before.

6

What are our lives, my father once remarked, in the grip of one of his especially gloomy Ages, but a series of arrivals and departures, greetings and leave-takings, framed on each side by their ultimate apotheoses. There may be some glum truth in that, and perhaps it's for this reason we attempt to make a mythology of certain first encounters, have people appear like Venus from the foam, so they might glint and glisten above the dull and uniform and relentless blue of the sea.

And I've tried this, Esther, each time I recall the next morning, watching in my mind's eye as a Montreal canoe makes its way towards where McLeod and I stand on the banks of the river, the morning bright and clear, the echoing cliffs all around us. But somehow, I cannot erase McLeod's voice, or artfully adjust the sequence of what happens next.

'Fucking Mackenzie,' he says, and will not stop saying it, whatever elisions my memory attempts.

And so it's always Mackenzie I see first, sitting in the middle of that canoe. This must be the Knight, I'd thought. The famous Sir Alexander Mackenzie. Author of the lauded *Travels*. The leader of our XY Company.

'And fucking Herse with him, too.'

And so it's always Herse I see second. An elegant gentleman, who looks like he might have stepped out of a London carriage rather than having travelled countless rough miles on a wild river.

Then it's not the voice of McLeod I'm aware of but instead his mouth gaping silently open, his face becoming as pale and stricken as a bowl of milk shuddered by an earthquake.

And so I do not see you arrive at all.

By the time I've made my way to the landing place, it's milling with new men – seven voyageurs and two Iroquois paddlers as well as Herse and Mackenzie. Who knows where McLeod is in these instants? I approach Mackenzie, a mightily plump man with the high soulful forehead you often see in portraits of Sirs and Authors and such. And it's this pictorial forehead that blinds me to the fact that Alexander Mackenzie, head of the XY Company, has seemingly arrived in a North West Company canoe, filled with NWC men.

'Sir Alexander,' I say. I think I may bow. Yes, I do bow. Narcisse smirks and begins to giggle. 'It is an honour to meet you, sir.'

The man lifts an eyebrow, scrunching the skin of his soulful forehead. Behind him, Herse breaks into an amused smile. 'I must say, these XY clerks are exceedingly well-mannered, George,' he says, his voice as English as his clothes suggest.

'Indeed,' says George, who is apparently not a Sir or an Alexander, and does not smile at all. 'They're certainly something. And you are?' he asks.

'Stanton. Arthur Stanton.'

From the corner of my eye, I catch Narcisse curtsying to one of the NWC men. 'Bonhomme,' he says effusively, 'what an honour!' By then, McLeod has come up behind me, looking like someone has hit him on the head with an axe and burnt the gardens of his childhood, and then killed his favourite dog.

'George,' he says, offering the faintest of nods.

'McLeod,' replies George Mackenzie, with a fainter one still. 'So, this is what's become of you. With the XY. Or with the rags and bones of it, at least,' he adds, looking us over.

There's a pause. One of the Iroquois paddlers slaps a mosquito on his shoulder. The men have stopped greeting each other; or, in various cases, glowering at each other.

'Herse,' McLeod mutters at last.

'Hello William. And excellent to see you again, too. We're travelling up to the New Fort from Montreal. We must have been behind you on the river.'

'We were expecting to be overtaken by the Knight,' says McLeod, as stiffly as tin.

'Ah, you haven't heard the news, then. You'll be waiting a long time. The Knight has business in the Assembly. He has been elected. He is now a Right Honourable Sir. Oh, and you'll see we have a guest travelling with us to the New Fort. No need for introductions, I think.'

I can see the veins throbbing in McLeod's neck, what he cannot say twitching through them. Except he's not looking at Mackenzie and Herse at all, but at a point behind them.

And it's only then, Esther, that I see you for the first time, standing at the landing place beside the Montreal canoe.

And here, I know, already delayed, already late, is where I should begin to build my mythology. How your face was like this and like that, how you moved this way and that way, how my heart began to beat in the fashion hearts are supposed to beat on such occasions, on such first sights. But the truth is, I only see your eyes. And they are black and hot with fury, and concentrated utterly on McLeod. The rest of us are scenery.

And like scenery we roll away, carted into dusty corners by

the stagehands, as McLeod begins to walk towards you – astonished, tentative, nervous, expectant, compelled – trying to find what words to say but not quite managing to say them, like a duellist not trusting his clunky pistol.

You don't move an inch. The men, unbidden, shuffle back and open a space around you.

'Esther,' says McLeod at last, almost croaking, as though each word is a rusty, weed-draped goblet retrieved from a wreck. 'Esther,' he says. 'What in God's name are you doing here? Why are you travelling with the NWC? Have you been in Montreal? Why have you been in Montreal? Esther, you must let me....'

Your voice is as sharp and clean and clear as a new-minted coin. 'Fuck you, William,' it says.

And that is that. One pipe later and everyone is back in the canoe – you and the Englishman Herse and the Mackenzie who is George not Alexander and the voyageurs and the Iroquois paddlers – heading before us on the river, between the echoing cliffs. Meanwhile, McLeod's big freckled hands are covering his face as he sits on the bank. The rest of us waiting, watching him, wondering when it will be time for us to follow.

Arrivals and departures, departures and arrivals, with births and deaths to act as Pillars and Posts. But it isn't like that, I'd tell my father, if I could. History – even the history of one small part of a little life – isn't a church register, or a book of appointments, or a succession of tidy epochs. It is not so easily parsed. Trying to fix one moment, we miss it. And what a jumble all the rest is, what a gallimaufry. One Age becomes another without us knowing: a half-painted picture in wet colours, forever overflowing its frame.

And soon after we will be on another river.

7

May 27th, 1804. Rain. Hyacinthe clubs porcupine.
We fix the canoe. Trees. We arrive at Mattawa River.

Which was much like the last river. More rapids, more pork grease and peas, more portages. We got up before the sun, paddled until it set, carried the canoe, fixed the canoe, moved from pipe to pipe to pipe. Crebassa told stories, Hyacinthe and Narcisse bickered, McLeod returned to silence and more deeply than ever into the bosom of Mistress Shrub. The only difference, it seemed, was a further deterioration in Seraphin's eyes and sense of direction. We now regularly overshot carrying places, came to land where there was no portage trail. But not knowing this country, our zig-zagging was only more scenery to me.

However, to avoid the confusion of the human scenery around me, the doubling names and new personages and proliferating Mackenzies – this perplexing world where men and boundaries and Companies were constantly shifting, as slippery as a player's paint – I now made a brief list in my journal to attempt to fix them. And how odd to see you in it, Esther, as a stranger.

> *The Sail (George Mackenzie, who is NOT Sir Alexander Mackenzie). A Big Wig in the NWC. The origin of his nickname is a simple one, according to Crebassa: him being*

considered as wide and full of wind as one. Or, in McLeod's words, 'He is all gammon and a hog.' Our rival.

The Englishman Herse, who is a trader for the NWC. Our rival.

A woman named Esther — who McLeod appears to know rather well.

Labrie — the dead man, who we were supposed to meet with.

Long Arm and Copperhead (MacDowell and Ross) — the XY traders we are supposed to meet with at the XY fort at the mouth of the Kaministiquia river on Lake Superior, to collect the second consignment of Missouri furs.

A man called Sugar, who they say McLeod abandoned on his expedition to the Athabasca country.

Beyond our gunwales, the land became hilly and then flat, lushly wooded and then pinched and rocky. And as the world altered around us, so the little one in our canoe began to strain and threaten to splinter.

The day Hyacinthe clubbed that porcupine and placed it to bake, gypsy-fashion, in the ashes, Young Godin and I were sitting at the far edge of the fire pit, speaking of the sea.

I'd put away my journal and was instead labouring over a page of the Xenophon my father had given me. I could barely decipher a word. My Greek was a very rusty sickle bumping dully against a very large forest.

What book was that? Godin asked.

I told him it was the story of a Greek soldier in Persia. An extremely old story.

And what happened in it?

Looking down at the impenetrable bark of the Greek, I tried to remember how my father had once explained the story, having despaired of my ever being able to read it myself. They have a battle, I told him. They have lots of battles. And the whole army becomes trapped in Persia, far away from home. And they must journey back through an unfamiliar country. Through many unfamiliar countries.

And did they get themselves back?

Some of them, I said. Most of them.

I told Godin the best part of the book was when they reached the sea and knew they'd be able to return home.

Could he see it?

See what?

The part where they reach the sea.

But it was in Greek.

He knew, he said. But he'd still like to see it.

So I turned to a page near the end and pointed at some words chosen completely at random, for I could no more translate them than Godin could read them. 'There,' I said. 'The men are calling out, "The Sea, The Sea".'

He looked at the words, marvelling, his crooked, smiling lips half-open.

But who knows if they were calling out anything at all, or what those words even meant? They might have described a field, or a shield, or the way the Colchians wore their hair.

'I'd like to see one too,' said Godin.

'See what?'

'A sea. They say the Great Lakes are like seas.'

I said I'd heard the same. Beside us, the porcupine, denuded of his quills, sizzled in the embers of the fire, which glowed more and more red as night began to fall.

As it did, McLeod's and my tent became a triangle of yellow light. A candle was burning inside, and his outline was visible through the illumined canvas. He was stooped over our camp table. Or perhaps collapsed there. Since his encounter with you, he'd taken to spending mealtimes alone, poring forlornly over his copy of the Knight's *Travels*, muttering despairingly about how you must have been in Montreal, beneath his very adjectival nose, and he had not a gnat's bollock of a clue why you'd been there, or for how long. Or else muttering darkly about how adjectival Herse and the adjectival Sail would not steal a single one of those Missouri furs from him.

Around the fire, despite the boon of the porcupine, the men were subdued, as though that yellow triangle were a beacon whose baleful light they couldn't cast off. McLeod's bad luck and depressed spirits seemed to emanate from it. Tempers flared. Arguments broke out. Hyacinthe threw his bowl of grease and peas at Narcisse. And added to this disquiet was the Great Hatching, the horror of a northern Spring. All around us was the shrill, constant, maddening thrum of mosquitoes, holding us together in the fire's protective smoke, even when we'd be better apart.

The conversation skipped its customary subjects – dogs and horses the men had favoured, wives they'd lost or wished for, hernias and ruptures of myriad sorts – and turned to their own disgruntled mutterings. Since being overtaken by the NWC canoe, the men no longer tried to hide these from me. They had their own Black Book for McLeod, and were adding chapters to it.

First, there was the fact of our having been overtaken. The men said that Herse, especially, was a sharp and astute trader, for an Englishman anyway, and they feared we'd have nothing to collect if the NWC connived to get their hands on our consignment of furs. Especially as Labrie, being dead, was not able to watch over them.

Second, Esther, there was you. Seraphin and Crebassa appeared to know of you well enough. Crebassa explained how your mother was a Saulteaux woman, originally from the South shore of Lake Superior, who'd died when you were still a child. Meanwhile your father – and at this my eyes began to widen – was none other than Long Arm. He also related the nature of your acquaintance with McLeod. There'd been rumours of an engagement between you, broken when McLeod had gone North to his disgrace.

Looking about the fire, I discovered Hyacinthe had been greatly moved by this suggestion of Romance. He had a sentimental heart for orphans and jilted lovers, as evidenced by the songs and ballads he preferred, in which lovers rarely found a happy end and Hyacinthe rarely had a dry eye.

Narcisse wondered why it was that you were travelling up from Montreal, if you'd previously lived in the country up there.

Hyacinthe said it was as plain as an Englishman's wretched beer to anyone who wasn't an idiot. You must have journeyed to Montreal to find the feckless McLeod, who'd so cruelly abandoned you. And McLeod, knowing this, had attempted to abscond once again. Invoking Hosts and Tabernacles and a Bishop's nether parts, he said he was tempted to go into the tent this very minute and punish the miscreant with his fists.

Crebassa said that judging from the recent encounter, he was sure Long Arm's daughter could tend to any bruised affections she might have well enough, suggesting it was our own hides and prospects we should be concerned with. How would Long Arm deal with McLeod? Would he give his furs over to the man who had jilted his daughter? And, if she was angry with McLeod – which she clearly was – and we had to deal with her mother's people, the Saulteaux, we'd have a hard time of it, for sure. Those Indian paddlers had been full of bad looks for us, he thought.

But they were Iroquois, I said.

Did I not hear them speak? said Crebassa.

I felt the weight of my ignorance, then. For all my blather about Xenophon and Persia, what little I knew of this world. The only Indians I'd been acquainted with in Sorel were Iroquois, and so I'd made all the Indians we'd met and traded with upon our way Iroquois, too. It seemed the kind of thing our neighbour Mr Bennington might do, which was not a happy comparison for me.

I would've asked more questions if it weren't for the necessities of Nature and the torment of the mosquitoes, which were so thick in the air, so multitudinous I'd begun to imagine them as moving, humming particles of the dark itself. While relieving myself in the river they swarmed onto my face and neck. My God, I thought when I was finished, they've made an itchy havoc of my member, too.

Back at the fire, the conversation had returned to McLeod's ill-fated journey. They'd run out of food, Crebassa said, except for a seagull they'd managed to kill.

And McLeod ate it all himself, leaving none for the other man, Sugar, Hyacinthe said.

And its eggs, added Narcisse.

They all shook their heads at this perfidy. The hoarding of food, and not sharing it, being considered an extraordinarily low and rascally thing, among the Frenchmen and Indians both. It could barely have been worse if McLeod had eaten Sugar.

What small breeze there was began to shift. The smoke of the fire thinned about me and it was like a door opening. In rushed the mosquitoes, settling around my eyes, in my ears, everywhere. I started to itch terribly, all of me, especially my most delicate parts.

It was said that McLeod took the only map, remarked Crebassa.

And the last paddle, said Hyacinthe.

And their single gun, said Narcisse.

And the tent, said Crebassa.

And Sugar's trousers, said Hyacinthe.

'Mr Arthur?' said Narcisse, for the torment of my itching had me scratching vigorously and helplessly. The rest of the men turned to look at me.

'The mosquitoes,' I gasped.

'Or maybe Cupid's Measles,' smirked Narcisse, seeing where I was scratching.

Unable to tolerate them, I sought refuge in the tent. Behind me, I heard Narcisse and Hyacinthe arguing over the liver of the porcupine.

Inside, McLeod was lying on his cot with his eyes closed. The candlelight flickered over his cheekbones and brow and again the doubts flickered uneasily in me. Who exactly did I sleep near every night? A cruel Rake. A feckless breaker of hearts. A rascally hoarder of eggs? A greedy devourer of scarce and precious fowls? The thief of men's trousers?

And then above the insect chorus rose the dull, heavy slap, slap of men's fists and men's faces meeting down by the fire, followed by a great commotion of voices, again full-stopped with slap, slap, slap.

'For the love of God in frigging Heaven,' said McLeod, opening his eyes. 'Hyacinthe and Narcisse.'

He was out of the tent before I'd had a chance to speak. From down by the fire came his utterances, short and abrupt, slightly Scottish and full of Anglo-Saxon, and all around them a sea of French oaths and accusations.

While this was happening the flap of the tent tentatively opened, and there was Godin, looking this way and that so much I feared his head might come loose from his shoulders. 'Mr Arthur,' he whispered. He informed me the other men were planning to desert, the moment we reached Sault Saint Marie, considering McLeod's character so low and his star so ill, that to follow it would be to risk misfortune and worse. Godin was greatly troubled. What would happen to him if he also deserted? Would McLeod inform his father and the Company? I tried to think what to say to put his mind at ease, but my own mind was in a similar tumult. What would my own father think? And my brothers? That I'd made half a journey and provoked a mutiny!

Outside the tent, the voices were quieting. Godin began to

edge backwards. He asked me if he should inform McLeod, though he feared doing this as the men would despise him.

I told him to say nothing for now. I'd think of something.

I was safely lying on my cot, pretending to slumber, when McLeod returned. He lay on his own with a heavy sigh.

'Arthur,' he said, 'what else do the men say about me?'

I let silence be my best answer.

McLeod, more fluent in that language, let it strengthen his question.

'That you killed a seagull and ate it all yourself. And its eggs, too.'

'Is that all?'

'And that you stole Sugar's trousers.'

'That is a damned lie.'

I said nothing.

'The other part is a damned lie too,' he said at last. 'About the eggs.'

Somewhere outside, an animal bellowed in the woods. One of the men's behinds answered it. I went to pinch out the candle, my mind in turmoil. Could I trust McLeod? Should I tell him about the planned desertion? Would it be better if I joined the men and deserted myself?

'McLeod,' I said.

'Yes, Arthur,' he replied wearily.

I asked why he hadn't thought to mention his particular connection to Long Arm, namely his engagement to his daughter?

McLeod let out a sigh. He hadn't mentioned it because it was none of anybody's adjectival business.

I said it appeared to be very much our business.

So be adjectival it, said McLeod. If he told me every adjectival thing, would I please oh please let him adverbially sleep?

To begin with, I was wrong entirely about that smudged circle around Rainy River.

Sitting up and relighting the candle as we huddled in the tent, McLeod took out his map, pointed to the circle, and began to speak. This was the place – Rainy River trading district, which encompassed an area West of Lake Superior along the banks of said river – where he'd come to know Long Arm. They were then in opposition: Long Arm with the XY, McLeod with the NWC. All this was two years ago, he continued, making it sound an epoch, and himself some sad Ancient recounting the bright meadows of his youth. Their two rival trading posts, each no more than a few log shacks, had faced each other – Long Arm's on the North bank of the river, McLeod's on the South – and their opposition had been a benign one, the rare sort that had them share New Year and Christmas and Saint's days together. Along with a few voyageurs, Long Arm had one clerk beneath him, Labrie. His daughter was also living with him. With this, McLeod's voice got sadder still. For a year they'd got along easily enough. And by that 'they' I was sure he meant you and him, Esther, and that 'easily enough' was McLeod's sparse way of describing wooing and Romance. And though it pains me to write it, in this Garden of Easily Enough he must have fared wonderfully well – for he was engaged to you before the end of the year.

In trade, it was another matter. McLeod admitted his

returns were dire. This wasn't because of the opposition of Long Arm and Labrie, who opposed him barely at all. No, his main rival was the NWC trader who ran the district next to his, around the southern shore of Lake of the Woods, and beat McLeod to every adjectival fur that came into the country.

And who was this?

I'd already met him. The Englishman Herse.

Here a certain perplexity must have shown on my face. But why should he have considered Herse a rival? If they both worked for the same Company?

Because he was proud and stupid and young, McLeod said, as though he were now fifty years older. How infuriating it had been, to see Herse fill up his warehouse with furs and be patted on the head by the Big Wigs, to become the darling of the NWC. Even his opponents admired him. Herse's XY opposition in the Lake of the Woods district was Copperhead, and they were bosom friends. They'd had their posts built right beside each other, and yet still managed to fill both their warehouses with furs. At this, some residue of McLeod's past frustration bubbled up briefly, and he took a moment to curse Herse for his trading prowess, and Herse's friend, Copperhead, for his damned reasonableness, and being so well liked by the voyageurs and Indians, etc.

It was towards the end of the year of Easily Enough, during the Spring and soon after his engagement, that Long Arm and Copperhead had arranged with the XY to explore the upper Missouri and its tributaries, leaving Labrie to take over the larger XY post at the Kaministiquia. It'd all been huggermugger, but Long Arm had confided in McLeod, saying that since he was to be married to his daughter, perhaps he might consider changing Companies and joining them. They'd be leaving early in the Autumn and McLeod might do better with them than he'd done with the NWC – a great deal better. He must keep this strictly to himself, but Long Arm and Copperhead were both sure there was a bonanza to be had out there, enough to make them sufficiently wealthy to do whatever they wished.

Soon afterwards, before he'd had a chance to decide, McLeod had been summoned by the Sail to the NWC's New Fort. He met him in his room, sitting behind a table freshly hacked from a tree. Without remark, the Sail had laid out a sheet of paper upon it, with McLeod's dire returns written there. When he did speak, it was to offer McLeod what he described as a fortunate opportunity – the chance to redeem himself and undertake a brief expedition up into the Athabasca country. What kind of expedition? The Sail had spread another piece of paper on the table – a roughly drawn map of the northern Districts, showing the route from Lake Winnipeg to the east of Athabasca Lake. There wasn't much on it.

Did he recognise this road?

By reputation, McLeod replied. It was the customary road to that country.

He was not to take it. The Sail pointed to a portion of the map with even less on it. He was to take this one instead, he said, placing his finger on a thin inky line leading through the scribbled shapes of two lakes.

But nobody took that road, said McLeod.

The Sail now unveiled his scheme. McLeod was to explore this other route and discover if it was navigable and practical for trade. For if so, it would shave several days off a long journey, and a healthy percentage from the Company's costs. McLeod might, at the same time, accomplish something in the way of exploration and improve his reputation. If he left immediately, he'd be there and back by Autumn. He'd be accompanied by a NWC man called Sugar, who'd act as his guide. This man had once been in the Hudson's Bay Company and claimed to have knowledge of the route.

'So go on, ask me,' McLeod said to me now, the sounds of the men's snoring drifting in through the flaps of our tent.

Ask him what?

Why he'd agreed to this. Why – if he was to be married, if Long Arm had offered him an opportunity to make a fortune – he'd risked this other journey.

Without waiting for my why, McLeod said he would direct me to those pesky and immemorial McLeods he'd mentioned, sitting in their beaver Heaven and looking down on him with shaking heads. He'd wanted to secure his good name in the trade, to make it burn a little brighter, at least bright enough to keep his ancestors happy. And besides, he was sure it was no risk at all. He'd be back from the Athabasca country in the Autumn, in time to resign his position in the NWC and join you and Long Arm and Copperhead. He would have everything. A good name in the trade. A bundle of furs. The woman he loved.

On his way down Rainy River, he'd stopped to tell Long Arm he'd be with him by early September. And to promise you, Esther, that you'd marry the day he returned. Come hell or high water, or whatever the northern countries pitted against him. If he still had a living breath, he'd be there.

And with that he'd headed North, towards the Athabasca country.

Making haste, as McLeod did, I'll skip past Lake of the Woods and Lake Winnipeg and join him as he stands on the banks of a river called the Missinippe. He looks briefly one way, at the road the traders usually take, and then heads reluctantly in the other direction, towards a river called the Reindeer and the road that nobody takes.

As they'd paddled up the Reindeer, McLeod had begun to suspect that this country was as familiar to Sugar as the moon. The river was slow-running and wide, and they eased along between its banks of sloping rock, its sandy bays, the soil becoming ever thinner and scarcer as they skirted the edge of what the map called the Great Stoney Ground.

Arriving at a lake also called Reindeer, they discovered it to be vast, with clear, deep water that the gentlest breeze turned instantly into long, treacherous rollers; in its more sheltered bays, there was still ice crumpled on the shore. Vast, and apparently empty. They paddled a hundred miles upon it and didn't meet with any Indians or see a single deer or moose. In places, wide swathes of the land were charred and burnt over, as if by a vengeful army in retreat. In this wretched emptiness, there were only gulls and loons and an occasional eagle, circling its own solitude.

At last, they came to a small river which led West and further north, in the direction of Athabasca. McLeod took the map he'd been given out of his pocket and showed it to Sugar, who scratched his ear. When had he been in the Hudson's Bay Company? McLeod asked. He'd been with the NWC for ten years, he replied. So before then? And when had he last taken this route? Sugar scratched his ear again and said nothing.

Following this river, they were for a while relieved to get off the turbulent waters of the lake. A very brief while. McLeod said that the next fifty miles were worth three hundred of the previous ones; the river turning into a multitude of rapids and ponds and carrying places, running through the lowest, rockiest, swampiest, most mosquito-tormented country he'd ever known. All Sugar seemed to know were the names of lakes and rivers he must have heard spoken long ago at the HBC posts around James' Bay, which he recited constantly, as though they were a magical spell that might guide them on their way. Reindeer River, Reindeer Lake, Manito Lake, Black River, Athabasca Lake. It wasn't the happiest sounding spell.

Nothing Sugar said was happy. He was one of those sour and embittered men who'd not risen in the NWC and had had too many lonely Winters to dwell on their resentments. McLeod supposed it was how he'd gotten his name: for, in the nomenclature of the trade, it was considered extremely witty to make the moniker either the apotheosis or the antithesis of the man. Sugar had grumbled about the NWC all the way from Lake Superior to the Missinippe, but the further they travelled this new road, the more these grumblings took on a darker, more mutinous air, with McLeod himself standing in for the entire NWC. McLeod began to sleep with his gun at night.

Fifty dreadful miles, and at the end of them they'd capsized in a rapid. Spared drowning, and still in possession of their canoe, they'd made a doleful inventory of what the river had left them, spreading their remaining outfit upon the stony bank. It consisted of the gun, thirty balls, four pounds of shot, three flints, five pounds of powder, one net of thirty fathoms, Sugar's spare trousers, one small axe, a tent of grey cotton, a bag of pemmican, and a few trifles to trade for provisions, such as beads, brass rings, and awls. These lands were inhabited by the Chipewyans, but they hadn't met with one. The sharp stones of the river had destroyed McLeod's trousers. He almost came to blows with Sugar, getting him to lend him his spare pair.

That night, as they sat by their fire, afflicted horribly as usual by mosquitoes, McLeod had tried to make a little speech. They'd had their difficulties, he admitted. But, he continued, pointing to a cluster of tiny birches on the bank, they should try to be like the roots of the trees up here, interlaced in their efforts to uphold each other on thin soil, and make the remainder of their journey a success. Sugar looked at him as though the river had taken something from his wits, or torn them like his trousers. 'Be your own fucking tree,' he said. He'd fashioned a mosquito mask out of a piece of deer hide, scraping it to parchment and cutting out holes for his mouth and eyes. McLeod could only see his glittering eyes and hear his foul breath whistling out of the hole.

The next day they arrived at the second lake.

'Manito Lake,' said Sugar.

And McLeod's spirits filled with unease. The word Manito, he explained, was what the Indians used to refer to spirits – those powers and beings they considered supernatural – and if there were such spirits residing at this lake, he didn't fancy they'd be kind ones, not for fur men, anyhow.

And so it turned out. The pair sat on the shore to discuss their predicament. Their bag of pemmican was half empty. The map said they had only to find a certain river to reach Athabasca Lake, but by now they trusted the map about as much as each other. McLeod suggested they explore the shoreline a while in search of the river and any game. Sugar suggested he tup himself and they turn straight back and head for the New Fort. McLeod reminded him forcefully who was head of the expedition. He thought their best course was to continue.

The name of that river was Black River, said McLeod, and the Pilgrim himself couldn't have named it better. For such were their humours as they set out to find it.

And when they found it, too.

They'd not followed Black River for one puff of a pipe before the second disaster struck. At the first rapid they encountered, over went the canoe, tumbling them into the water, while the canoe vanished over the lip of a small falls. McLeod found it in the pool below and thanked God for small mercies.

And small they turned out to be. After scouring the pool and searching the banks, they made a second doleful inventory. The river had taken their powder, the last of their pemmican, their trading goods, their net, their shot and McLeod's paddle. They were left with a gun with a single load of shot, an axe, an awl, and a small piece of grey canvas. The canoe had a gash stretching from its bow to its mid-section like a monstrous grin.

From this point on, McLeod could offer no proper reckoning of days. They may have been at that place for three or six or eight, who knew? They spent them trying to patch the canoe and find food. They boiled the black lichen that grew on the rocks, they boiled their moccasins, they searched for bearberries, they tried to eat the mosquitoes that were eating them. McLeod made forays along the riverbank with the gun and its one precious shot, but the only thing he found were a few gulls' nests with some eggs that were already embryos. They devoured these raw.

By a miracle of bark, pine gum, the piece of canvas and the single awl, they managed at last to make a patch of sorts for the canoe. That night, as they sat by the fire, drinking a broth made from his second moccasin, McLeod announced that, perilous though it was, they should attempt to float the canoe, and he'd try to lead them on to Lake Athabasca.

Lead us? Sugar retorted. He was sick to his adjectival bones of being led by the likes of McLeod. They should have turned back at the lake. And out it had come, then: how ten years hadn't lifted him above the lowest clerk in the Company; how he must follow such a succession of fools as McLeod, and make them rich ones, and grin and nod the while; how hard it was to rise in the trade if you weren't a Scotsman, or weren't related to one, at least. While if you were a MacThis or a MacThat, then you might be a Partner and Big Wig though you were so young and green you were trailing your camp blanket after you like afterbirth. But all those Dorichs and Doreens, he exclaimed bitterly, in a voice put on to sound like heath and heather, what adjectival good were they here?

McLeod said he'd rarely seen such fury in a pair of eyes, and directed entirely at him as though he were the embodiment of every MacThis and MacThat who'd ever thwarted Sugar.

That night he took the gun and went to sleep away from their camp, hidden in some bushes.

The next morning, McLeod was deep in the grip of a fever. The leaves of a tiny birch tree played above him. Two clouds drifted by, shaped like elephants and giraffes and other animals he'd never seen except in pictures. He'd thought, *I will die here.* He'd thought, *I don't want to die here.* He'd thought, *I must be back at Rainy River by Autumn.* Then he was ranting and raving and begging. Sugar was standing above him. Sometimes he was two feet tall. Sometimes he was ten feet tall. McLeod told him he'd give him anything if he could get him away from there and back to Rainy River. He told him about the Missouri Eldorado Long Arm was planning to explore, and all the furs they'd find there. If he could just get him to Rainy River, he'd make sure Sugar had a share of them.

When he next came to, the fever had abated somewhat.

He heard the faint splash of Sugar's feet in the river.

In the seconds it took him to drag himself onto his feet, Sugar was already sitting in the stern of the floating canoe. McLeod was about to ask him what he was doing, but it was obvious what he was doing: he was abandoning him there. He'd already begun to paddle furiously backwards, trying to get the canoe into the current. McLeod saved his breath, and with legs like tadpole tails staggered to the bank. As the bow began to slide into the current, he plunged into the water, groping desperately toward the stern. He missed it and caught hold of Sugar's paddle instead.

By all rights, McLeod said, Sugar should have cast him off in the struggle that followed. But somehow he'd kept his hold and, conjoined by the paddle, they were swept along to where the hackles of the river began to rise. Inch by desperate inch, McLeod pulled himself closer to the canoe, until at last he grabbed hold of the gunwale and pulled with all his might. It tilted. It swayed. It flipped. And suddenly he was holding onto the bottom of the stern with one hand and the paddle with the other, and Sugar was floating in the river. The current divided, pulling McLeod and the canoe into an eddy where its patch was ripped away, while Sugar was drawn into the frothing centre of the river, where he bobbed and reared like a cork. And all the while keeping his gaze fixed on McLeod, Sugar's eyes burning out from the holes in the soaking mask. And beyond the cold, and beyond his exhaustion, McLeod was aware that these were the eyes of a man who truly and absolutely hated him. And then he was gone, and there was only McLeod and the useless canoe.

It was now he entered his most desperate straits. Returning to the accursed bank of that accursed river, he began to despair. Even if he could repair the canoe a second time, which was doubtful, how far could he get with no provisions, through a country he didn't know? It was while sunk in such reflections that he'd heard the cry of a gull, which out there might as well have been the caterwauling of Grace and Providence.

There it floated, only a few yards from the bank. McLeod took a trembling aim and fired. The gull lay dead in the water, and he thanked God, and the Saints he wasn't supposed to worship, and any other gods that might be nearby. Then he opened the bird and ate the precious fat in its belly. It was the worst thing he'd ever tasted, a foul quintessence of fish and rot. Not even starvation could improve it.

But he must have left some Deity out of his thanks, for within the hour his stomach began to churn and ache. There was no need, said McLeod, to go into the subsequent details of his distress, except to say it was a terrible sort of efflux. He weakened and sickened. He tried to fortify himself with mouthfuls of the gull's flesh, but the more gull he put in, the more of himself came out.

This continued for days, until there wasn't much left of himself to expel. At some point, he crawled over to where the axe and his empty gun lay on the ground. He used the axe to cut a few willow boughs to lie on, and then settled himself down to die.

The rest was delirium. He watched the seagull crawl out of his arse and stand screeching by his head. A raven sat on a tree above him and winked and sang a sad Scottish song. An Indian appeared and lit a fire. McLeod smelt the scent of pine gum boiling. The Indian poured some water into his mouth, placed a scrap of gull flesh in there too, saying something in a language he didn't understand. McLeod said a man's dying thoughts were for himself and God, but he'd share one of them with me. It was this: that he was not an immemorial McLeod and would not go to rest with his ancestors in a Heaven lined with furs. During those hours on the bank, he realised he didn't give a damn about this trade, not truly, and now he was about to die for the sake of his reputation in it. Out there on Black River, his ambition shrivelled smaller than a grain of dirt. He would like to stay alive. He wished he hadn't listened to the Sail. He wished he'd never left Rainy River. By which he meant the Land of Easily Enough. By which he meant you.

The next thing he remembered was waking up in the bottom of a Montreal canoe, beside a voyageur's moccasin. Where was he? he'd groaned. Near Sault Saint Marie, the voyageur answered. But that was impossible. It was very possible, the man said. McLeod had been sent down to Montreal and that was where they were taking him. Though, having heard the story of his disgrace, the voyageur would happily leave him on a rock somewhere for the ravens to pick.

But how had he even got here? The voyageur told him some Indians had returned him to one of the Northern posts, using his own canoe. The clerk there said the Indians had told him they'd discovered McLeod surrounded by eggshells, with a gun and an axe and a paddle and a half-eaten seagull. They'd found no sign of his companion, though it appeared McLeod was wearing his trousers.

But he'd been given them, McLeod had said.

Who gave a man his own trousers? exclaimed the voyageur, unable to hide his disgust.

He'd not left anybody anywhere, McLeod had tried to say. The canoe was staved and useless. It was the other man who'd tried to abandon him. But nobody was listening.

And then it was as though he'd run off a cliff. My God, he thought, he must get back to Rainy River. He'd tried to jump out of the canoe and swim but was barely strong enough to stand, and the voyageur had hit him on the head with his paddle. When he next came to, they were approaching the Ottawa river, and they'd bound his arms and legs like a pig about to be sticked. They didn't release him until they were nearing Lachine.

There was no getting back then. It was too close to Winter,

and he had no Company. And so he'd had to wait to find a new one and return.

And he'd never known that you, Esther, were also in Montreal?

Known! By adjectival Christ, what did I adverbially think!

And I saw it then, as clear as day: McLeod in his pinched garret in Montreal, running his sooty finger around and around the not quite perfect circle of his Golden Age – his time with you up there – repeating on paper the revolving torment of his thoughts and memories. And I knew why he'd come back here. It wasn't to restore a broken reputation, or make a bundle for the XY, but to mend the consequences of that missed rendezvous at Rainy River.

8

I'd learnt there were three ways to get a canoe up a strong current. You could carry it around that current on land, you could push it with poles, or you could tie ropes and pull or 'line' it from land. Or you could employ a combination. At the Portage des Décharges, we'd taken half the packs out of the canoe to carry on land (the décharge the place was named for) while Narcisse and Godin lined the canoe from the shore. McLeod was ahead of me on the portage trail.

'Oh fuck,' I heard him call. 'Oh fucking fuck.'

The trail ran close by the bank, and – turning around – I glimpsed, through the trees an arm in the current, and then quickly after a torso, and then a leg, and then only the swift water. How easily the river might make a mere instant of us. The men who were carrying packs hardly had time to lift their stooped heads, blinking in surprise as McLeod, on land, came bounding past in a blur of elbows and knees and Anglo-Saxon.

'Hold that line,' he called to Narcisse, who was scrabbling backwards along the bank, as though he'd harpooned a whale. 'Somebody help him hold that fucking line.'

Hyacinthe began running towards Narcisse. I followed McLeod down the trail.

We came upon Godin's back in a pool at the bottom of the rapids, turning in slow circles, his hair slick and black against the back of his skull. Crebassa and Seraphin were behind me.

Further up the bank, Hyacinthe and Narcisse had secured the canoe and were staring at the pool in horror. The current was strong on either side of it. There appeared no way to reach Godin without being swept away.

Without a pause, McLeod ran into the river. Soon it was up nearly to his chest, surging against him, and it seemed certain the current would overpower him. Below where he stood, the water seethed and broke over ledges and boulders, as if practising for what it would do to his bones.

But somehow, he kept on his feet. Reaching the edge of the eddying water, he grabbed hold of Godin's shoulder, turned him over, and moved slowly backwards with small, precarious steps, until the water was at his waist. Then he scooped Godin up in his long arms. Godin's face was ghastly pale. A brown rivulet of water dribbled from the corner of his mouth.

By now we were all gathered on the bank and formed a circle around where McLeod placed Godin on the ground. He punched the boy twice on the chest before he gasped and drew breath. The rest of us remained silent, not wishing to take his air. By the time Godin had drawn enough of it into his lungs, he began to scream.

In looking at his mouth and chest, we'd not seen his leg. It was as crooked as a thorn tree. Below the knee, the bone pushed jaggedly out against the skin, stretching it as a spoon would the surface of a cold pudding.

McLeod sent Narcisse and Hyacinthe to cut birch poles for a splint. 'Godin,' he said, staring directly into his panicked eyes. 'Can you see those other canoes that are coming?' Crebassa and Seraphin peered down the river, but there were no canoes. Godin's eyes rolled in his head; a foamy white spittle had replaced the river water at the corners of his mouth. 'How many of them are there?' McLeod asked firmly. Godin's eyes rolled slightly in that direction. Without shifting his own gaze, McLeod gestured to Seraphin and Crebassa to hold his arms.

Godin screamed again, more loudly, as McLeod snapped back the leg bone, and then fell silent. Godin looked as though he were sleeping.

May 30th, 1804. Les Vases. Mud. Vanished beavers. The whole trade.

The river next became a vast swamp or bog. This might be the world, I thought, if God had not got around to separating the waters from the earth. It was all mud. Beneath the moss there was mud, beneath the reeds there was mud, beneath the roots of the bushes and trees there was mud. Beneath the mud there was mud. It found its way into our boots, our shirts, our britches. Any semblance of solid ground was counterfeit: a player's greasepaint, Mr Punch's smile. The composite beetle of our party had become a salamander, a water snake – the men's legs sunk down past their knees, the air loud with their oaths. There was much mention of the privy parts of Cardinals and Bishops. And in between the Cocks and Cods of the Divines, came the triumphant chorus of frogs, the maddening thrum and whine of mosquitoes, the pitiful moans and whimpers of Young Godin as he was dragged through the mire.

There was not solid ground enough to pitch a tent. When night came, we made our beds on mats of willow boughs and rushes, falling asleep to the sound of bubbles of air escaping up through the wet folds of the earth, dreaming of mud.

Eventually, the river diminished to a narrow channel running through abandoned beaver ponds, their lodges and dams reduced to mounds of mud and sticks, crumbling into mystery like the pyramids of the desert; the animals themselves long dead and skinned and nothing remaining to tend to the unruly waterways. We could barely force our canoe through.

'Are we nearer the lakes?' Godin asked me weakly.

I said we must be getting very close. Since his injury, in the moments his fever left him lucid, he'd been much concerned about us reaching the Great Lakes, as though being on their open waters would somehow help ease him.

He was lying beside me on a bed made from the packs. The men had strapped his legs together with the lining rope. The injured leg had become monstrously bloated and brown-black, as though his toes had been gulping from the bog. McLeod had taken his place with the paddle. The other men did not avoid him now. There was no more talk of desertion.

The Mattawa narrowed and narrowed, until it was little more than a maze through lily pads and cattails and the flashing blue of irises. How Seraphin chose a route through this was a mystery to me. And a mystery to him, too, it seemed, for we tracked endlessly back and forth, our progress painfully slow.

Here and there, McLeod would stop for a moment to moon over the signs – a few burnt sticks and flattened reeds, remnants of peas and grease – of where you and Herse and the NWC canoe had passed through before us. But since Godin's accident, he'd put away his shrub.

At last, the Mattawa became a creek, hardly wide enough for the canoe to pass through. 'To think all the trade comes through this stream,' ruminated McLeod the Philosopher when we stopped here for a pipe. 'To Mackinac. To the New Fort. To the Grande Portage. To Athabasca. And back. The whole endeavour, all those big houses in Montreal, depend on this.' 'A frigging puddle in a swamp,' added McLeod the mud-smeared XY trader. 'A Quag of Perplexity,' concluded McLeod the Pilgrim.

And within this mazy swamp a transformation, a boundary crossed. For the water, where it was flowing at all, was now flowing West. Somewhere, we'd crossed a Height of Land, one of those dark shadings on the map. The men attempted a ceremony of sorts to mark the change. They tossed away the poles they used to push the canoe, and McLeod took out a keg of rum to offer them a dram. But it was a limp, half-hearted huzzah. Our hearts were not in it.

June 1st, 1804. Lake Nippissing. The Sea.

The puddle became a trickle, and then a channel, and then a lake where you could barely see the farthest shore. I knew from the Knight's map that this body of water was a presaging one: an easing of the eye and mind towards the great inland seas of Huron and Superior.

I pretended to Godin we had reached those lakes.

'It is like an ocean, Mr Arthur,' he told me.

It truly was, I said, in tones as awed as I could make them.

But before we were halfway across, his fever had returned, and he was back on his father's farm in Berthier, where a cow had escaped from its pasture and he must find it before his father discovered it gone. And in some wise this was fortunate: it at least spared him the sight of a small rocky island topped with crosses.

June 3rd, 1804. French River. L'Enfant Perdu.

On the other side of the lake we joined French River, where the current ran strongly with us. The Height of Land we'd passed over, barely noticing, here made all the difference in the world. Where before we'd splashed and strained and poled and lined, we were now carried. One pipe equalled ten times the leagues and miles it had before. Seraphin took one beaky glance and said we'd reach Huron by the end of the next day.

We camped that evening at a place the men called L'Enfant Perdu. I wrote the name in my journal and wandered over to where Crebassa was staring into the kettle, to ask its origin. He looked about him, to check where Godin had been placed, and whispered that the Indians also called it Crying Child, after the tale of a young Indian boy who was pulled under the water here while bathing in sight of his parents. They'd searched for him along the banks and dove into the river to search for him there, but all to no purpose. There was no sign of him.

But later that day they heard him.

Crying and moaning, Crebassa said – squinting into the steam of grease and peas and pressing the toe of his moccasin into the dirt – right here beneath the ground of our camp. They began to dig with their paddles, the crying and moaning seeming to come from just below the surface. But however deep they dug, they only found dirt. At this point he lowered his voice still further. Sometimes the cries would move, he whispered, until they appeared to be coming from beneath the rocky hills behind us, as if the child were wandering under the earth. For six days they'd dug, following the cries of the child, until the fear and sadness became too much for them and they departed.

Later that evening it began to snow. The day had started humid, with drops of rain in the air, but as it went on had cooled until the rain turned into thick, wet flakes. They rested for a while on the skinny needles of the pines and then were gone.

Afterwards, the sky cleared, and it became colder still. The awful thrumming of the mosquitoes disappeared, and McLeod and I stayed for a while outside of our tent while the men slept soundly beneath their canoe. We sat with crossed legs, tailor fashion, at the side of a small fire. McLeod sipped some water from a cup and passed it to me. The night was very large around us.

Did he believe in spirits? I asked.

Spirits. Such as ghosts?

Ghosts and other things. Some of the men did, I thought.

'Ah,' he said, 'the Lost Child. I understand now. They believe in holy relics and miracles too, Arthur. They believe the Virgin Mary came all the way down from Heaven to the Ottawa river to save a boat of Frenchmen from the Iroquois.'

I would have liked to tell him then about the little people my mother had told me lived in her old country, and the floating candles she believed presaged a person's death. And how these were no stranger to her than breathing air, far less strange than all the alterations she'd had in her life. But I was used to keeping this to myself. In Sorel, and in front of my father, it'd been best not to talk openly about corpse candles and fairies.

And I would've liked to tell him about the hearth of our kitchen, where in Winter – with snow covering the fields and my father in his study worrying the brains of wealthy farmers' sons – my mother would tell me stories about the island where she was born. How very green it was; how her father had ground corn in a windmill, the tower of which, on clear days, she'd climb to the top and look out across the sea towards Ireland; a Faraway as rich and exotic to me as the lands and oceans Sinbad flew over on his carpet. And how sometimes these got mixed up with the older stories she told, of ancient Princes and Princesses, huge boars and Giants, and terrible floods – villages and courts engulfed magically and awfully by the sea, their church bells ringing beneath the waves, royal pennants on towers swaying in the current like seaweed, bubbles of horribly surprised breath floating to the surface. And how it was there, with her, where I was safest and happiest, that I'd learnt to fear drowning.

But instead I asked him if he was afraid, sometimes? Of the river? Of the Great Lakes?

'I don't think I'll die on this river, Arthur. Or those lakes. But I'm not sure I won't, either.'

'Do you believe that Indian boy disappeared beneath the ground?'

McLeod took a long swig from the cup. He looked over to where the men's legs stuck restlessly out from the oilcloth, some of them flexing and pushing over dreamed portages. Godin's leg looked like a fallen log.

'I believe it can snow in June,' he said.

The next day the sun rose red and warm, and Godin's leg began to stink. The men paddled at a quicker tempo, as if they might outpace the stench.

His head lolled against my shoulder in the canoe, as hot as a potash furnace. He was muttering again about the cow that had broken out of its pasture, much afraid of his father's wrath if he couldn't find her. He began to call out to it. The men increased their tempo once again and broke out into a joyless version of a song – about a millwheel and a pie made of three pigeons – to cover up the sound. This turned ominously into a song about being very afraid of the wolves. I reached across and took hold of Godin's hand. The fever, and the fear of his father, had made it tremble.

'Don't worry,' I whispered into his hot ear. 'We'll find it.'

We passed down a rapid and I kept my eyes wide open. 'I see it,' I told Godin, referring to his cow, for what he was seeing was real enough to him. 'It's there at the edge of the woods.'

'See what?' he suddenly asked, as though waking.

I thought he must be back with us now, out of his father's pasture.

'The sea,' I said, 'the sea.'

He had been dead for an hour before we reached Lake Huron.

June 6th, 1804. Lake Huron.

We buried Young Godin in a small meadow on the shore of that great lake. This meadow appeared a green patch transported from another, softer, place – for everywhere around and about was formed of granite shelves and slabs, topped here and there by stunted, wind-bent pines. The lake itself was hiding under a blanket of fog, though I could sense its waters slowly heaving.

After we'd dug the pit, McLeod gave us all a dram of rum. Narcisse poured a drop of his onto Godin lying in his blanket there. Hyacinthe, Seraphin and Crebassa sprinkled some tobacco.

McLeod and I stood back a few paces. I asked him if this is what they did for their Last Rites and such.

'Up here, they make their own rites and rituals,' said McLeod. 'Away from their priests. Do you know what they probably see in there?'

I said I didn't. Except if he meant poor Godin.

'They probably see Old Nick's foot on the treadle of the loom,' he said. 'Because it's easier to be afraid of the Devil than a river or a lake. And most likely better, too. Otherwise, there'd only be bad luck and weather and water.'

The fog had almost cleared when Seraphin called a start. What a wide horizon it was. What an expanse of sky and light, slipping West all the way over the edge of the watery world.

This water was wonderfully clear. You could see the lake's bed far below, quilted with the sleek green backs of fishes, which, to those who didn't perpetually imagine themselves lying dead there, would have seemed quite beautiful. Behind us was Godin's little cross sitting in its stranded meadow.

A breeze was baffling the surface of the lake, shifting one way and then another. Crebassa said we should hoist a sail.

We'd need a better wind for that, said Seraphin.

Crebassa nodded, and then began a strange conjuring; a jonglerie, as the men called it.

He dropped a penny into the water, and after it a pinch of tobacco and a flint. 'For the Old Woman,' he said in a low voice, half whisper, half incantation. 'For the Mother of the Winds.' We waited, Seraphin studying the lake's surface, McLeod shifting his long limbs. Crebassa dropped a gun worm into the lake and repeated the incantation.

We waited again, until eventually the men reluctantly took up their paddles.

Yet within an hour the wind had settled and blew briskly westward. We hoisted a small tarpaulin as a sail and were soon moving swiftly over this inland sea, which was indeed a wonder – immense, brightly sparkling, dotted with a multitude of islands. And, looking back, I think it was then I began to realise I no longer had any clear notion of whose foot was on the treadle of what loom.

But let me skip forward, Esther, aided by that brisk wind, past all this. Because I find an abiding sadness in it, for that boy Godin, who you may only have seen for a second or two, but who I think of now, with his crooked, gentle smile and errant cow and violent father. Moths to candles are young men, and then two sticks in a lonely nowhere.

And off we sail, in search of furs and the mystery of a dead man and the pangs of a bruised and broken heart. Dead skins and live skins, and everything in between.

PART TWO

Opposition

1

How miraculously quick is ink. I've crossed Lake Huron and Lake Superior with one dip of a quill, where it would have taken ten thousand of them with a paddle.

And here we are, at the mouth of Kaministiquia River, ogling the wooden palisades and bastions of the NWC fort, which has yet to be re-baptised with the name of a Company Big Wig and is still called only New. Everywhere is hustle-bustle and hellow-bellow: canoes arriving, canoes departing; shots fired Indian-fashion in greeting, shots fired Indian-fashion in farewell; packs being unloaded onto the wharves; Northmen and Porkeaters and Indians and Clerks and Partners shouting greetings and curses and whoops in all their languages. Milch cows low, brick kilns puff, carpenters hammer and saw, blacksmiths beat spikes of red iron. In the air hangs the scent of wood chippings, wood smoke, wood sap; of tobacco, rum, high wines; of the hides of dead beasts and drying meat. The New Fort, the great Emporium of the Pays d'en Haut, fresh-risen from the forest. I marvel at it then, I marvel at it now, and we paddle on straight past it.

'Not our fort,' says McLeod, ruefully. 'Our fort,' he says, some minutes later.

On the other bank of the river is a bundle of sagging logs and a warehouse that slants leftwards into the marshy earth. Several stones have absented themselves from the chimneys.

The sagging bundle plays badly at being a cabin, with invitations in the walls and roof for any living creature who desires to fly or crawl or creep through them. A dilapidated mule chews its gummy cud in a clearing the forest wants back. Behind it, at a distance, rise the cliffs of that high undulating plateau the Saulteaux claim is a Giant in repose. And so indeed it appears: his chest swelled with piney breath; his stony, sleepy eyes pointed Heavenward.

Crebassa, reading my expression, explains that this is only a minor fort – that the XY's main rendezvous place remains to the South of us, at the Grande Portage, where the old NWC fort also is.

And that XY fort at the Grande Portage is more like the New Fort?

Oh no, he says, not at all. It is much smaller. And less grand. And not so well made. But the Knight says some day in the future this fort here might be like the New Fort.

I say this barely looks like a fort at all.

'And what do you see?' Crebassa asks Narcisse, gesturing to our buildings.

'I see the rain dripping on my head when I sleep tonight.'

'You see,' Crebassa says. 'He envisions the future.'

'The Fort of Decrepitude,' McLeod remarks bleakly to himself.

But if our first sighting of the XY fort is glum, it is a Halcyon Day compared to what waits for us inside.

There was nothing in our warehouse but mosquitoes, mice, and spider's webs.

I recall McLeod as he walked through its door, and then as

he walked silently back out again. He might have been Mr Janus: one face was writ with grim determination, the second only with grim.

The rest of us were waiting beside the wreck of our cabin. 'What of the Missouri furs?' I asked.

'There are no furs in there,' he replied.

'No furs in there,' the men repeated, as though it were the chorus of some forlorn Normandy ballad.

It was easy to read what was written on their faces: the wish that they'd turned back at Sault Saint Marie and were paddling home to Montreal. They looked at McLeod as though his luck were a deformity, a horrid goitre growing on his neck. But since the accident with Godin, and making their unspoken decision to stay with him, this goitre was now on all their necks. There was no need for anyone to say a word.

How could there be no furs? I said.

McLeod stared down at me as if I'd crawled out of a slop bucket. Adjectival, adverbial, Arthur, adjectival. Either the beavers had risen on the Resurrection Day, got back their bodies, and returned to live in the forest, or else he would suggest no adjectival furs had been delivered here.

But Mr Ogilvy had said the first cargo –

He knew what Ogilvy had adverbially said. But Ogilvy was a thousand miles away, in Montreal, and it was clear as day Long Arm and Copperhead hadn't set foot here. Nobody had for a long, long while. It would have been better to have discovered that the Sail and Herse and the NWC had pilfered them. At least then there'd be a chance of pilfering them back.

So what would we do?

We'd wait. What else could we adverbially do? And with

that, McLeod turned to retire with Mistress Shrub to our tent. The men did the same to the leaky cabin. And thinking it best to leave McLeod alone, I joined them.

Our immediate future was much as Narcisse had prognosticated. The rain came tumbling through the roof that first night. And the next one, too. During the day, the clouds swelled and fattened over the Giant's belly, erupting in plump drops, and the fearsome, rumbling din of that thunder which, you told me later, the bay at the mouth of the river was famous for, the Saulteaux believing it the noise made by gigantic birds. Thunder teaches fatalism. Here it comes, and here it is, and you are helpless to do anything but be in it. But where it comes from is all muddy water to me now. God told Job he made it, and spoke through it, too. But that was in the country where Job lived. It was the Thunder Birds who lived up in this country, so why shouldn't it have been the mighty flapping of their wings?

The men were subdued and hardly spoke, as if the storm were holding their tongues and deciding their Fates. For it was clear enough what they'd hoped and been half-promised – that they'd be done with the Missouri furs by Summer's end and paddling home before the freeze – had become far less certain. There were anxious, chilly looks in every eye. Voyageurs are experts in anticipating Winter. Even as the rivers thaw in Spring, they picture them freezing.

On the third day, the storm cleared. On the other bank of the river, so many packs of furs arrived it seemed that every animal North and West of us must surely be naked. And while nobody else arrived at our fort, it appeared as though everybody in the whole of the North West countries were coming and going and jawing there across the water: the Caesars of the NWC, the Chiefs of the Saulteaux and Cree, the Athabasca brigades, the Red River brigades, the Rainy River brigades. For this NWC fort was the centre point or pause of that great relay which led the thousands of miles from a beaver swimming in a faraway pond to becoming a hat on a gentleman's head. First, the Indians would hunt the animals and gather their furs. Then they would exchange these furs with the nearest trader in return for goods. Then the traders would transport these furs in packs from all the far-flung corners of the North West countries to the New Fort. And then the Porkeaters would transport them in their Montreal canoes from the New Fort to Lachine (and hence to Montreal). This fort was the hub of an enormous wheel, a place of gathering and convergence, the site of the Great Rendezvous.

Meanwhile, on our side of the river, McLeod was slumped on a tree stump at the edge of the forest. Down by the bank, Narcisse was whittling a woman out of a cedar bough. Seraphin had begun planting squash seeds in the clearing.

And where were you, Esther? This, I knew, was the question that lodged unspoken and uppermost in McLeod's mind – and had been lodged secretly there, all along, from my first glimpse of him at Lachine through every silent minute I'd spent beside him in our canoe. With this tormenting addition: namely, your reasons for having been in Montreal (which he feared might be connected to some other suitor). As for our Company errand – securing the Missouri furs Labrie had been supposed to be protecting, and our rendezvous with your father and Copperhead to secure the rest — these had always been secondary to his true purpose: the opportunity to find you and plead his case, to beg for a reconciliation.

And now, like Tantalus, just when he thought the fruit nearly in his grasp, it eluded him. When he'd told the men we must wait here at the mouth of the Kaministiquia for your father to arrive, McLeod's primary thought must have been that this was precisely why you had also travelled here. And since you'd travelled in an NWC canoe, it was logical to suppose you were lodged right there across the river, in the New Fort — a place which, for reasons that were soon to become apparent, was as impenetrable to him as the Tower of London.

I joined McLeod at his tree stump, and after several minutes of silence, during which he appeared to be constantly veering between vacant, hopeless staring, and lovelorn glances at the New Fort, and eying our stores of rum, I asked him what he thought it might be best to do, considering our predicament.

He told me that at this present moment, he was contemplating whether it might be best to throw himself in the river.

Our XY Company predicament, I added pointedly, suggesting that in consideration of Ogilvy's instructions it might be better for us to be discovering what exactly had happened to Labrie and the first consignment of furs. And if anybody had any knowledge of the whereabouts of Long Arm and Copperhead.

But of course, he said, leaping from his stump. Why hadn't he thought of it before! The solution to all our woes. *Perhaps* I'd like to paddle over and ask one of those NWC fellows at the New Fort. They'd surely be eager to help us locate our furs. They'd no doubt invite us merrily through the gates to share a dram. *Perhaps* that one on the bank who was kindly showing us his todger.

I looked across the river, and sure enough, he was.

In my defence, I was only then learning the nature of the Companies, and that there were stones that gave up blood more easily than the NWC gave up anything. Somewhere very far away, I suppose that Napoleon was considering Nelson's ships, and Nelson, Napoleon's. The history books will tell it was a year of famous oppositions. But I was still an infant in the cradle when it came to how we Companies 'opposed' each other, as it was termed – making it sound the grand and noble equipoise of Armies and Parliaments, but which only meant we scrambled and fought and wooed and connived for furs, and for the custom and favour of the Indians who procured them for us. The NWC and XY had become mirrors of each other (with our own XY the fainter reflection), so that a trader from one Company need only put up a woebegone post on some distant, lonely river before the other Company would erect their own post – like here – on the other bank. And then the two would settle in to glare at and menace each other. It was half the japing rivalry of schoolboys and half the deadly earnest of hard and grasping men, and was neither a pretty nor grand nor a noble thing.

The NWC men called us 'Potties', and many other names too, and would sometimes gather on their bank to shout these out to us, miming and mumming their meaning with their hands on their behinds and privy parts. That man and his member had been a mild introduction. On subsequent afternoons, they were far more vigorous in their pantomime, and made an entire line of moons on the bank: some smooth, some hairy, some cratered, some pocked and patterned with pox.

All of which is to say, it was no easy thing to ask them anything. And the gates of their fort, which had opened for the trade of the whole surrounding country, were closed as fast as a coffin lid against us.

McLeod sat back down morosely on his stump, and so I left him and joined Narcisse. Hyacinthe was sitting amongst some reeds on the bank, staring at the river. He'd been staring at the river ever since the storm relented. I asked Narcisse what he was looking for. 'He's watching for the man who robbed him of his nose. He is always watching for him, wherever we go. Always.'

I asked him who his sculpture was meant to be. He told me she was the woman who'd be his wife. Her name was Anna-Marie, and he'd marry her when we returned. But first he'd make her bigger, he said with a smile, and set about carving the knot in the wood that would be her bosom.

It was quite the sight, I said.

It was, he said, without looking up, his attention fixed on the intricate work of fashioning a nipple.

The NWC fort, I said.

Yes, he said, that too.

Meanwhile, high above the fort's palisades, on the watchtower, pacing in orderly circles, his coat and hat gleaming like raven feathers, was the Englishman Herse – the sunlight glinting from the surface of the looking glass he was holding, as if he were a Cyclops with its one refulgent eye. I wondered what it was he was looking out for, and supposed it was probably the same as us – the arrival of Long Arm and Copperhead with their consignment of furs. Except, as our opposition, he would be intent on taking them from us. I recalled Ogilvy's talk then, about Loose Fish and Fast Fish, and felt how everything here now seemed like a Loose Fish. And our vessel a leaky tub. And our Captain a besotted drunk, with barely half an eye on our intended quarry. And the water about us filled with sharks.

2

One happy illusion of this scribbling, Esther, is that I'm speaking to you; that these dead letters are alive in a mouth. I imagine your ear hearing them as much as your eye seeing them.

Did I ever tell you about Old Crebassa's ear? How he'd sometimes take it out of its leather purse and hold it up to his living one? I asked him once why he did this, and he said it was like those shells that wash up on an ocean strand and give back the remembered melody of waves. He said if he listened carefully, he could hear echoes of his past in it, everything his ear had once heard – the sounds of his happier days, and his sadder ones, too. He told me he often heard the voice of his wife in it. And who was she? He said she was a Saulteaux woman, who he'd not seen for many, many years. They'd met and married when he was a younger man but had quarrelled. It was she who'd bitten off his ear. And that was why they'd parted? Oh no, he replied, that wasn't the reason at all – he'd loved her dearly, more than enough to forgive her for an ear. He'd left her to go back to Montreal, and then hadn't had the chance to return to where she and her people lived. It was because of the trade, he said. The constant coming and going of it. And because he was a younger man then and thought the world would be full of women he'd love just as dearly. It hadn't been. He said when he heard her speak through his ear, she was often asking him again why he was leaving, and he no longer had an answer for her.

I wish I could hear your voice on this piece of paper. I wish I had an ear that spoke. So let me try, in my clod-hopping way, to make one.

It was during this time, as we waited opposite the New Fort, that I learnt to enjoy the pursuit of game. McLeod lent me his old NWC gun, with a twisted fox inlaid in silver on its stock, and after mastering the measuring of powder, the placement of flints, the choices of shot and ball, and all the other intricacies of its use, I'd range the woods beyond our fort in search of nutritious victims to lay low. And lay low they did, in a different fashion and of their own volition, for surely the presence of all those hungry men in the New Fort had made even the crows in these parts nervous. I became expert in the hindquarters of various beasts and fowls: the white of deer tails, like linen towels in the wind; the lanky gait of moose; the whirring backside-feathers of partridges.

One afternoon, after discharging a vast quantity of shot at the behinds of some geese – and feeling that silver fox to be shaking his head at me – I discovered you standing close by at the edge of the pond. The sun was shining down warmly upon us, driving the mosquitoes into the shade beneath the trees.

'At least the geese are safe,' you said. 'I'm not so certain about my frigging ears.'

It was the second time I'd heard you speak, Esther. The first to me. And hope you won't mind me putting you down unexpurgated. Perhaps you'll remember my reddening face, as I replied, 'The geese are amazingly nervous in these parts.'

'Yes,' you said. 'I'm sure they're unusually so. Your name is Arthur, isn't it?'

At this point, to my dismay, the geese circled back and flew directly and fearlessly over where we stood, with a terrific hooting and flapping.

Let me be like Narcisse for a second, with his whittling knife and his wooden love. Your black hair was tied tightly back from your forehead, revealing the small scar that runs down the side of your left cheek, between a little constellation of freckles. I could see the slight gap between your front teeth. I thought it very beautiful. I do.

A bundle of fur lay at your feet. 'Some amazingly nervous hares,' you said, seeing me looking there. You'd taken them with snares and showed me one of these, describing the best ways and places to set them (having witnessed my efforts with the gun). I'd seen snares before – the boys had used them on the farms near our house – but mooned over this one as though peering into the workings of an intricate clock.

'It's just a snare, Arthur,' you said.

I asked how you'd become so expert in their use.

Your mother had taught you. And needing to adverbially eat was an excellent schoolmaster, too.

As we spoke, you picked up one of the hares and with a few deft flicks and easings of a knife, slipped it effortlessly out of its skin with a faint shushing sound as the membranes parted, as if it were a sigh of relief and what the hare had wanted all along. You ran a hand down over its new nakedness and with a quick movement of your long fingers had its innards lying steaming on the grass.

Again, the geese made a hooting circle around us, impatient

to return to their pond. 'Here, you try,' you said, passing one to me.

'No Arthur, now you've pierced the flesh.'

'No, no, not there.'

'It's a knife, Arthur, not a frigging stone.'

Taking it from me, you slipped it out of its hare's form and into another as easily as an alchemist. 'Like this.'

And as you turned hares into meat, we talked a little. I asked about your mother, who'd taught you about snares. You told me she'd died when you were still a child and, afterwards, you'd been raised by your father, with some help from your mother's family when they were living close by. I tried imagining a younger Esther then, living in a fort like the NWC one perhaps, for many of the voyageurs and traders had Indian wives, and their children were often to be seen playing about the New Fort. But this wasn't a path I could properly follow, being one so ignorant as to have recently confused Saulteaux and Iroquois.

I asked if you had a Saulteaux name.

You said it wasn't polite to ask for names.

For a third time the geese circled over us. From somewhere came the tok tok tok of a woodpecker, terrifying grubs. Frogs chirruped in the pond. 'You know, your Frenchmen have a name for *you*,' you said, with a wry creasing of the skin about your eyes.

It seemed they had names for everybody, I said. It was Old This or Young That. The Red Haired, the Heron-legged, the Moose-nosed, the Fat, the Thin, the Short. I could only imagine what they'd found for me.

Indeed, you said, and began to place the bodies and skins of the hares in a bag that hung around your shoulders.

But what was it?

Maybe it was better if I didn't ask. You had to get back to the river, you said, taking four or five paces before turning back to me. 'Arthur,' you said, 'next time, aim a little in front of them.'

'In front of who?'

'The geese. When they're flying away.'

They'd flown over my head a fourth and fifth time before it occurred to me that I hadn't asked a single question about what had taken you to Montreal, or why you'd travelled up here to the New Fort with Herse and the Sail in the NWC canoe, or why you were now lodged in the New Fort, or where your father and Copperhead might be, or indeed anything that McLeod would have pulled his eyes out to know.

3

My journal is empty for the next weeks. One day might have substituted for the others thus: *June/July, all of them.*

No sign or word of Long Arm or Copperhead. I looked at animal tails. McLeod sat on his stump, trying to catch sight of Esther. Or else tried lurking outside the New Fort's walls, hoping he might encounter her, or that the sight of him would get her to soften and relent and come out to speak with him. But he is poorly constructed for lurking. The NWC men who spotted him hurled insults, and anything else to hand. Narcisse made Anna-Marie so heavy bosomed that if she'd come to life she would've fallen directly onto her face. Seraphin worked on his squashes. Hyacinthe surveyed the river for the thief of his nose. Crebassa smoked and chatted with his ear.

Eventually, McLeod's efforts to speak to you reached that Nadir I'm sure you recall well enough. The sight of him lurking constantly outside the NWC walls, under a rain of NWC insults, and offal, and myriad rotten things, must have indeed softened your heart a little, for one afternoon you came out and stood at the walls above him. Being not so very far away, off on one of my hunting jaunts, I caught vague fragments and snatches of the interview that followed. McLeod, staggered by his success, began insisting how though it looked like he had broken his engagement, by not coming to you at Rainy River, this had all been a terrible misunderstanding, and that anything you might have heard of his expedition was mostly a calumny. Unfortunately, Mistress Shrub had hardly improved his eloquence and turned him into a Pyramus at that wall. His pleas and excuses came out garbled, a slurry porridge of words, spreading confusion rather than understanding, and moreover prompted McLeod to make a disastrous detour, led on by the green-eyed beast. For instead of continuing to make his own case, he began asking why it was you had been in Montreal? If it was to be with some other suitor? And who might that be? Etc. But even so, he would be prepared to forgive you that.... I caught the strong gist of your next words, adverbial and adjectival, about the outrageous notion, more adverbial and adjectival, *of him forgiving you*. And then you were gone. And McLeod was back on his stump, his opportunity squandered, more firmly contemplating throwing himself in the river.

And continued so, for several days, until at last one morning, under the pale glare of the NWC arses, he roused himself from his Stump of Despond, summoning me to our tent. He told me he'd been trying to figure what Herse was up to on that adjectival watchtower, and why you'd been travelling with him and the NWC. This was where his mighty cogitations had led him. He still hadn't a mosquito's member of a clue what had taken you to Montreal in the first place, but as you were staying in the New Fort, it was clear you must now be waiting for your father, the same as us. As for Herse, the obvious conclusion was he was also watching for Long Arm – with the hope of getting his damned English hands on the Missouri furs before we could. That was why he and the NWC had provided you passage from Montreal to the New Fort. You must be a sort of bait or lure. For wherever Long Arm might be, eventually he'd come to collect his daughter.

All that time on the stump had clearly taken McLeod's reflections down roads aplenty, however tangled and shrub-scented they seemed to me. For he now added to these imagined conspiracies, saying he was sure Herse must have a further scheme to hatch. His guess was he was watching equally for Long Arm's partner, Copperhead.

When I asked why this might be, McLeod reminded me of what he'd told me back on the river – that Copperhead and Herse were great friends, though employed by different Companies. I should understand that during the entire time he'd known Herse and Copperhead, during his time at the Rainy River district, he'd never been able to think of the one without the other. He'd often had to remind himself they were with opposing Companies. If all opposition had been like theirs, then Napoleon would have given Nelson a glass of Madeira and a cigar at the Nile and that whole mighty Fisticuffs would've been a jovial slap on the back instead. It all seemed obvious to McLeod, now: Herse must be trying to discard even that notional opposition by getting Copperhead – or him and Long Arm both – to abscond the XY and join him in the NWC. It made perfect sense for all the parties involved. The NWC would get the Missouri furs, together with the even more valuable knowledge of their exact source (he was sure they'd offer Copperhead – and Long Arm too, if he chose – the most generous of terms). And Herse would have his friend in the same Company as him.

I could barely follow him down all these roads, so replied if this was true then what could we do? For a start, he said, we could make sure to find Long Arm and Copperhead first. Labrie must have had some notion of their whereabouts, or perhaps he'd been planning on joining them, when whatever had happened had happened to him. We could start there. And with this he summoned the men and told them he had a plan.

Which, it turned out, was exactly my original plan from before, and wouldn't have taken a Pythagoras to figure. He said it was imperative we discover what had happened to Labrie, and who had delivered him to the New Fort. And we must shake every tree in this forest to discover any rumours there might be about the whereabouts of Long Arm and Copperhead. It was no longer enough to simply wait on their arrival.

And how did he suggest we go about this, I asked, gesturing across the river, the same way he'd done to me several weeks ago.

One of us must try to get into the New Fort and pretend to be with the NWC. There they could ask subtle questions.

He meant they could be a spy, said Hyacinthe.

Somebody to glean information, said McLeod.

And who might this fortunate somebody-to-glean-information be, asked Hyacinthe? Why didn't McLeod go himself?

Look at him, said McLeod, indicating his own conspicuous height, which would have made him a Lop-Stick stalking amongst alder bushes. There was also the question of his former employ and current reputation. There was barely an NWC man in there who didn't know, and despise, him. There was no way to disguise himself. Lord knows, he'd thought of every means he might get in there, and there wasn't one.

'The same,' said Hyacinthe, pointing to his nose.

'The same,' said Crebassa, pointing to his ear.

All eyes now turned to me.

'Excellent,' said McLeod. 'Then it's settled. You can take Narcisse with you, Arthur.'

And that was that. Off Narcisse and I went, to play at Greeks and wooden horses.

As it was, fortune was briefly on our side and we didn't need a horse; we barely needed a disguise. A brigade of canoes arrived just as we crossed the river, and in the hubbub we ambled through the gates of the New Fort with scarcely a nod in our direction.

In the way of forts, I'd say I began my experience of them with a Capital, like a country bumpkin for whom the first city he sees is Rome (I didn't count our own XY one, as that was more Rome after the Visigoths had had their frolic in it). There were buildings for almost everything. Stores for trade goods, shops where you might buy silk scarves and beef boots, corn and grease sheds standing on their stilts. In its centre was a grassy square and a large house, which might have been a modest enough mansion in Montreal but here, magnified as it was by distance and lack of comparison, had been given the name Great Hall.

Narcisse had begun to enjoy our piece of subterfuge, acting as if we were two Swells on an outing. While I fretted and pulled my father's hat down close over my head, he stopped to linger around the carpenters at their sawing, to eye the blacksmith's wares, to ogle the contents of the shops. He had a joy in manufactures, in made things. And after a while I began to enjoy them myself, for it appeared objects from the entire world had made their way to this distant place: Vermillion from the Orient, Brazilian tobacco, Holland twine, Venetian beads, knives from Sheffield, axes from Birmingham. And while we gawped, Narcisse went about our secret work. In a voice made rougher than it was, with a touch of frostbite and starvation put into it, he asked whoever was near whether they'd heard of this dead fellow from the Winter, and who might have delivered his corpse? And if the questions turned back on us, he'd look down his nose at the questioner and mention Athabasca and say no more, imitating the lordly, aloof ways of the Athabasca men.

The spaces between the buildings acted as streets, and in them all types and ranks of men mingled – guides, clerks, voyageurs, Saulteaux, partners, agents. What I'd never anticipated was such an array of finery. There was hardly one of them that was not done up in his own version of Dandy: the voyageurs with their brightest sashes, caps and shirts, the partners in their top hats and tailcoats, the Saulteaux and Cree in their scarlet chief's coats and silver brooches. It was all push and press and preen and puff, a thronging of peacocks and hardly a hen.

While Narcisse was admiring the twine of a sturgeon net, I got jostled along in this current of fops and lost sight of him, finding myself outside the raw wooden walls of a newly erected building. Two burly Frenchmen with sawdust in their beards caught me eyeing it, and one said in a winking kind of voice, 'Looking for quarters, are you?'

I told him I had no need of accommodation.

And then the questions came. Where had I come from?

What brigade was I with? I attempted Narcisse's ruse. 'Athabasca,' I said, trying to puff out my chest, though it had no air left in it.

They looked me over like a piece of spoiling meat – my cheeks, my lips, my hands, my back – and found me not spoiled enough.

'And I've just come from Josephine Bonaparte's bedchamber,' said the first.

The other couldn't think of a witty phrase, so moved towards me instead. He had very large hands.

'These Porkeaters,' came a voice from behind me. 'They can't even fib properly. He's with me, gentlemen. A green fellow, straight from Montreal.'

I turned around.

Herse winked at me.

'A bold excursion, Mr Stanton, if I might say so,' said Herse. 'For an XY man.'

I thanked him and said he might call me Arthur.

'I wouldn't thank me quite yet, Arthur,' he said, a glint in his green ironical eyes.

We strolled away from the gaol, for that is what the building was (and wouldn't you agree that Herse was a man who always appeared to stroll, in any setting), passing the kitchens of the Great Hall and the powder store with its turf roof, the scent of roast fowls and brimstone mingling. He asked how my time had been since we'd first met.

I said it had had its difficulties.

It had been the same for him on his first outing, he said.

As we spoke, I admired his hat. An extremely fine and sleek

beaver had perished to make its felt. And then felt poorly for my own, which had been much battered and bruised along the road. By this time, we'd reached the base of the watchtower. Herse asked if I'd like to ascend it with him to enjoy the view. And while climbing the ladder, I considered what subtle questions I'd ask; subtle enough to uncover the schemes McLeod had attributed to him, subtle enough to evade the suspicions of even a man with Herse's reputation for sharpness and astuteness.

From the tower's summit, all the fort was visible, including the small fields outside the palisades where the corn and vegetables were grown and the milch cows grazed. And beyond this, the whole country. On one side of us, Lake Superior, with its headlands and islands and slumbering Giants; on the other, the river snaking away into the forest. Across it, our XY hovel appeared some botched and abandoned experiment in fort-making.

A bird's eye view being a rare commodity up there, it enlarged my questions. I asked him why it was the NWC had moved here, since they already had a fort at the Grande Portage. Herse said it was because the Grande Portage was in the United States, and the Americans had finally got around to realising this and would tax us if they could.

So where exactly was the border?

Herse adjusted his hat a careful inch and said they hadn't decided for certain. It remained a notional sort of border. But we were probably on the right side of it now, though many of the NWC and XY posts still traded in the country below it as if it were their own.

And the Americans?

The Americans were busy laying claim to everywhere they happened to walk. And were trying to walk as far and wide as they could. As far as the Pacific Ocean, just as the Knight had journeyed on his famous travels. There was an expedition afoot even as we spoke, he said.

But these were really the Indian countries?

They were. Though certain Indian nations claimed use of one part, and others the same part. For instance, where we stood was the land of the Saulteaux, but to the South and West of us it was the land of both the Saulteaux and the Sioux, portions of which were contended and known as the Debated Lands. Such was the way of territories and countries up here, he said. People could all lay claim to them without having the power to possess them entirely – or, instead, had a philosophy that wished their use rather than their possession. And why was that such a bad thing, he added, as though anticipating an objection. Men kicked and shouted at horses they owned but must coax and whisper and persuade and barter with the horses they only wished the use of. You might have a leaf, he said, without pulling up the root and walking away with the tree.

And that was the end of my lesson on the geography of the North West countries, which, all be told, left me little the wiser.

But I enjoyed the view, nevertheless. From up here there was nothing in it trying to bite or fool or drown me. Moreover, Herse did not seem like a shark, at all. To the contrary, standing beside him in his fine hat and frock coat – which appeared miraculously immune from the dust and dirt of the fort – it felt as though we were two gentlemen gazing upon an Alp and noting our feelings about it. And in much the same fashion he might have elegantly remarked on the sublimity of a crag or gorge, Herse spread his hands before him and said was this not an extremely large haystack in which to be searching for a needle?

It was, I said, caught up in higher sentiments, and disinclined to grubby them by asking what needle that might be.

Had Mr Ogilvy given me his speech about bones? He must have given it to everybody in Montreal. 'We must be concerned with what is covering them,' he said, expertly mimicking Mr Ogilvy's voice. 'You might discover a new continent, etc, etc.'

Yes, I laughed, the very same speech.

And doubtless there had been a whole oration about those furs from the Missouri country as well.

Yes, that too.

But what a tragedy about poor Labrie. McLeod had heard nothing yet of who'd delivered him to the fort? Or what might have happened to him?

None, I said, still caught up in the civilised converse of two like-minded gentlemen. I admitted McLeod had been more preoccupied lately by issues of the Heart.

But Labrie, said Herse, more insistent now, his eyes boring into mine. Had I been there when the voyageurs delivered him? If so, had something been discovered on his person? Some letter or note perhaps? Had McLeod not mentioned anything?

Not a thing, I said. We'd heard nothing about the whereabouts of Long Arm, either. Or Copperhead. Perhaps he himself had heard something, what with them being such fast friends?

Herse's smile disappeared. He said that good man's proper name was Ross, and I'd do well to use it in his hearing. Down below, a fracas had broken out about a chicken. A man was chasing a dog with a stick. There was only so long you could stand above it, he said sadly.

He next spoke at the bottom of the tower, as we were approaching the gate of the fort.

'You do understand that we are in opposition, Arthur?' he said.

I told him I did. And regretted it should be this way.

This was an imperfect world, he said. XY this and NWC that and HBC another. It was very tiring. The way he saw it, there were lots of kinds of men in this world and not enough alphabet for them all. While, though – in a better place – we wouldn't be XY or NWC, in this fort we must.

And with that, he took hold of me firmly by the collar of my coat and pushed me roughly towards the gate, making sure this action was plainly visible to everyone around us. At its threshold, he paused and whispered in my ear, 'My apologies, Arthur. An imperfect world,' and then kicked me very elegantly, and very hard, on my behind.

Out I tumbled, into the dirt.

Back on our side of the river, McLeod and the men asked what we'd discovered.

Narcisse had discovered plenty. The word was that Labrie's body had been received at the New Fort by the doctor fellow who oversaw it during the Winter. He was currently tending some injured men at the Rat Portage fort but was due to return in a week or two. Ah, said McLeod. That must be Munro.

Narcisse's next words sent a chill through all the men. He said there was a rumour in the fort that Long Arm and Copperhead had never intended to return to the Kaministiquia with their furs. This rumour had it they'd cached them somewhere else entirely. At a Secret Post. Somewhere between here and the Missouri country. As for where exactly that might be, nobody seemed sure. Some said the Great Mire, others the Mandan Villages, others the Debated Lands.

The men looked as though Mr Winter had come to grimly shake their hands. They stood in silence, as though half frozen already.

And what had I discovered in the fort? McLeod asked.

I told him I'd had less success in my espionage.

Meaning adjectivally none. Then we'd have to wait and see what the doctor, Munro, had to say.

4

A week or so after my expulsion from the New Fort I'd gone to our own warehouse to make an inventory of our supplies of rum and shrub and high wines (for that year the whole forest was awash in liquors; it had become the cruel and disastrous lubricant of all transactions), only to discover several of our barrels breached and mostly empty.

'Those fuckers,' exploded McLeod when I showed him. 'Those rascally fuckers.'

Crebassa and Hyacinthe joined us, staring at the wet earth beneath the barrels as though it was their blood that had been spilled. There was much profane mention of communion wafers.

McLeod paddled immediately across the river and – navigating the smirks and winks and behinds of some of the NWC men – approached the gate of the fort. Three times he battered it with his bony fist, calling for one of the gentlemen there to come out to him. None did. But a few hours later the Sail appeared at the gates and, accompanied by several men, paddled over to where we'd gathered on the bank. One of the staved barrels lay before us like a toppled and blasphemed god, while the crew sniffed morosely at its departed fumes. A gristly, enraged rasping came from where Hyacinthe's nose had once been.

I shall condense the discussion that followed and offer its

gist, to wit: (McLeod) they had staved our barrels; (the Sail) they hadn't staved our barrels. At last, to avoid the spilling of real blood, a compromise was settled upon: we would all swear on the Bible that no more barrels would be staved in the future.

'Somebody fetch a copy of the Book,' the Sail called out to us.

We stood in silence. There wasn't a Bible among us.

'By God. Well, somebody bring me *a* book then.'

All eyes now turned to me. I went to fetch my journal.

'No, no,' said McLeod. 'It must be a real book. We can't be swearing on Arthur's scribbles.'

Again, all eyes were upon me. I went reluctantly to fetch my copy of Xenophon.

The Sail stood by the riverbank, my father's book in his plump hand, and one by one the men came forward to place their grubby fingers on it, swearing, by all the Saints who hadn't existed when it had been written, that nobody would touch the others' liquor. Hyacinthe and Narcisse were the last to swear but began arguing who'd go first, grabbing at the book as though battling over marbles in a schoolyard, until at last it came free of any grasp and span into the air, landing in the shallow water by the bank. Xenophon, who had forded the Tigris, now sank slowly onto the bed of the Kaministiquia.

I looked on aghast. But the rest of the men paid no heed to it and at last departed to their various places.

And I was left sitting on a log by the edge of the river, holding the pulped and dripping remains, pulling my father's battered hat more tightly onto my head. What would he think if he could see this? *Of course* – that is what he'd think. *Of course*.

This pulp was a perfect Emblem of my neglect of the Greeks and my studies and everything else that had shaped his lack of hope in my prospects.

Still deep in such dreary ruminations, I found myself asked what it was about this sopping mess that made me sad.

It was you, Esther, who'd come to sit beside me on the log.

As the pages dripped onto my lap, I explained how the book was an Emblem of how I'd disappointed my father's expectations of me.

So, my father had wanted me to be a dry book, you said.

Oh no, it was merely a Symbol.

You were smiling. Ah, the book was merely a Symbol. Who would have thought such a thing.

I told you how it was in Greek but I'd never had the skill and learning to read it.

Perhaps then, if it was making me sad, it was better not to think of it as a Symbol or Emblem at all, but as a book that had fallen into a river. And besides, you added, sweeping your hand before us, this was not Greece. It was, I thought, a very lovely hand. Across the river, beneath the palisades of the NWC fort, two men were bludgeoning each other with their fists. On our side, Hyacinthe was plucking a baby swan he'd killed with a club.

No, I said, it wasn't Greece.

And there were many other languages here to learn, you said. Which might prove more useful to me in my profession.

We sat for some time on this log, lost in our own thoughts. My own were now not inconsiderably concerned with you sitting beside me.

This question of fathers and expectations was a difficult

one, you said at last. Take your own father, MacDowell (or Long Arm, as I'd doubtless learnt to call him), and his expectations for you. It had never been a question while your mother lived, but then lately he'd become concerned with what Scottish men should think such things should be, and decided the proper thing to do would be to go to Montreal and getting you a young lady's education, similar to the one that his great aunt had had, forty years before, in Inverness.

I said it was just like fathers to be bound by what they'd known themselves as children. I fancied my own would've liked me to be a country parson in Sussex. For even in the realm of Imagined Lives, my brothers would have run the ancestral family estate. But perhaps I might have tended to their spiritual needs, if only I could have read the New Testament in Greek.

You said Imagined Lives were your own father's difficulty. Before this notion of what Scottish men might expect from their daughters had popped into his head, you'd been happy enough with your Actual Life.

So it was your father who'd made you go to Montreal?

No, or not exactly. You'd had an arrangement with *another*, but had made a promise to your father that if this arrangement didn't turn out as you expected, then you'd try Montreal. For one season at least.

And how had your time there been?

What was there to say. Adjectivally woeful. You'd been lodged with some dry old stick of a Scotswoman distantly related to your father, who'd taken it upon herself to act as a sort of governess. One much like his great aunt in Inverness, you supposed. Perhaps she'd been exhumed.

And what'd she wanted you to learn?

You took a moment to consider.

Mostly how to draw flowers you'd never adverbially seen.

Another moment.

And to sew patterns of those flowers. And to read poems about those flowers. And to pretend to forget all the flowers you knew about. You'd refused even to touch the adjectival piano.

I blushed. For isn't there a certain intimacy in the sharing of anger? More so than laughter, even? Not sure exactly what to say, I said nothing. And knowing there is a good chance you'll never ask me, Esther, let me say it began in that moment, on that log: a fizzing, jangling sort of feeling in my belly, a sudden wanting to say the right things, which I hardly knew then was desire, which after all is wanting, and wanting. I continued to say nothing.

'You're shy, aren't you Arthur?' you said.

We sat and watched as the feathers from Hyacinthe's murdered swan blew over the bank of the river and the clouds skirted the top of the Giant's belly. My heart had begun to beat very fast.

And now you were returning to live with your father?

Yes, wherever that might be. He was a restless man, always searching for somewhere new – or at least had been since your mother died.

And what would you do? Wait for him to arrive here at the Kaministiquia?

You'd probably be better off finding him than waiting for him, you said. It had been some weeks already, with no sign or word. Had I heard anything?

Only what I thought you'd probably already heard in the New Fort. That there were rumours he'd never intended to cache his furs here. And then, following on from the fizzing, jangling feeling that was so new to me, another novel feeling – the guilt of feeling it for another's beloved. Prompted by this, I forced myself to mention McLeod. I said he was eager to know your intentions. He was rather desperate for another hearing.

Adjectival McLeod could mind his own adjectival business. And it would be balmy day in January, in Athabasca, before you listened to another adjectival word of what he had to say.

And then, as if conjured, as if jongleried, McLeod appeared, walking towards the riverbank through the snowstorm of swan feathers. When I looked back, you were already disappearing into the trees. This was the way of it at the New Fort – to McLeod, you remained carefully invisible, however much he lurked about trying to encounter you; while you were happy to appear to me (though looking back, perhaps these first meetings might have been more in the way of gleaning information).

Afterwards, I went down to the edge of the river and returned the *Anabasis* to the Kaministiquia. To begin its journey to another sea.

5

I was now being hoisted on the horns of a dilemma, one that might have twisted the wits of even a clerk less green. On that wretched piece of paper in my pocket, I was contracted to serve the XY Company and its interests. More immediately, I was responsible for our men and their interests. But it was clear enough by this point that somewise we were all of us become mere instruments of McLeod's single interest – the cogs and wheels which would allow him to follow the path of his besottedness, namely the means to reconcile with you. And yet, McLeod had risked his skin for poor Godin, which counted for a great deal up there, and had joined the men to him, however reluctantly. As did the prospect of getting their hands on the Missouri furs, which would deliver them what counted for riches in a voyageur's world. The rest of the men were not blind – they had realised McLeod's true object, just as I had – and here was the uneasy and unvoiced bargain, I think, that had been struck between them: that as long as McLeod's quest might also lead to the accomplishment of what they hoped to obtain, then they would follow him. McLeod had said Herse and the NWC were using you as a bait to draw your father, and hence his furs. I would use a gentler analogy, Esther, and say that in the eyes of our XY crew, you were either the honeycomb the precious bee would be drawn to, or else the bee we must follow in order to find the honeycomb.

As for me, during those weeks I realised that however airy and dreamy my reasons for joining the XY had been, I had now at least some semblance of an obligation to it – or more properly, the Company men I'd journeyed with. And then of course there was that fizzing in my breast (but that was another set of horns, which would become sharper soon enough).

It wasn't long after the episode of the staved barrels that McLeod, having drained a considerable portion of one of those remaining, confided in me the scheme he'd hatched in his cups, presenting it as though it were a Revelation sent in a cloud. His current predicament presented nothing less than a Miraculous Solution. Since we'd had no sign or word of Long Arm, and you would not hear his entreaties, he'd prove his love for you by finding him. Making it his quest, like a Knight of Old. To his last adjectival breath. It would prove him True and Devoted, wipe away all misunderstandings. And so on, and so forth.

But wouldn't we have to find Long Arm anyway, I reminded him, in order to collect the Missouri furs.

What pettifogging, cold and clerkly views I had, he said, bellowing shrub-vapours into my face. I had no adjectival clue of the Travails of the Heart. And then, after all this high chivalric babble, added more quietly this prosy addendum: since, Esther, you wouldn't hear him out properly, and didn't believe what he'd already told you, and now refused to even see him, perhaps he might get access to your father's ear first and convince him what had truly happened, with the hope that Long Arm would help him plead McLeod's case with you. But first he would make one more attempt with you. With this, he stomped off and paddled over to the New Fort, to announce his intentions. By now the others had joined me and we watched from our side of the bank as he staggered drunkenly beneath its palisades. He was shouting up at them and, there being no wind, we could make out his words. Esther, he kept calling out, slurring every 's' like a man half-paralysed by snake venom. You must believe me, Esther. This is madness, Esther. You must understand, Esther. But I'll find him for you, I swear, Esther. I'll prove myself, Esther. I'll make this right, Esther. I never changed my mind, Esther. Never. Etc. Etc.

Needless to say, the NWC men within the fort found this spectacle extremely amusing. Several climbed up the walls to shout back at him in rough mockeries of a lady's voice. Oh, McLeod, if only your member were not so small, etc. Oh, McLeod, I never came, etc. Oh, McLeod, take these gifts as proof of my heart's affections. And down rained a box of cabbages upon his head.

'Our noble leader,' said Narcisse.

Hyacinthe punched the horsefly sitting on his thigh.

The next morning, we caught sight of the Rat Portage brigade gliding toward the wharves of the New Fort, their songs drifting before them down the river. McLeod staggered out of his tent and ran towards us, shouting, 'Get that damned canoe in the water.'

When we arrived on the other bank, the brigade was unloading packs of fur onto the wharf and the gentleman leading it, who must be the doctor fellow, Munro, was approaching the gate. McLeod ran after him. Herse, I noted, had departed his eyrie on the watchtower.

Meanwhile, Hyacinthe's gaze had become fixed on one of the Rat Portage voyageurs.

'Uh oh,' said Narcisse.

Hyacinthe leapt onto the wharf. 'It's him,' he announced.

'Who?' I asked.

Crebassa exhaled a cloud of smoke. 'It doesn't matter who. It's always him or him or him,' he said, gesturing to each of the voyageurs with the stem of his pipe. It was barely returned to his mouth before Hyacinthe had bolted forward, grabbing hold of the voyageur standing nearest him. The collision of his forehead upon this man's nose made a fleshy thud and in the next instant the two of them were coiled and grunting in the grass. As the other voyageurs tried to disentangle them, they became twined together, until they were a growing ball of men, a writhing composite, like snakes gathering for warmth in the first frosts of Autumn.

'We should fetch him, I suppose,' said Narcisse.

Crebassa puffed thoughtfully on his pipe. 'Give him a minute or two,' he said. 'He's better company, afterwards.'

When, at last, the ball of men had become single men again, McLeod had returned, and Hyacinthe, with new blood dripping over his old wound, was attempting to hide an elated grin.

Turning to McLeod, I inquired whether he'd managed to speak with Munro. He had.

And what had he discovered?

'We go,' he called out to the men in reply, clambering back into the canoe.

'To where?' asked Narcisse.

'To the falls.'

'What falls?' I asked in alarm.

After some delay, occasioned by tending to Hyacinthe's injured face, we left Seraphin to oversee the fort and set out, paddling upriver all through the afternoon, and through a moonlit night too, only slowing our strokes as the sky began to lighten, revealing a great plume of mist. A low rumble had been building for several pipes, the current strengthening against us. Eventually, we were forced to land the canoe and line it from the shore. The rumble blossomed to a terrific din, and the trees parted to reveal the Kakabeka Falls.

I've read much of waterfalls recently, mostly written by mooning, frock-coated Englishmen, considering them as they might a vintage of port or a painting on a wall – with this one having just so much Majesty and that one a little less Sublimity, and usually housed like a pearl in (always careful not to glance at the paths and roads and footprints) a forest Primeval, surrounded by a hush Immemorial, and so on and so on. I'll not add to their parlour-room raptures. You know what that falls looks like, Esther, and what you saw in it. As for me, it looked like an awful lot of water, falling an awful long way down, and what I saw in it was this: the damp, green shadows of old nightmares; the sleek, sad back of Godin's head, turning around and around in a pool.

McLeod, who for the duration of the journey had reverted to Mute, now informed us we were in search of a house.

'A house?' said Crebassa. In every direction there was nothing but trees and rocks and mist. 'Whose house?'

'A man they call the Governor.'

'The governor of what?'

He had no time to explain every adjectival thing. According to the doctor, Munro, this was where Labrie had been found.

He'd been delivered to the New Fort by an island Scotsman. Though what Labrie was doing travelling past here in the Winter, he didn't adverbially know.

McLeod told the others to keep guard of the canoe. I was to go with him. Crebassa sat down and lit a pipe. Hyacinthe and Narcisse took their paddles and tried to bludgeon the vast armoured backs of some sturgeon that were milling in the shallower pools.

We found the house nestled in the lee of the falls. It was fashioned out of pieces of driftwood, intricately knotted around a jagged outcrop of granite. This wood was as smooth and pale as bone, of all different shapes and lengths, like a heaped ossuary, an edifice of ribs, femurs, spines, gigantic knuckles. The skeletons of Ogilvy's antediluvian beasts. Above it, smoke snaked out from a crude stone chimney, twisting and knotting skyward as though it were the driftwood metamorphosing into an airy form.

'It's like Crusoe's Island house,' I said.

'Not like a book,' said McLeod, though he didn't sound half so sure now.

We found a hide door, gave it a shake, and called out hello.

'Come in, come in,' replied a voice from within, the way a distracted parson might usher you in for tea.

McLeod turned to me and whispered, 'Best call him Mr Governor.'

'Mr Governor, sir,' I said.

In front of us loomed a corpulent, claret-faced man, his belly pushing out against the buttons of a faded red waistcoat. His head, flanked by long cascades of white hair, separated by a pink, bald circle, almost touched the low roof. 'Ah,' he said, as though I were an underling whose name he'd temporarily misplaced, 'and you are?'

'Arthur,' I said.

'And McLeod, Mr Governor.'

'Well, take a seat, boys.'

There were no seats except a throne made of driftwood, which he sat on. We sat on the floor. Behind him, a pile of leather-bound almanacs was half-toppled against the wall. The names of English counties wrestled with the mildew on their covers. Inside them, a wet Spring and poor harvest would be prognosticated for Wiltshire, fifty years ago.

'McLeod,' said the Governor. 'You must be one of our Orkney men? Though not my absconded one. That rascal, Spey.'

'I am Scottish, sir, but my family are not from those parts.'

'Yes, yes. Fine men from those islands. Except for your parsimony, of course. But that is understandable. I remember stopping there on my first voyage to the Bay. They were all collecting seaweed. And burning seaweed. And not a tree in sight. What an awful smell it made. I often told Spey that this place was a Paradise in comparison.'

'My family,' McLeod began, but then thought better of it. 'I was wondering if I might ask your assistance, sir.'

'With the trade?'

'After a fashion.'

The back of the dwelling was formed out of the granite outcrop, pocked by a small cave. From this there erupted a sudden shuffling and snorting, rising over the faint rumbling of the falls. The Governor, unperturbed, and unprompted, fell into reminiscence, recalling his first years with the Hudson's Bay Company at Prince of Wales Fort. How they battled the French, he said, his eyes lighting up. How the Cree brought them furs to be sent to London. How they were easier days. The volume of the shuffling and snorting increased. A gloomy, greenish light struggled in through a parchment window.

'But to return to the business at hand,' said McLeod.

'Oh, I'm no longer in the world of business,' replied the Governor, the claret skin creasing around his eyes. 'I'm a countryman now. Retired. In his little castle.' He gazed plaintively up at the window, as though he might saunter outside into an orchard escaped from his mouldy almanacs, to pick some Wiltshire pears.

'It's about a visitor you might've had,' said McLeod, 'during the Winter. A Frenchman. A trader named Labrie.'

'Samuel!' exclaimed the Governor.

McLeod and I turned at the same moment, to witness a large pig emerge from the mouth of the cave. It looked thoughtfully up at its master, its small piggy eyes shaded by long lashes, and then stepped delicately around McLeod's feet and out the door.

'He has excellent manners,' said the Governor, pointedly. 'Unlike many in the trade.'

'Indeed,' said McLeod.

'I let him wander where he wishes, like his namesake, Mr Hearne. In the Bay, the white bears would have taken him, but here he's a formidable fellow.'

'I have no doubt of it, sir,' said McLeod, 'but to return to the Frenchman –' The veins in his neck had begun to throb.

'When the French came against us at Prince of Wales Fort,

I had the canons ready,' cried the Governor, leaping abruptly from his chair. His trousers had gone in the knees, revealing caps as red and knobbly as over-ripe crab apples. For a second, he appeared ready to set light to a fuse. 'But we didn't fire a single shot,' he said, falling back despondently onto his throne, his white, hairless shins expressing all the melancholy of old and thwarted men. 'Hearne wouldn't give the order. He was our Governor then. I called him what he was – a coward!'

As if summoned, the pig reappeared. He eyed McLeod and me suspiciously before returning to his cave.

'I am sorry to press, sir, but this man –'

'Ah, you must mean the frozen fellow. My servant Spey discovered him above the falls.'

'That would be him,' exclaimed McLeod. 'Could he speak when he was discovered? Did he say where he'd travelled from?'

The Governor became thoughtful. He was thoughtful for quite a long while. He tilted his head back and ran his fingers through one side of his white hair.

'What are you thinking, sir?'

'I'm thinking how odd this world is. For that's exactly what the Englishman asked.'

'Englishman?'

'Yes. The Englishman who was here an hour ago, with his country wife.'

McLeod expelled his breath slowly, over grinding teeth. 'A man named Herse?'

'Indeed.'

'That was not his wife!'

Some men have faces that cannot help making a pantomime

of their thoughts. McLeod was among them. The little muscles and sinews of his were padding frantically this way and that, like a dog who's had three bones tossed his way and can't decide which one to take. Had this frozen man said anything at all? he asked.

How would he know, replied the Governor. The frozen French fellow could barely speak, being half-dead with the cold, and beset by the sort of delusions that being frozen often gave men – that sheets of ice were warm blankets and banks of snow sunny meadows and the like. He thought for a second. But there was something about a place.

'What place?' McLeod said, his voice rising.

The Governor now raised himself, on both his chair and his dignity, and declared he wouldn't be spoken to like this by an Orkney man.

I interceded, mimicking as best I could my father's Sussex Gentleman and glowering at McLeod as if he'd made a pig of his Latin. 'Forgive him, Mr Governor, sir. If I might press a bit further on the matter of this place. Do you recollect its name?'

'A French name. The folle something.'

'The Folle Avoine?' said McLeod.

'That's the very name the Englishman suggested. And his wife, whose language was quite foul. There was a lake, too. I think it was called Yellow.'

I won't describe the various antics of McLeod's face over the next minutes. It's enough to relate what the Governor, in his zig-zagging way, eventually told us: namely, that his servant, the Orkney man named Spey, had delivered Labrie, who by that time was a frozen body, to the New Fort. And that the Governor had provided six Spanish dollars to pay for the poor fellow's remains to be returned to Montreal.

I asked where this servant was now.

The rascal had absconded, said the Governor. Had never returned from the New Fort. He glared at McLeod. 'You have no loyalty, you Orkney men.' And then he was back, arguing with Hearne about those cannons, one Age overflowing and interrupting the other. And since there was no returning him entire to this present one, we offered our farewells.

Outside, a breeze was beginning to blow, swirling the mist of the falls around us, putting the air in motion, which was a great relief, for inside, it had begun to seem as though we were in a green shadow where time and season were as stalled and mildewed as Wiltshire in the almanacs. The Governor had followed us to the doorway and stood there, the two flanks of his hair trailing behind him. An old man from a book in the Bible. A Bardic man. Samuel's nose poked around the edge of the door.

'As cracked as a fucking pot,' muttered McLeod, striding quickly ahead. And then began cursing Herse for having got there before us. And then ranting about how Herse must have struck some kind of bargain with you, to accompany him. The bait and the hook together. And now, damn it all, they had the same information and direction as us. By this time he was some distance ahead.

And what did we do now? I called after him.

We should go South, he said. Immediately. It being imperative we reach Yellow Lake before you and Herse. Lord knew, if you found your father before McLeod himself, you and Long Arm would probably be off straight away, who knew where, leaving my companion's hopes royally scuppered. And if Herse was to find Copperhead and your father, the furs would most likely be away too, directly into an NWC warehouse.

And so it was settled. This is what McLeod told the men: that Labrie, with his final words, had mentioned Yellow Lake and the Folle Avoine district. Therefore, he was almost certain, this was where the Secret Post was, and within it the Missouri furs. We'd search for it, taking our goods to trade with in the meantime. And if luck was with us, we might yet be away before the Winter and back to Lachine before the ice came.

And was anybody else privy to these last words? Hyacinthe asked.

Perhaps, said McLeod, after a pause.

Perhaps someone from the NWC? Perhaps the lady who'd been travelling with them? Perhaps Herse?

We would be there first, said McLeod. He was sure of that.

Back at the fort, as we made our preparations swiftly to embark, I cornered McLeod in his tent and insisted he show me on the Knight's map where we were headed. He unfolded it with a huff and moved his finger impatiently down the western shore of Superior, past the Grande Portage, until it came to a halt near the southwestern corner of the lake. Beneath it, the map was almost entirely unmarked except for a few scribbled rivers. He traced a brief circle over the blank space. This was the Folle Avoine, he said. The upper reaches of the Missouri and the Mandan villages were over to the west. And the Debated Lands? He traced another circle, covering almost exactly the same blank space. It seemed a rather risky place for any post, secret or otherwise, he remarked. Personally, he would have chosen somewhere to the North. Why risky? I asked. Oh, I shouldn't dwell on that. Probably not so risky for traders, he thought. When pressed, he refused to elaborate and so I asked about Yellow Lake instead, it being nowhere on this map. Had he been there before? No. But he had a notion where it was. A notion! Enough to get us there, he said. Before anyone else adverbially did. And with that strode out the door.

But before we depart, let me say a brief farewell to Seraphin. For as the rest of us hurriedly gathered the packs and prepared the canoe, he paced around the clearing where his squashes were planted. When McLeod approached him, he looked down at the ground and apologised. For what? said McLeod.

Seraphin replied it was for him not wanting to join us. He wished to watch his squashes grow.

'The squashes? You want to watch the squashes grow?'

'Yes, Mr McLeod.'

'You realise the XY will probably send you down to Montreal, with no wages?'

'I know,' he said. 'But in truth, I'm tired of looking at water. I want to watch them grow.'

'Then I hope they do grow, Seraphin,' McLeod said, and shook his hand.

And with that we headed South, without a guide or steersman, toward the blank spaces beyond the Grande Portage – which were in Saulteaux country and Sioux country and United States country and NWC country and XY country.

PART THREE

Debated Lands

1

The first time I heard an owl hooting on the shores of Yellow Lake, I thought it merely an owl; that hooting was what owls did at night, while perching in trees and contemplating mice. It was the last time I'd have such a thought. For in the Folle Avoine, which was also the Debated Lands, nothing was one thing alone. There wouldn't even be a first time for the eerie laments of the wolves or the keening of the loons.

But we're not there yet.

Our present journey was a prefiguring one, an antechamber where Lake Superior played its own tricks. For nervous day after nervous day, we hugged its shores – the tree-topped islands, the granite cliffs, the steep headlands, and whatever Giants or Thunder Birds slumbered upon them. The rest of the men took upon themselves the anxiety of Seraphin's watching, eyeing the changing winds and water, fearing waves that could, in an instant, run like young mountains. But the truth is, I noted this new scenery more with my innards than my eyes.

Our diet had changed with the terrain. We'd run out of peas and grease, and what little flour we had was saved for special occasions. We ate meat and fish, which we traded for with the Saulteaux we encountered on our way. And more meat and fish. We boiled it, we roasted it, we burnt it. The men prospered. My own stomach fell into a miry ruin. For league after league it came out, each time in volumes and stenches more prolific and awful. My insides had become Les Vases. McLeod explained this wasn't unusual for novices in the trade; that a diet of meat with no bread or corn or vegetables took some adjustment. He made me sleep outside the tent at night.

During the day, having taken Seraphin's place in the stern, McLeod navigated. I'll be generous, and say we made a halting progress. In his absence, Seraphin had begun to seem like Magellan. Each morning, in the half-light, McLeod would take out the Knight's much creased and folded map and, running his finger firmly along it, announce confidently we'd reach this place or that. And the end of each day would find us becalmed at the mouth of a river that turned out to be a bay, or some mysteriously wandering isle, and his spirits would have become as crumpled as his map, and he would have become convinced you and Herse were going to overtake us. The day and the territory split him in two: there was a Dawn and Dusk McLeod; one that felt himself one step ahead, the other about to be one step behind.

The bewildering course of our route, and the prospect of being second to the NWC, had also begun to make the men nervous. For, especially after the spectacle under the palisades of the New Fort, they had begun grumbling to the effect that McLeod's heart (and alas, when I say 'his heart' they said his member) should not be our sole compass needle. As I've said, they'd made their uneasy bargain with him: that they would help him follow his desire if he led them to theirs – which was to get those furs and then get home. While McLeod fumbled with his map, they'd started scanning the horizon anxiously, looking for NWC canoes.

It was a great relief then when we arrived at last at a sandy promontory on the southern shore, near the mouth of a river. This was the Brule, which should lead to the St Croix, which would most certainly lead us to Yellow River and then to Yellow Lake, announced a confident Dawn McLeod. And soon enough that Dawn and its rosy fingers spread over us all.

It was Crebassa who brought the news. He'd been trading for *wattap* with an elderly Saulteaux woman, who'd told him of a rumour about a Scottish man living in a shack some miles away in the forest.

A Scottish man, Narcisse and Hyacinthe exclaimed. Only one, or maybe two? And how long was this fellow's right arm? What colour was his hair? A shack. *Or a post?* Crebassa said he knew no more than what he'd been told, but it was easy to see they were already half-lifting those Missouri furs onto their backs. As for McLeod, he was brightening and brightening, the pantomime of his face saying clearly: at last, a stroke of adjectival luck!

And where was this post?

Crebassa gave him some directions.

Leading from this road?

Crebassa nodded and McLeod told me to fetch my pipe. The two of us would follow it immediately.

But what road? I asked.

This one, he said, indicating the forest with his hand.

He meant this *forest*.

The Indian roads were a great mystery to me then, as those water roads and graveyard roads had been before. To the Indians, and the more experienced Winterers, they were as clear and plain as the cobbles of the Rue Saint-Paul. But for one not accustomed to them, they were no more than a few stray leaves being disturbed here, an exposed root there, maybe a broken stick further on. It seemed to me a thunderstorm, or a rutting moose, or almost anything, could make signs identical to these roads.

McLeod stamped and stomped his way ahead and was almost out of sight after the first mile. Eventually, he paused for a pipe and shared Crebassa's directions with me. We should follow this road until we reached a beaver pond and – keeping it on the side of the sun – follow its shore thus and thus until we reached a swale, and after that an eagle's nest, and then a pine which had been struck by lightning, and after that… and on and on in a litany of features that were all Alpha and Omega to me.

Stamp, stomp, went McLeod, with me stumbling in his wake, until after about an hour he stopped again. 'We've reached the eagle's nest.'

I couldn't see any eagle's nest. There were trees. And then more trees.

Stomp, stamp, stomp. More trees. A beaver pond. Another beaver pond. A swale. Another swale.

It was getting rather dark, I remarked after several more miles.

There was plenty of day, said McLeod. Now where was that burnt tree?

Soon it was easy enough to track McLeod: I need only listen for his voice. 'Where is that frigging tree?' 'Where is that fucking swale?' The whole forest turned adjectival. At some point, we came to the edge of a large spruce swamp that didn't appear part of the directions at all. The light faded further as we stumbled around it. 'The Swamp of Crebassa's Ear,' muttered a McLeod fast approaching Dusk. 'These directions are useless. His good ear hears Saulteaux about as well as the missing one.' It'd be best if we camped here and gave ourselves a fresh start in the morning, he decided, his tempers edging further into their melancholy Hemisphere. He told me to light a fire and reached into his pack to fetch a small keg of rum.

The flames lit up the trunks of the trees and licked the deep shadows between them. A thousand miles of shadows, I thought, in every direction. Ohio and the Mississippi below, Athabasca and the Hyperborean Sea above. To one side the mountains and rivers the Knight had written of, on the other my father in his study reading Thucydides. The vastness made your heart pound two ways at once: one for the marvel of it, the other for the fear of it.

McLeod passed me the rum and I remarked that Herse was right – this was a very large haystack.

Herse, exclaimed McLeod, sitting up straighter beside the fire. When had I been speaking to Herse? What had I said to him?

Only a few words in the fort, I told him.

Speaking to Herse! Why hadn't I mentioned this before?

I hadn't considered it important and saw no harm in it. Our conversation had mostly concerned geographical matters.

McLeod's next words had vehemence enough to lift him to his feet. No harm in it! If Herse turned Long Arm and Copperhead into NWC men, we wouldn't get a single fur. And besides, if Herse helped Esther to find her father before he did, all his hopes were turned to excrement. And a great deal more of this, accompanied by some rough treatment of a large stick of firewood with his boot, which stick he hurled onto the fire, stamping and stomping around the rising flames and sparks as though it were a heathen ceremony. Until, at last, they settled, and with them his temper. He sat back down and took a morose swig from the keg.

If you would only believe him, Esther, McLeod lamented. If he could only get you to see that going to Montreal had been forced upon him, that it'd never been in his power to come to you at Rainy River. It was the only reason he'd returned to this damned place.

And what if you wouldn't believe him?

That he didn't adjectivally know. That, he couldn't even bring himself to think about. His best chance was finding your father, Long Arm. His search itself would prove his devotion. And if he could convince Long Arm about the true debacle of his expedition, and how it had ended, he might speak up for him. Surely, you would listen to your father.

We drank for a pipe more in silence, before McLeod looked up despairingly at me, despairingly at the fire, and then despairingly at the enormous night. What if Esther were to find her father before him, he sighed? What if they left together, for who knew where? He might search for them until the End of Days in this great wilderness. 'That would be my Siberia,' he said. And perhaps this Siberia was also a part of his Pilgrim geography, some Land of the Broken-hearted. Though I'm not sure the famous Pilgrim ever travelled there.

The next morning, I woke with a pile of pinecones on my head and McLeod's stale breath in my ear. He was going to find the road again, he was saying, and would return for me as soon as he did. In the meantime, I was to stay put.

After he'd been gone an hour or so, I rekindled the fire and sat back against a tree to enjoy the silence, the flames dancing safely in their circle of stones, watching the squirrel that had covered my head with its pinecones and wondering at its tameness. Could I be the first man it had ever seen? Or the first white man, at least?

Or the most simple-minded, blockheaded, dunce of a man! For it hadn't occurred to me until that moment the seriousness of my predicament if McLeod didn't return for me. McLeod of the seagull and its eggs. McLeod of the false river mouths and wandering islands. McLeod who couldn't find the burnt tree. I tried to recall our directions – a swale, a beaver pond, an eagle's nest, the sun on this side or the other – and my head began to swim. My father might as well have handed me a page of his Thucydides to translate.

Another hour went by, or so it seemed. And then another. And it was then that those bleak footnotes coffined in Travels began to rise and whisper in my ear with their cracked lips. A grisly, pinched, gut-foundered, thin-ribbed parade. There were those unfortunate wretches forced to draw lots for whose heart and liver and buttocks would be devoured; those who perished of cold in sight of the fires of their camps; those who came to blame their misfortunes on each other, turning upon themselves like wolverines in a sack; those who abandoned the weak or halt or slow or stupid to a terrible Fate. Round and round these spectres danced. A few pine needles fell from the branches above, the flames of the fire faltered against the stones. The squirrel had disappeared. There were trees, the spaces between them, and me. There was no more comfort in this silence than there'd been at the bottom of Godin's pit.

Overwhelmed by these spectres, I became convinced it was near certain McLeod wouldn't return. And for no other reason than the sun, which was all that was familiar, I decided to go South and try to discover the road myself. In my path was a small stream, and as one fear can swallow up another, in I went, neck or nothing, and was soon up to my waist in the water. The instant my feet touched the solid earth again, I began to run. And run. How far? You might as well have asked a frightened deer to calculate the miles of its flight. When my breath gave out, the trees, beaver ponds, swales, ridges around me seemed all oddly familiar and entirely unknown. Some broken twigs became a road, a crumpled leaf a footprint. A second later they were only the forest floor. And who knows how many panicked circles I might have run in if I'd not then looked up to discover the dark, mouldering logs of a hovel squatting in a clearing ahead, like the very worst kind of fairy tale.

Gathering what shreds of courage were left in me, and pulling my father's hat firmly over my head, as though it were the paternal embrace I'd never known, I inched towards it. This building was so dilapidated that even the Companies would've baulked at calling it anything but a ruin. It was with some horror then that I watched the crooked oblong of its door begin to open.

The man that walked out was dressed in a ragged blanket, that might once have been white but was now some other shade entirely. Dismayingly, the little haystack of filthy hair heaped upon their head was straw-coloured, not copper. The pale green eyes beneath it looked one way, fearfully, then another, then directly at me. It was impossible to tell how long his right arm was.

We remained frozen in this position for several moments, both calculating in what direction we might flee, before at last I called out in a croaky voice, 'My name is Arthur.' Adding – for what else was I there? – 'I am with the XY Company.'

Silence.

'Are you with the NWC?'

More silence.

'I'm not with anybody,' he said at last. 'Is this the way to America?' The voice was Scottish, but a different kind of Scottish to the ones I knew.

'MacDowell?'

By some trick of the forest, it seemed the reply now came from behind me. 'No, it is not frigging Long Arm,' it said. 'Or Copperhead.'

Turning, I found McLeod glowering down at me. What part of 'stay put' was such an adjectival mystery to me, he remarked.

Another look made my error obvious. Beneath the mask of dirt was a boyish face, a peach that had been rolled in the mud. This was your father thirty years ago, or not at all.

With a far better ear for Scottish, McLeod said, 'You are an Orkney man, I think?'

He nodded.

'The Governor's man, Spey?'

Another nod.

And what was there in this post?

There was nothing in this wretched place but misery.

And with that, McLeod invited him to return with us to our camp, and the forest quickly became a road again – a gentle, green and dappled glade. As we walked, McLeod questioned the poor fellow. He told us he'd barely been on this continent beyond a full year. Having arrived at an HBC post on the shore of Hudson's Bay, he'd found work there as the personal servant of the Governor, though by then he wasn't even a deputy Governor, being kept on by that Company as a sort of relic. After barely a month, the Governor had decided on his retirement. At first, Spey thought this was his Ticket, as for some time he'd considered himself escaped from a poor, pinched place on one side of the ocean into the jaws of a woeful, barren, freezing place on the other. His great hope had been to get, eventually, to the United States. Somewhere with farms, a village, perhaps an apple orchard. Somewhere he might be himself. This is what he'd imagined when the Governor spoke of his own retirement. But instead, they'd only journeyed as far as those damp and freezing falls, where he'd spent almost a year in bondage to a madman and his infernal pig.

And then he'd found the man above the falls, lying curled like a baby in the snow. A set of footprints showed he'd come from the West, the direction of the Rainy Lake fort. He'd laid this man out in front of the fire at the Governor's place, where at first he'd seemed quite dead. But then, to Spey's astonishment, he'd opened his eyes and begun to speak. None of it made much sense, either to Spey or the Governor. He'd said his name was Labrie, and he'd brought word from them (without saying who they were). They would be somewhere in the Folle Avoine... something, something Yellow Lake.

And then something about an Evil Shadow following him. And then something about his mother. And then something about a woman named Annette. He'd pay her six pence for handwork, not a penny more. And then more of this gibberish, before slipping into a moaning sleep.

An hour later, the Governor had gone out to relieve himself when Labrie had suddenly opened his eyes again and sat up, demanding his hat. Spey handed it to him. Reaching into its crown, he'd said, 'Give this to the doctor, Munro. To keep for him.'

Reached for what? Keep for whom? McLeod exclaimed.

Who knew, Spey said. 'But where is it?' the man had kept saying, tearing at his hat. At last, he stared into its crown in despair. 'The Shadow has taken it,' he said, before falling back into sleep. He was dead by nightfall.

The Governor, moved by the man's demise, had decided he should be taken to the New Fort and delivered to Munro, so he could arrange for his body to be returned to Montreal. Perhaps they might find his mother or Annette there, that they could bury him. He let Spey take his four dogs, a sled, and six Spanish dollars for the frozen man's passage home.

Once he'd delivered Labrie and the six Spanish dollars to the New Fort, Spey had made a decision. Since he had the dogs and the sled, and Munro had said America wasn't far away – and was in fact getting closer every year – he'd escape the Governor and carry on until he reached it. He'd had an extremely hard and dreadful time thereafter, and eventually reached this ruin, as lost and forsaken as L'Enfant Perdu. And if nothing else, I would learn this from my time up there, and never stop learning it: that you could be lost a footstep from where you might be safe; and where you thought yourself safe could be a footstep from where you might be lost.

Anywhere could become your Siberia. Anywhere can.

And what had become of the dogs? I asked.

Spey said he didn't wish to speak of that time. None of it.

By this time, we'd reached our main camp. The others rushed eagerly over the sand towards us and, seeing Spey's straw-coloured hair and boyish cheeks and symmetrical arms, fell immediately into a subdued despond. A despond quickly deepened when McLeod announced they must prepare to ascend the river, and to arrange another place in the canoe for the Orkney man, Spey. As they did, I asked McLeod what he'd gleaned from Spey's account. He told me his guess was that what had been in Labrie's hat – or had not been in Labrie's hat! – was a set of directions of some kind, drawn up by Long Arm and Copperhead. He was convinced it gave the location of the Secret Post, though who it had been intended for was a vexing adjectival riddle to him.

To assuage the men's disappointment, which was also his own, he then called for a dram to be had. And as we bid farewell to the waters of Lake Superior, a canoe appeared on the horizon, moving quickly in our direction. As it approached closer, we could see it was paddled by six men. And as it got closer still, five men and one woman. And closer. Herse, four NWC voyageurs, and you, Esther. It swept right past the promontory and into the mouth of the river, on the road to Yellow Lake, with Herse offering a wave, you staring severely ahead, and the voyageurs making a motion with their hands simulating the act of self-pleasure.

'No, no,' said McLeod, holding his half-drunk dram in his hand, appearing as though he'd found a piece of coal in his Christmas pudding, as if his whole Christmas pudding were a piece of coal.

And with that, Esther, you were up the river and out of sight. McLeod looked as though he were again contemplating throwing himself into it. And I was concealing a secret smile, to know that you were ahead of us on our journey and not behind.

2

But where was I with that owl? Yes, there it is, hooting on the shore of Yellow Lake. And hearing it in memory, I consider it a sort of Halcyon Owl, an Owl of the Innocents. Perhaps it was that glimpse of you on the river, but those first days at the lake felt as golden as the sandy bed which gave it its name. I often try to recall it as it was in those brief moments, a small mote of time, poised and preserved in the honey of wild bees. There is the beach we step out of our canoe onto. There is the long, forested point, open to the late Summer breezes. There are the ponds near our camp, Yellow River flowing into the lake from the West, and then out again to the North. There are the three islands. There are the groves of fir and elm and maple, the wild plums, the pure, clear, glittering water. But then the honey jar begins to tip and spill, and the honeycomb itself is beset by chisels and axes.

For we'd hardly taken a sip of clear, glittering water, or picked a single plum, before McLeod had us building. He said there was no way of knowing how long we'd be here and so we must make some preparations.

For the Winter?

For that as well, if it came to it.

So, we hacked down the groves and erected crude log walls; we gathered stones for a chimney; we stripped bark and made shingles for a roof. Two buildings began to take shape: a squat, misshapen living-quarters for us, and a squat, misshapen warehouse for trade goods and furs. It seemed to me that wherever we went, we made the world a little uglier.

The prime reason for our building became apparent soon enough. Amid our labours, we were visited by several bands of Saulteaux wishing to trade. McLeod asked each of them if they knew of another post in the vicinity, or had heard of any traders passing through, gesturing to his arm and hair. One of these bands, made up of a group of hunters accompanied by their children and wives, included a woman who had blackened her face. I asked McLeod what the meaning of this was. He said it was a mourning custom, adding that one of the band had recently been killed by a Sioux raiding party – the husband of this woman. They'd recovered his body and buried it close to the lake. Or rather housed it, he said, for the Saulteaux often erected a kind of mausoleum above their graves, provisioned with what they might need for the journey they must take to reach their Heaven. For that journey....

And did he think these Sioux might still be nearby?

Oh, quite possibly. They might be watching us this very second. We'd be none the wiser.

And this didn't concern him?

It did. That was why we must build this post, for our protection.

But it wasn't much of a post. Definitely not a fort.

'They only rarely kill traders, Arthur.'

'Only rarely?'

'Occasionally,' he said. 'At least, not very often.'

Perhaps McLeod was so heartsore that the prospect of being

flayed and burnt and murdered played lightly on him. For if I knew very little about the Saulteaux, then I knew nothing at all about the Sioux, except for this matter of flaying and burning and murdering (and possibly eating too) – which picture I'd had drawn for me by Crebassa and several of the Saulteaux hunters, who I later learnt were their enemies by long custom, and used the Sioux on occasion to frighten errant children, in the same manner as the English did Old Nick and Frenchmen, or Frenchmen did Englishmen.

The rest of the men showed less phlegm in this matter of the Sioux than McLeod. The mausoleum of the Widow's husband was close by in the forest and, once we'd finished with our hacking and hammering and despoiling for the day, we'd hear her voice there, sometimes raised, sometimes gentle, sometimes dipping into cooing whispers. I asked Crebassa what it was she was saying, and to whom, and he told me this was the manner of her grieving, her keening, her converse with the dead; that she would berate her husband for having put himself in the way of that raiding party and being killed, and then say how much she loved him, and then how much she would miss him. For the Saulteaux dead did not always depart immediately on their journeys.

These hunters and their families remained with us a week and I recall how on the third night that owl returned to his hooting. It caused great consternation among them; the men leaping to their feet with guns and knives, the women pushing their children behind them. The next morning, I asked Crebassa what this might mean. He puffed on his pipe and shook his head, saying wasn't it clear and plain? When the Sioux called out to each other, it wouldn't be in Sioux – it would be in the voices of owls, and loons, and wolves, and any other creature they chose to imitate.

And so that was the last time an owl was only an owl for me.

The Widow (for such the men named her) stayed on with us, to attend her husband's grave, and together with the Orkney man, Spey, made two new members of our crew. The poor fellow had hardly uttered a word since offering us his account. With the rest of the men this was understandable; he only had a few rags and bones of French, though Narcisse had offered himself eagerly enough as his teacher. McLeod thought his Upper Storey broken ('It's just my frigging luck, Arthur – the man is as dilly as his master'), but to me his quietness appeared more a symptom of his general habit of privacy and nervousness. He wouldn't share the living hovel with the men and had instead fashioned a dwelling made of branches outside its walls. He was an odd, secretive fellow, but so were many fellows. As for the nervousness, well, we were all nervous in that place.

But in all of this I've forgotten a third addition. One afternoon, soon after the Saulteaux hunters had departed, Narcisse and Hyacinthe emerged from the woods with a young bear.

And what was this? McLeod asked.

A bear, said Narcisse.

That he could see, but why was it here?

Narcisse explained how its mother had been taken by one of the hunters, who'd adopted the cub, holding bears as they did in the greatest esteem, as they might a wise uncle or grandfather.

McLeod asked what they'd exchanged for it.

Some rum, Narcisse said.

McLeod said he didn't consider some rum a good exchange, unless this bear had been cut into steaks and chops. But in truth, it would've taken the most wizened of hearts not to take to this creature. He was a tremendously scruffy little fellow, with brown-black hair that stuck up here, there, and everywhere, as though a herd of cows had licked a village drunkard sleeping in a haystack. He was missing an eye, which greatly endeared him to Crebassa, who'd forgive him any of his antics. He had a habit of licking his hind feet and making a purring noise, like a cat, and was much in love with the drams the men gave him. They named him Bruno.

3

All the while we were making our beggarly castle, McLeod was frantic to begin his quest for Long Arm and Copperhead – or for the Missouri furs, as he was careful to describe this to the other men. He was sure you and Herse were somewhere nearby, combing the surrounding country, and dreaded you might discover your father first. And also that Herse would finagle his friend Copperhead, and the furs, into the NWC's pocket. He'd searched the forest around the lake, in the hope of stumbling on the Secret Post, but to no avail. And since I'd come to see the building of our post as a general battening of the hatches, the securing of a tiny ship in the wide and dangerous sea of the Debated Lands, it gave me no joy when he announced the two of us were to make a journey.

And when was this?

Tomorrow, he said.

It was still dark when he woke me, saying we must ready a small canoe he'd purchased from one of the Saulteaux hunters, which was so battered and threadbare it appeared as if much of its bark had returned to its Natal tree. A heavy rain beat a dismal tattoo on the half-finished shingles of the roof. 'Load three kegs of rum, and two trade packs,' he said impatiently. 'We don't want to miss the best part of the day.'

I had one keg and two packs of trading goods secured beneath an oilcloth, and was about to fetch the others, when a gap appeared in the clouds, showing the moon. We must depart immediately, said McLeod. But the rest? Except by then he'd already jumped into the stern. We were across the lake and some way up Yellow River before we stopped for a pipe in the first grey light. I asked him where we were going.

McLeod gestured to the oilcloth. To trade, he said. There was a fellow he knew staying not so many miles up the river, so one of the hunters had said.

Would the Saulteaux not come to us to trade?

McLeod shook his head, telling me I was much mistaken in my conception of this Indian trade. For the most part it was us that went to them. We were the Tinkers. And this whole country was the door of their house.

And whose house might we be going to? What fellow?

But McLeod had already emptied his pipe and begun to paddle.

It was past midday when we arrived at a Saulteaux camp. I counted seven wigwams. All around there were deer carcasses being cut into strips, hides drying in smoke, wild rice being beaten, dogs growling and cowering, children playing, preparations being made for the coming season. My journal says this was in September, and I was learning quickly a lesson about time in the northern Summer and Autumn, viz that there was never enough of it.

We entered the largest of the wigwams and joined a circle of four men. There were several women also inside, and a few younger men, but they continued about their business – fixing moccasins, discussing the events of the day, preparing fish and meat – as though each space was a separate room with imagined walls.

The six of us shared a pipe and, after a pause, McLeod and a man in a red capot exchanged speeches, which I understood not a word of, only that they followed a certain formality and etiquette, and that McLeod's grasp of the language was as creaky as a rusty hinge. The light from the smoke-hole glittered upon the silver brooches in the man in the red capot's hair and the gorget at his neck, catching the engraved shoulders of a lynx.

McLeod then ordered me to bring in the packs, as though he were a Chief. The men appraised their contents, clearly unimpressed.

McLeod then ordered me to fetch the kegs, again in chiefly fashion.

And the others, he said?

I explained that there was only the one.

His eyes widened. 'You only brought one?'

The others stared at us, and then at the solitary keg, and then at each other.

'You brought one keg,' repeated McLeod outside the wigwam after we'd been bundled out of it, enunciating each word with an appalled amazement, much as when Narcisse had discovered a leech on his member at Les Vases.

The man in the red capot now joined us. McLeod addressed him as the Two Birds and, to my surprise, did so in English. He'd been brought up near the Grande Portage, as I'd discover later, and learnt it from the Scottish traders who wintered there. He asked McLeod what he thought he was doing, bringing these crappy goods, and one keg. He knew very well the NWC would offer four. What would the Knight (who was well known in these parts as a trader and head of the XY) think of this shameful, absurd, insulting miserliness? The men inside were shitting themselves with laughter at the offer of this one keg. The women too. And the children. And the dogs.

McLeod replied that it had been a mistake, lifting his chin in my direction. Some of his men were greener than lily-pads. Then he should tell this lily-pad, said the Two Birds, that if he was to bring shit to trade then it should not be astounding if he got shit in return.

There was a lengthy silence, before the Two Birds informed McLeod that his own niece had already been here, with an NWC trader – the Englishman Herse.

Esther, I exclaimed. Both men ignored me.

His niece had been eager to inquire after her father's whereabouts, he continued. And Herse had spoken about a cache of furs. Both had said the Two Birds might expect a visit from McLeod, inquiring about the same.

McLeod's face had become a drunken bear at a country fair: one thought lurching this way, another veering that.

The Two Birds added that perhaps this information was what McLeod had really come to trade for.

McLeod offered a faint and cowed nod. And had Esther mentioned him in some way? he remarked forlornly.

Now he thought about it, she had mentioned him. That he was a coward and a piece of manure. For breaking his engagement. For his cruel fecklessness. For scarpering to Montreal. And for having left that man behind, too. And eating the only food himself. A seagull and its eggs. And that she would not listen to his excuses, though he crawled over a hundred knife blades to make them.

He'd never broken his engagement, McLeod protested. He'd done everything in his power. It was all a misunderstanding... etc. And he had not eaten them. None of it was true. The Two Birds knew him better than that.

Know him! Who did he know? A cruel rake who had abandoned his niece. A man who brought him one abysmal keg. If McLeod was trying to find Long Arm to make Esther less angry with him, to return to her good graces, it would have been easier to just say so. He could tell him what he knew about that. Esther hadn't told him he shouldn't. And we could leave behind our one pitiful keg as payment for this knowledge.

Another cowed nod from McLeod.

He'd met both Long Arm and Copperhead early in the Spring, no more than fifty miles West from here. The men had been transporting a large cache of furs from somewhere in the West.

Well, this was something, said McLeod, brightening. And had they mentioned where they were headed? Had he heard anything about a post they might have established?

They hadn't, and he'd heard nothing about a post. But they had said they'd be returning later in the Summer, and he could tell McLeod the direction they'd been going in when he met them. The Two Birds then gave out some Indian-road directions, the usual swales and creeks and hills and trees with eagle nests and the like. McLeod thanked him.

The Two Birds shook his head. 'I am embarrassed for you, Tall Tree,' he said. 'For this one laughable keg, for abandoning my niece, for the seagull and its eggs. For all of it.'

And had the Two Birds mentioned all this to the Englishman Herse, McLeod asked nervously?

He had. Esther had said it was fine for Herse to know, as he was helping her. And besides, the Two Birds had known both Herse and Copperhead in past times, when they'd traded for opposing Companies in the Lake of the Woods district. They were both fine fellows, especially Copperhead. Generous and fair, he said pointedly. In fact, it baffled him that Copperhead – and Long Arm, too – should continue in our XY Company, if it had apparently descended to such beggarly, one-keg, ways. At this, all of McLeod's brightness vanished.

We'd returned some two or three silent pipes down the river before he would speak to me. I said I hadn't realised he also had a North West country name.

It was better than the name the voyageurs had for me, he replied, rather unpleasantly.

And what was that?

The White Frog.

While we smoked our pipes, water began to trickle into the bottom of the canoe. McLeod decided we had no other choice than to make our way as best we could with this leak, he paddling in the stern while I used my small tin eating dish to bail out the water as fast as I could. But before long, the trickles became torrents, and I was sitting in a puddle.

We'd sloshed our way a few more miles when hunger began to weaken us considerably. Pulling to shore, McLeod took his gun and went to hunt, returning with a dead eagle which we roasted over a fire. It seemed a sorrowful thing, seeing such a majestic bird reduced to this. I remarked on it to McLeod. 'Oh lah de dah,' said he. 'My profound apologies, Mr Stanton. I should have asked before I pulled the trigger.

Would you prefer beefsteaks? Or perhaps some mutton? And what wines would suit you best?'

I ate my piece of eagle, but the thought of its diminished majesty continued to trouble me as I washed the remains from my dish, comforting myself with the thought that there was a great difference between the idea of the eagle and the meat of the eagle, just as how my father's Greeks might interpret it. There were Actual eagles and more perfect Ideas of eagles. As I pondered this, the dish fell from my fingers and sank into the swift-moving murk of the current. McLeod was staring at me.

'Where is the dish, Arthur?'

'I think it's in the river.'

'You think it's in the river.' A pause. 'So how do you suggest we remove the water from the canoe?'

I had no answer. McLeod looked at the top of my head and lifted his eyebrows.

'No,' I said. 'Not that.'

'Yes, *that*.'

And so we continued on our way, with me using my hat to bail the water from the canoe. And there was all the difference in the world between the Idea of my hat – that it represented my father's regard for me, his love and concern – and the Actual pulpy mass it slowly became.

We'd gone no more than a pipe when the remains of my hat gave out and the canoe began to sink. We barely made it to the bank. And then discovered we were on the wrong bank and would have to carry the packs of untraded goods across the river and walk the rest of the way. McLeod decided he'd take our two packs of goods and the gun, and I'd carry the clothes we had been wearing, to keep them dry.

The water swirled around my shins and knees. It touched my thighs, my buttocks, the tip of my member, as cold as the lick of a salamander's tongue. There were slippery things beneath my toes. Poplar leaves floated on the surface. Who knew where the river took them? The shores of Superior? Beyond? They were pale against the dark and the image came to me of Young Godin, turning over and over in the current, the cold water flowing from the side of his mouth. The branches of the cedars and alders were like arms reaching down to me. I rushed towards them. I held out my hands to grasp them.

'Where are our clothes, Arthur?' said McLeod on the other side, the water dripping in rivulets down his neck and chest.

The river has taken them, I replied meekly.

The River of Adjectival Ineptitude, he said, and began to kick an unfortunate willow.

Our packs contained no cloth or blankets, and so we had to return naked through the forest. When at last we approached our own post, we were as blue as indigo with cold. I told McLeod we should at least try to cover our private selves.

'With what, Arthur? You've given every frigging thing to the river.'

Amongst other items, our packs contained many of the silver brooches the Saulteaux used to decorate their hair and persons. If we tied these on a string, I suggested, we could make a kind of breechclout of them. And so, with a pack to the front of us, and our buttocks ringed with silver, we ran tinkling and jangling the rest of the way.

'Who goes there?' demanded Hyacinthe from inside the living hovel.

'Open the fucking door,' shouted McLeod. 'It is us.'

How to describe the look of shock and chagrin on McLeod's face when we discovered Herse waiting for us inside? Ink wouldn't do it justice. 'Well, well,' he said. 'What a picture this is! It seems you're always losing your trousers, William.'

Bruno ran up and licked my knee.

4

There is no need to draw a picture of McLeod's added chagrin on discovering that Herse and his four NWC brutes had begun to construct a post less than two hundred yards from ours, leaving the two Companies almost as close on the ground as they were in the alphabet. Or how we were forced to watch these NWC brutes at their building and it was as though we'd gone back in time and were watching a mightier and more capable version of ourselves in the mirror, hacking down more trees, making better walls, gathering larger stones for their chimney. And how this became the lopsided nature of our opposition: they did what we did, better, and we watched them; and then we did what they did, worse, and they watched us.

But the greatest torment for McLeod was finding that you'd settled on the nearest of the three islands, some hundred yards from the shore. A hundred yards of water that might as well have been the Pacific Ocean. Three times he paddled out to it to say his piece, and on each occasion was very forcibly rebuffed. Thereafter, he took to gawping at that island like Tantalus at a bowl of figs, until one evening, deep in his cups, he hatched one of his schemes and beseeched me to act as his intermediary. I must explain to her, he said. I must tell her what had happened. I must make her believe it… etc, etc. The usual lament.

And with his bruised and yearning heart there before me, I pledged I would.

His scheme was that I volunteer myself for fishing duties and set the nets directly out from the shore of the island. But, in fact, I would be the bait. If you were to happen to speak to me as I tended the nets, then I could make his case. And sure enough, one afternoon I found you sitting on a flat rock, watching me.

'There are no fish there, you know, Arthur.'

I said I was sure there were plenty of pike and pickerel below.

Amazingly nervous pike and pickerel, you'd guess, from the perpetual emptiness of my nets, and then invited me for tea.

Back from the shore, your wigwam stood in a clearing surrounded by poplars. Their yellowing leaves hung silent in the stillness of the afternoon, and the sounds from the mainland, made large by this stillness, slipped over to us across the water. Hyacinthe and Narcisse were locked in some dispute concerning the touching of the wooden Anna-Marie; an NWC axe chuck-chuck-chucked at the trunk of a pine; Bruno let out an inexplicable and mournful groan.

A golden light shone through the wigwam's smoke-hole. Who knows what that tea was made from, but it might have been Mandrake or Wolfsbane, for all I cared. It was delicious to me. I'd often imagined living on an island myself, I remarked. Like Crusoe's deserted one. You said it seemed men like Crusoe were always turning up on islands and deciding they were deserted. The smoke of twenty cook fires might be in their eyes, but they'd rub them and say, 'Behold this empty place.'

I asked why you'd chosen to stay here and not with your uncle – your mother's brother, the Two Birds – who I'd recently met.

You said it was important you be at this lake, for reasons it wasn't important for me to know.

Golden light, golden minutes. What did we talk of? About the places you'd lived as a child. You brought out a hide bag, embroidered with beads, full of things you'd gathered from them: a silver gorget, engraved with the same lynx as your uncle's; a buffalo horn from Red River; a Cree arrowhead from Bas de la Rivière. Like a cabinet of curiosities a traveller might gather, your Ages made incarnate.

It seemed you'd lived in a lot of places, I said.

You said your father was a restless man. A great Here and Thereian. And after your mother had died, he had become more restless still.

And you'd always gone with him?

Yes. You'd always loved travelling and living with him. You had always loved your father, despite his recent perturbations about what Scottish fathers should expect, and Montreal, etc.

You told me a story. Once, when you were eleven years old, your father had left you with your uncle's family for a few weeks while he went to trade somewhere along Rainy River, near where it entered Lake of the Woods. Stealing a canoe from your uncle, you'd travelled over thirty miles along the river on your own before reaching him at a post along its banks. Searching in the bag, you took out a tiny bone. The Muskrat Jaw place. How astonished he'd been to see you! And happy that you'd found him! And secretly, despite his gentle chastisements, delighted you'd followed him.

The light fell on your freckles. The bickering voices of Narcisse and Hyacinthe faded, the axe fell silent. And I thought I noted a small and wondrous shift in the air: a poised, expectant hush; an awareness – how to put it? – that my hand was *this* far from your hand, or perhaps *that* close, or maybe....

You brought out a caribou bone from Isle La Crosse, a piece of quartz, saying how much you'd liked travelling to new districts and territories, had liked living that life. The trading posts were in-between sorts of places, where people might live in-between lives. And you supposed the origin of your father's recent worries, him wanting you to try out Montreal, was that the growing opposition between the Companies, and between the Nations too, would one day pinch these in-between places into one-thing-or-another places. And what would you do then?

And had you had any luck discovering your father's whereabouts this time? McLeod was also looking for him, I admitted. Your uncle had mentioned a direction, a road....

Adjectival McLeod. As if you couldn't find your own father yourself. As for roads, there were a hundred of them through this country, any of which your uncle may have suggested. There were ways of finding that were much better than blundering naked through the forest, frightening the animals with your jangling arse.

But I must tell you, I suddenly blurted, how the Orkney man named Spey, the Governor's servant who had joined us, had mentioned...

You knew. Labrie's hat. The missing message or document.

Herse had already persuaded the whole account out of Spey. Not that McLeod had mentioned it. Not that McLeod....

McLeod, McLeod. It was as though he'd stomped into the wigwam, and any shift in the air or expectant anything had gone scarpering off into the trees. And worse. At the mention of his name you'd looked into the dregs of your tea, as if beneath all the adjectival this and that was something much sadder. My stomach fizzed and lurched in a whole new fashion. And here was the first appearance of the Other Arthur, who, alas, will soon enough make his ugly, misshapen way onto the stage. The golden light had begun to turn green. Meanwhile, somewhere from the mainland shore, a voice was calling out.

Here was my opportunity to make McLeod's case and fulfil my pledge, to tell the story he'd told me. But instead, the Other Arthur now flapped my tongue for me. I said the breaking of an engagement seemed a very low and dastardly thing.

You didn't want to even adverbially think about your engagement.

The voice from the shore was becoming louder. And because the gods enjoy their fun and games with us, it was the voice I least wanted to hear, McLeod's, and it was calling my name.

Back on the mainland, McLeod was impatiently arranging an expedition to search the road the Two Birds had described. It was all straightforward, he informed me. There was every chance this road would lead directly to the Secret Post and, if Long Arm and Copperhead weren't there already, they'd surely be returning soon with the next consignment of the

Missouri furs. He'd leave the next day and make his way to a river, a lake, myriad beaver ponds, swales innumerable, etc, etc. But where had I been?

Checking the fishing nets.

And?

There were no fish.

He wasn't talking about the damned fish. Had I had the chance to speak to you?

No.

But he'd not seen me in the canoe, and thought I must have landed on the island.

Did he not believe me?

Not seeing me in the canoe, he'd assumed....

He could believe me or not, as he wished. But for now he'd have to excuse me as I must attend to my journal.

McLeod said he couldn't figure what ants had got into my trousers to cause this harrumphing. And I'd written barely an adjectival word in that journal this past month, he added.

Off I stomped to the living hovel, to spend the evening contemplating the shoddy roof above me and the turmoil within. That fizzing and jangling in my belly, I was now sure, must be love – though my knowledge of it then came mostly from books, where it appeared a fine and noble sentiment, which prompted you to perform fine and noble actions, not something you had for somebody else's once betrothed and that made you suddenly a schemer and liar. McLeod was in love with you. McLeod had once been engaged to you. You'd once been in love with McLeod. McLeod was my companion and master in the trade. I'd promised to make his case for him. I hadn't. I had begun to fall in love with you. I wished I'd never met McLeod. I wished you'd never met McLeod. But what did it matter. You'd never share my affections, anyhow. I'd seen the way you'd looked at your tea. Around and around these thoughts swirled, like checker pieces tossed into a maelstrom.

They swirled me, through a sleepless night, right into the next morning. Outside, a heavy dew had soaked the grass. All the time we'd been building, the season had been turning. The maple leaves were reddening. Sometimes in the woods you might hear the partridges thumping their feathers like drums. If partridges they were.

Still in the tentacles of my greener, baser thoughts, I wandered to the shore. The sun was yet to rise, and the whole world appeared to be waiting for it. A fantastical mist shrouded the lake, with nothing moving except the legs of water-walking insects, making momentary runes on its surface. With each step, the details of this tranquil scene began to make a mockery of all base and huffy thoughts, and the tentacles loosened.

McLeod was already sitting near the water. As if animated by an unfelt breeze, his shoulders rose and slumped, his hand lifted and dropped back to the sand, his body tensed. And then, appearing out of the nowhere of the mist, was you, standing on the far shore. You splashed some water on your face and untied your hair, combed it, and tied it back, so for a second it was as if a little part of the night had snuck back across its threshold. All this occurred in silence, but if a whole body could groan, then McLeod's would have echoed across the lake, bouncing from island to island and on to the inland seas. A Dusk McLeod smoked a stricken pipe, trapped in the brightening light. Turning back, I left him there undisturbed, feeling like Brutus in the new and hidden places of my heart.

The checker pieces had fallen into place then, the board solid and clear: the expectant hush and shift of air were phantasms, something conjured out of foolish hopes. I'd made you a figure of Romance. I was just like my father, trying to metamorphose the world in front of him into the world he dreamed and desired, turning mosquitoes into Nymphs and Dryads, spruce swamps into ancient olive groves. My jealousy was madness; my thoughts of you were disloyal and low and impossible.

I resolved there and then to put aside my treacherous affections.

By the time he returned to the hovel, McLeod was Dawn again, announcing he'd be leaving immediately.

I told him I'd go fetch my things and be ready to depart.

Oh no, there was no need for that, he said.

No need? But why?

The River of Ineptitude flowed eloquently between us.

Eventually, I asked who'd be in charge when he was gone.

'You will, Arthur,' he replied, and then appeared surprised this was the case, as if it had just occurred to him. He thought a moment. While he was gone, I should trade whatever I could for provisions. He thought some more. 'Do whatever Crebassa tells you to do,' he said, before walking towards the trading hovel to collect some supplies.

A minute later, he returned. 'Do nothing Narcisse or Hyacinthe tell you to do.'

He was gone two more minutes before returning a second

time. 'And do absolutely fucking nothing Herse tells you to do. And don't blab anything to him, either. Keep the old bone-box shut.'

His canoe was barely out of sight, and I was thinking, such are the wages of Loyalty, when Herse sauntered over towards our living hovel, carrying a keg of shrub. Since we were both close to finishing our posts, he suggested the two Companies might come together to celebrate when we were done.

I said I'd have to ask Crebassa what he thought.

Crebassa took one look at the keg of shrub and said he thought it an excellent idea.

5

My journal – or what scant pages of it I filled during that time – now says it is turning into October. Some people picture the North West countries and think it mostly snow. But if somebody asked me, I'd say I picture it most often as Autumn, when it seemed that every season might poke its head out. Some days the sun was as hot as Summer, others there was a touch of frost on the grass, a thought of ice at the edges of the lake. Leaves turned and fell, but sometimes you might find a waterlily late in its blooming, rushing to flower like a tardy schoolboy, and then dying the next day. Some things too early, some things too late, and some things beautifully just so.

Beyond our post, Yellow Lake played wondrous little tricks. Windless mornings and evenings brought out more of the fantastical mists, and beneath them the lake appeared to multiply itself. A raft of sticks and weeds from its bed floated up to the surface and made a new sort of island, which wandered daily from point to point. Meanwhile, with the water flat as glass, the permanent islands doubled themselves on its surface, so there were upside-down islands and right-side-up islands and wandering islands and stationary islands.

It was a pause, a lull, a pipe, though there were still comings and goings. A few bands of Saulteaux came from their wild rice places to our trading hovel. The Widow had put up her wigwam between the posts, and Crebassa had taken to promenading with her along the lakeshore in a cloud of pipe smoke and his best red sash. Narcisse continued to teach Spey French, by way of songs, and each day they paddled the lake singing about Normandy swains in love, and such. Hyacinthe, with nobody to grumble at, grumbled to himself about having nobody to grumble at. Herse's NWC men went out to hack and haul the last logs for their post. And as for you, Esther... well, I was trying very hard not to notice what you were doing. I was trying very hard not to notice you at all.

It was during this time, when McLeod was away and I was trying to distract myself from Normandy-swain-type-thoughts, that I began to learn my profession, or as much of it as I ever would at least. It is there in my journal, which now takes on a business aspect, with bills of lading, items of provision, the names of trading Chiefs.

And furs. Furs in lists, furs in ledgers, furs in thought, furs in deed. One sentence says, *I learn to see the world in beavers*. And so, for a short while, I did.

Money, as I'd known it, was quite useless here. All value was judged by the skins of beavers – they were British pounds and Halifax shillings and Spanish dollars and everything else. In ink, and in our trading hovel, and beside fires, and in wigwams, and everywhere trading took place, we turned things into beaver skins, whether they be on paper as debts or credit, or as objects in exchange. Mr Smith of Edinburgh would himself have wondered at it. So, I think that that year a carrot of tobacco was five beaver skins, and for one, you might have a pound of musket balls. A verge of ribbon was half a beaver, a package of beads was four. You might have fifteen large brooches for one beaver, or a brass kettle for seven. Fifteen pounds of bear grease could be had for four beaver skins, a sack of Indian rice for two, one hundred whitefish for six. A prepared beaver skin was a Made Beaver. MB was our shilling sign.

And last, because not all animals could be beavers, we turned their skins into equivalents. And so, the fur of a deer was worth half the fur of a beaver; the poor muskrat a mere tenth of one. An otter skin was worth two, as was a lynx. A marten would get you half, but a fisher a whole.

All this turning of animals into dead beavers and Made Beavers and paper beavers had a strange effect. For a while, each time I saw a creature, instead of looking at it as it was, I'd translate it into portions of another. A deer would step into a glade, and I'd see half a beaver. A muskrat slipping into the water would become the head of a beaver. A glimpse of a fisher, two beavers. A bear ambling through the woods, two beavers and the hind portion of another.

During those weeks I quite mangled and mutilated the woods with my seeing, chopping and slicing this, doubling that, quartering another, but it was perhaps a sign of my poor choice of vocation that eventually this faded. The men who prospered were those who always kept beavers in their eyes, who had eyes shaped like beavers, who woke up thinking about beavers, and closed those beaver-shaped eyes at night like the slap of a beaver's tail. For them, the forest was full of walking, bounding, gnawing, swimming, scampering money. But I was never one of them.

Perhaps, even despite this, I might have fared better as a trader if the estimation of our Company in the eyes of the

Saulteaux hadn't fallen so low. They might have been well enough inclined towards us to begin with (although the episode of the One Keg – where it had been heard – told badly against us) but once they'd passed by the NWC post – which I now realised Herse had positioned cunningly, so that they *must* pass by it to reach us – and met with one of the NWC brutes, then the situation would be altered.

Their slanders were numerous. I append a list of the gentler ones:

That we were cheats and hogs.

That our goods (which were the same as theirs) were inferior, nay useless, nay an insult to any Indian.

That we yearned and conspired to trade with their enemies, the Sioux.

That because we were a beggarly, pitiful, raggedy, rascally Company, in choosing to deal with us they'd only incur the enmity of the NWC and gain nothing in return, viz that they'd be backing the wrong horse, some spavined nag in a race of thoroughbreds.

That we were led by that infamous devourer of seagulls and eggs and abandoner of men (and women too), McLeod, who wasn't even here to attend them, and had left in his stead this… but why add what character they gave to me.

Opposition, Arthur. An imperfect world, Arthur. Needs be what must, Arthur.

So said Herse. For, in McLeod's absence, we'd begun to meet at regular intervals for our own little rendezvous, to enjoy a cup of tea of some variety. For Herse was uncommonly knowledgeable about plants and their properties and uses –

whether for tea or purges or unguents or purgatives. You'd often find him deep in conversation with the Widow after an afternoon of botanising, wagging chins like two old-time apothecaries comparing their wares.

At our teas we'd talk of this and that, and Herse would give me advice enough to avoid disaster, but not so much that there was any risk of us prospering.

This and that, but what exactly? It's odd that even now, as I write, I cannot properly give a character for Herse. I knew he was English, but I wouldn't be able to tell his origins beyond that. I knew he had an interest in plants. And I knew that this imperfect world, where everything was the value of a beaver, was distasteful to him, an unpleasantness to be tolerated.

But if Herse played the trader reluctantly, he nevertheless played it extraordinarily well. Take that outer Herse, the one we knew best – the garments of Herse. Though a trading clerk, he was as well turned out as any Big Wig, with an extra shine to his boots and a shirt whose cleanliness was as miraculous in that place as the Shroud of Turin. This was no mere dandiness. He was well respected for it amongst the Saulteaux, whose men especially took great pride in their appearance and finery and looked down on the general slovenliness of traders, considering the most of us, when we weren't dolled up for a dance or arrival at a fort, an unkempt, beardy, reeking sort of men. All of which is to say he excelled at a profession he didn't like. And if it felt I only knew him in bits and pieces, offcuts that couldn't be stitched into a single garment, then at least it felt certain he felt kindly towards me and meant me well. Meanwhile, McLeod's antipathy towards him, based on their time before as rivals, was as clear as day to me: Herse had been much better at a trade his heart wasn't in than McLeod had been at a trade he'd once thought was his very destiny.

This and that – though if I ever tried to move our convo towards what had led him to this place, or mentioned Copperhead or Long Arm, or anything connected to them, he'd pirouette elegantly away from it like a Spanish man avoiding a bull.

At one of our teas, he asked me frankly what had led me here. We were sitting, as we usually did, in a pleasant grove of birch trees near the lakeshore. Herse handed me a tisane, purported to be excellent for the bowels.

I explained how I'd heard stories of the country up here and thought it an adventurous kind of life. And then there was Crusoe and Sinbad and Gulliver.

And I'd imagined myself suited to it?

Perhaps.

He left a long pause, and as I was then like water, which cannot stop itself flowing into an empty space, I began to add how my father hadn't considered me suited for alternative professions. And still the pause endured, and more poured out – about my disappointment of my father's expectations, etc, etc.

Herse replied at last. He said I wasn't alone in this. He said that this trade was a refuge for many others who hadn't chosen it.

And had he wished for another kind of life?

We all wished for those, he said, and then here we were in this one, and must try to do as best we could. But if he had to say what he'd most wish for, then it might not be so far away from what my Mr Crusoe had had: some secluded place where the world wasn't looking, where they might live in a Sovereign kind of way – in any fashion, and by any law, they chose.

Which was as close as I ever came to grasping his Philosophy and hopes, and was followed by the closest I ever got to the story of his life. He told me he'd learnt the hard rules of the trade in his first year. No easy months at the Grande Portage for him. He was sent straight up to winter at Lake Winnipeg, to work under a dour old Scotsman called Cuthbert.

He remembered well the instruction he was given when he was sent into the woods to fetch the meat of a slaughtered moose.

Mr Cuthbert, what do I do if I can't find my way back?

You will probably die from the cold, Herse.

When he was sent to short-change a band of Cree with some barrels of diluted rum.

What will I do if they realise?

They will probably kill you, Herse.

When Cuthbert sent him down Red River in flood.

What if the water is too high?

You will probably drown, Herse.

How many deaths had Cuthbert predicted for him! He might as well have been apprenticed to the Reaper. But he'd lived. And learning how to stay alive wasn't the worst thing to learn up here.

He said I shouldn't be too hard on my father. Herse was himself an orphan, he said, and had spent most of his life alone in this world, with hardly a thing he'd done in it but by his own efforts. But to have one person to whom to present your accomplishments, or even failures – whether for applause or censure or anything – was worth every beaver on this continent.

And so, the Autumn crept on, in its piecemeal way, with bits of Summer and bits of Winter mixed in. There was tea with Herse, there were the escapades of Bruno, there were beavers, there were the NWC brutes with their slanders, there were our fears of being flayed and murdered by the Sioux, there were the islands doubled in their morning mists, and sometimes you were on yours and sometimes not, and sometimes, despite my better resolutions, I would take McLeod's place on the shore and sigh.

6

Of all the voices in those woods, the ones I considered most true were those of ducks. With them I was the hunter, and even attempted to mimic them, with a poor and strangled quacking. During these fowling expeditions, I made a sort of Indian road of familiar landmarks and features, never straying too far from the notional safety of our post. To the West of us was a creek, with a crossing place of stones, which flowed into Yellow River near where it entered the lake. Beyond this were the two ponds, bounded by a ridge topped with firs and a tall lightning-blasted pine. This was the limit of my fowling Kingdom, due to the far side of the ridge being thick with alders, and a general premonition that the chances of my being murdered/devoured/flayed by the Sioux were greater there.

One October morning, after perching on the trading hovel's roof, watching the ducks fly past, I issued out like one of Gil Blas' cronies towards the creek. Crossing at the stones, I discovered a whole flock snickering in the first of the ponds and – with a single shot – laid two of them low where they sat on the water. A third was wounded and, the blood up in me as much as it was leaking out of the duck, I sprinted up the ridge towards where it'd floundered. There is a peculiar and temporary derangement of the mind that comes in the pursuit of game – a sudden panicked blankness that has you pouring gunpowder into your pocket rather than your gun, or making a piece of bark seem an excellent flint – and it was this temporary flustering of Reason which had me scrambling after that duck before stopping, stepping back into my senses, and realising I'd strayed beyond the *ne plus ultra* of my Kingdom, deep into the alders. And if my reading of Defoe had taught me anything, I shouldn't have been surprised to discover a footprint.

But there it was. And there was another, and another still, leading towards the second pond. It must be Narcisse or Hyacinthe, I thought, or else Herse or one of the NWC brutes. Except surely I'd have seen them from the roof?

I looked again and had never tried so hard at translation. What did they say? It seemed they'd come from the river and gone over the ridge towards the second pond. But what of the stride of the man who'd made them? It appeared to me a very small and short stride, perhaps of some voyageur reduced to his ideal shape, his Platonic form: a mere torso with two ant-like legs appended to scurry over portages.

Short legs? Or short, soundless and stealthy steps? Sioux steps. Staring at those footprints, I now began to play a solitary and terrified game of 'What would you do?' What would you do if you were surrounded by a band of Sioux who planned to flay/murder/perhaps-devour you? And my answer came loudly: run away as fast as I could. I relayed this to my legs, except they were trembling too much to listen. Pillars and Posts, as my father would have mournfully remarked, though I'd never pictured my own Post as the blade of a Tommy-haw dripping with my brains. I would run, I repeated to my legs. And this time they heard me.

Ridge, lightning-blasted tree, second pond, first pond, and

then at the crossing point of stones what I'd not expected – a sighting of the agent of my bloody End. There, stepping from the last of the stones, the first I'd seen, and quite probably the last – a Sioux.

'Bail up,' I cried, pointing my fowling gun at him. 'Bail up!' As though this Sioux fellow would miraculously understand English and drop his weapon and lift his hands. Except that he did stop, and slowly turned around, and seemed to have indeed dropped his weapon for he had none in his hand. 'Stand still or I will shoot you,' I croaked.

'Arthur, put down that fucking gun,' replied McLeod, his decidedly long stride taking him onto the bank.

So here is McLeod, returned from his pursuit of your father, and looking as if he has been himself pursued by every mosquito and fly in the North West countries. His face is a blotchy mass of bites, a pin cushion of bites, an inflated udder of bites. The rest of him looks as though it's been vomited from Les Vases, and then rolled in briars. He is all mud and tatters. At the mouth of the creek lies his canoe in a similar condition.

When I ask if he's had any success, out pours a stream adjectival and adverbial, strongly indicating not. He greatly suspects the Two Birds' road might have been meant for chasing wild geese and hunting snipe and fishing for red herrings. The only thing he's discovered is word from a Saulteaux hunter about a recent sighting of a trader passing through the country.

Did he ask about this trader's arm and hair?

Of course he adverbially did. But the sighting was from afar and he was wearing an adjectival hat.

And more streams adjectival and adverbial, which carry us back to our post, where Crebassa and Hyacinthe are smoking pipes and Narcisse is teaching Spey the words to a song about hunting partridges.

And there, by chance, stepping around the corner of our living hovel, presumably headed for the NWC post to speak with Herse, and pursued by a scampering Bruno, are you, Esther. Since the trajectories are set, there is no opportunity for your paths to avoid each other and face to face you and McLeod come, at last. And here we are, us three, in our awkward Triangle, with one bear in addition.

'Esther,' says McLeod with great formality, as though you are meeting in some Montreal garden and not the shore of Yellow Lake, with him in his ruined garments, carefully composing his devoured face.

'Mr McLeod,' you reply in kind, with pines and birches standing in for cherry orchards.

'Arthur,' you add with a nod, in afterthought.

'Esther,' I say, with you my only thought.

'Well then,' says McLeod.

'Well,' says you.

'Well indeed,' says McLeod. Followed by many other variations of 'Well', until at last you ask him if he's had any success on his journey.

It has gone well enough, he replies.

Meaning he has found nothing.

Neither of you state the purpose of said journey. There is no mention of your father. The language is unaccustomedly stiff and pristine, cleaving to origins Latin rather than Saxon. He is doing everything in his power, begins McLeod, to find... Interrupted by your, Well, perhaps it would be better if he attended to his own business and left you to pursue yours; followed by his, Well, what do I have to do to show you, to make you believe... and your, Well, it might have been better for him to have considered that, when what he did mattered to you, etc. And all the while the language teetering, straining, becoming a thin, taut thread with no more gentle versions of Well to hide behind, until Well itself becomes a more Saxon kind of word.

Well, maybe he will damn well continue looking anyway.

Well, he is very welcome to continue his bungling pursuit wherever he wishes. He is excellent at finding nothing. And at least if he travels alone, he might eat all the seagulls and eggs himself.... Well, verb me, says McLeod, his dudgeon hatching, his dudgeon fledging, his dudgeon rising, until it is an eagle (in its ideal rather than edible form) soaring up and up through the clouds and skies. Perhaps his search is for his own Honour and you shouldn't flatter yourself it is merely to return to your good Graces; perhaps it is for the restoration of his good name etc, etc. Then pity the name McLeod, you say, if its reputation depends on his feckless, bungling, etc, etc.

Well, maybe I will find him... etc.

Well, maybe you couldn't find a... etc.

Well, maybe I will... etc.

Through a long circumnavigation, we are back at your very first reunion on Deep River. 'Fuck you, William.'

And then McLeod is stamping and stomping his way into the trading hovel. When he emerges, several minutes later, he's carrying a pack of fresh supplies. Since his face speaks thunder, none of us say a word, not wanting to find out how loud the thunder speaks. He stands looking towards your island a moment, aims a kick at Bruno – who's been trying to lick his boot – before turning on his heels and stamping and stomping his way back towards his canoe and disappearing back up the river.

And now we have arrived at that moment I wish dearly I could slow and stall and place gently in amber – the night of the party.

It turned out to be a happy occasion, in the precarious way we had them up there. Both Companies' posts had been completed; our own men still hoped there was yet a sliver of a chance we'd find the Missouri furs before the snow; the cooling days and nights had banished the mosquitoes. Herse provided the keg of shrub, with one of high wine in addition. The men had their regales and drams and cooked cakes with our precious remnant of flour. They made a fire in the space between the posts and joined with the NWC brutes there, falling into a dowsed and gently stupefied detente in which they danced and sang and told stories, and had not yet begun to think of punching one another. Bruno drank a pint of rum and frolicked and licked his feet and purred. Narcisse, sotted with high wine, began to waltz with his wooden Anna-Marie. Spey sang a song in French. Crebassa sortied out in his sash and finest neckerchief and chivalrously presented his flour-cakes to the Widow. Hyacinthe forgave the masticator of his nose for a spell and stopped eyeing the teeth of the NWC brutes. We even gave them their names for an hour or two.

Only Herse didn't seem to share in the merriment, though he filled everyone's cups. He sat alone at the edge of the fire's light, watching the sparks fly up into the dark, as though remembering sad stories from the edge of the world. Or else happy ones the world had made sad.

And there also, at the edge of this light, were you. I can't say if you were merry or sad. I'm not certain what you saw in that rising, flittering, fire-bat flock of sparks. I can only say what I saw – which was your lips and teeth, wet with high wine, and above them a dome of stars made clearer by the cooling night, and possessed with a vanquishing clarity that seemed to take away all memory of how I'd arrived there beneath it, as though there were skies and nights that you were born into, carrying nothing but a pair of astonished eyes. All my resolutions dissolved beneath it. And then we were sharing high wine from your cup and I was glad to find it no longer tasted of shrub, as all liquors had since Lachine. What did we speak about then? Who knows. Who cares. We watched the men jig and reel, we watched Herse filling cups, we watched Bruno totter on his hind legs. One of the NWC men played a fiddle with its three surviving strings and it was a symphony.

As the voices around us got louder, and Hyacinthe began to tell the story of how he'd lost his nose, and the high wine performed its better alchemies, I decided I might try to eke out a few more pipes of this happy lull.

I told you I was going to go sit by the lake.

And why was that? you asked.

Because I already knew the story of Hyacinthe losing his nose.

We made our way to the promontory of sand, opposite the

second of the islands, and watched the glittering water, which looked like moonlight and starlight, and nobody had ever drowned in moonlight and starlight.

It was a very fine moon tonight, I said.

You told me this was called the Falling Leaves Moon, then laughed and said you didn't know what they called it in Greece.

Nor did I, I said, laughing also.

And then began to wish I could describe the fantastical mists that covered the lake each morning – to you, who'd already seen a thousand such fantastical mists on lakes, including these – and wondered why everything I now saw made me wonder what you would see in it, as if I had lent some part of my eyes to you, perhaps that part that gave things meaning.

Instead, I said I wondered where McLeod was.

You said you would prefer not to spend one second of this evening talking about adjectival McLeod.

And nor did I but couldn't help myself. There I was with you, only to discover him lumbering roughly and unbidden into my guilty thoughts. I waited for the quiet lapping of the water to take him away.

You took a long swig from the tin cup and asked me about my mother. I told you how she was from an island across the ocean that I often imagined, though I'd never seen it. It was very green, I thought. And full of castles.

'I think you're rather kind, Arthur,' you said, and looked at me curiously, as though realising something you'd not quite expected. You asked me why I was afraid of water.

I explained how I'd been raised with stories about floods

and inundations. That was another thing about my mother's island: its castles often seemed to be underwater.

Your mother had also told you such stories, you said. About floods and inundations. But they hadn't made you afraid. In your stories, they were how the world had started.

I said in mine they were usually how it ended.

'Come with me,' you said then, taking my hand.

We walked along the shore until we reached a small crescent of sand, fringed by cedars, opposite the third island. Away in the distance, the firelight flickered against the pale bark of poplars and birches, making night-bones of them. Sparks eddied up into the dark. The voices of the men had been loud in the still, clear air, but now seemed to gentle as they came across the water towards us, until they were hardly even whispers. We might have been in another country from them.

We removed our capots and moccasins, and took one step, and then another, into the lake, whose golden bed was invisible. The water was cool, and your hand was warm. Its fingers were long and smooth, the skin hard at the heel and then smoothing again in the fleshy palm. I'd never considered a hand in such detail. If it had been a Greek verb, I might have been a Professor.

The water pressed and wetted our flannel shirts against us, as if they were skin. The cedars cast moon shadows from shore, dark blending into glittering dark. 'Are you afraid of this,' you said, letting go of my hand and swirling the water with yours.

I said I wasn't, and in that moment it was the truth.

You asked me to kneel, and so I did, the water coming up to my chest.

'Or this,' you said, cupping some in your hands and pouring

it over my head. Above me, your face became a liquid oval. Somewhere out on the lake a loon began its nightly lament, and each note of it was liquid too.

'Or this,' you said, kneeling in front of me, so we were face to face, and I could see your lips parted over your teeth, with that little gap as deep and promising as any sky. We were so close I could feel your breath, warm and cool at once, and then feel your lips too, which were as liquid and smooth as the water which dripped over us.

'Or this,' you whispered, reaching down and unbuttoning my trousers. Your long fingers felt like your breath and lips, and all my body seemed lodged in that one part of me, touched by skin and then by water and then by skin.

And then you wrapped your legs around me, and everything was warm and cool and smooth and liquid.

And how happily I would end this flow of recollection here and have that as my single Age. One would have been enough, without succession, without decline. To be with you in Yellow Lake, swaddled in wet flannel, discovering how this went miraculously there, and what it felt like.

But it will not stay still. Even that night will fracture into little epochs, its own declines and falls. Away from us, where it seems another country – yet one to which we must return – the high wine will begin its befuddling work. Hyacinthe will punch one of the NWC men, turned brute again; the Widow will reject Crebassa's gallant advances; Narcisse will wish his lover wasn't wooden; and Bruno will frolic too near the coals of the fire and singe his feet.

And so the night will end with bruises and yearnings and regrets and a bear forlornly weeping.

7

The next morning it began to snow.

By the time the men had dragged themselves from their cocoons of wool and shrub-sweat it had already begun to settle, and the land was beginning to appear much like those customary pictures of the North West countries – as though it would not stop being Winter for a long, long time. And while my own hopes had leap-frogged the moon the evening before, so now those slender hopes the men had clung to – that they might be away from here before the end of the Autumn – were extinguished.

We'd been woken by the din of Spey banging a kettle against the wall of the living hovel. What in the name of various ecclesiastical Cods and Members was this, demanded Hyacinthe?

'A bear,' called Spey in alarm.

'It is only Bruno,' groaned Narcisse.

'Not Bruno,' came Spey's reply. 'Bruno's with me.'

We tumbled out the door, shielding our gaze from the newly glittering world, which offered myriad sharp and tiny spearpoints to our eyes. And sure enough there was Bruno, hopping from singed foot to singed foot, glowering and growling in the direction of the first pond.

The bear had been right there, said Spey. Watching from the trees.

Perhaps he'd been after our food supplies in the trading hovel, I said.

What supplies, remarked Crebassa mournfully. We'd made the last of our flour into cakes. And we'd hardly traded enough to live on.

What should I do?

I should find that bear and shoot him, Spey said. And then turn him into steaks.

Indeed, I said, taking up my gun somewhat nervously (for a bear was not a duck) and, accompanied by Hyacinthe and Narcisse, set off in pursuit.

The new snow was like the opening of a book. We could see bits and pieces of animal stories everywhere in it. The bear's recent story was this: he'd been watching our post from the treeline; he'd fled across the creek (making use, curiously, of the stepping stones) and around the first and second ponds; he'd gone over the ridge – which we now descended in his wake, moving through the alders, my heart beating faster as we left my fowling Kingdom behind.

We'd gone no more than a few hundred yards and were approaching the river, when we came upon the ashes of a small fire. It was hard to tell how old they were. Hyacinthe suggested weeks. I suggested days. Narcisse suggested the more pressing question was the meaning of the sticks.

And sure enough, some sticks had been planted in a circle around the ashes. We counted six of them.

'Who would –' I began. Narcisse looked at Hyacinthe, Hyacinthe looked at me, and we all, wordlessly, decided it might be better to contemplate the meaning of this page of the book from the safety of the post and began walking swiftly back towards it.

As for the bear, he could have these woods to himself.

After Crebassa had told her what we'd seen, the Widow suggested we'd have been better advised to run back to the post. For it was customary, she explained, for the Sioux to leave such sticks by their fires, to mark their presence and number and show they were not afraid to enter this country.

How quickly everything altered. The alarm spread over to the NWC brutes, everyone rushing to arm themselves, Hyacinthe perching on the roof of our living hovel to act as sentry, Narcisse insisting to Spey that he move into it for his safety. Meanwhile, I searched for Herse, to discuss our joint predicament, but couldn't find him. And then puffed out my chest and announced I'd go immediately to rescue you from the island.

What a different lake it was that morning: the scene of my recent joy turned into one of fear and anxiety. But even so, I considered how momentous the previous night had been, how it had changed everything. In what manner would I explain to McLeod our new situation? That you'd chosen me; that love could not be staunched but flowed like rivers etc; that we must discuss this development like gentlemen, with civility. Meanwhile, I wondered where we'd live, had a family for us, pictured us in our happy dotage, holding hands.

Finding you outside your wigwam, contemplating the snow, I informed you of the discovery of the sticks and gallantly announced I'd come to escort you to the safety of the post.

Ah, so I was here to save you. How very sweet. But you'd be quite fine on the island, you thought. A great deal safer than at the post, most probably.

And about last night?

It had been a very nice night.

A nice night! It had been a momentous night. And I was eager to run directly and passionately into the arms of its consequences and responsibilities. Esther, I said, tremblingly, falling to my knee. Since we had done the thing, nothing would make me happier and more full of joy than to do the other thing. We would be engaged.

Oh dear.

Oh dear?

Please stand up, Arthur, you said.

I didn't. Though my knee was becoming wet in the snow and I was more frozen than the snowflakes. *Oh dear?*

Oh, Arthur. You'd enjoyed doing that with me. You were fond of me, and were not a spinster aunt from Inverness. But there would be no engagement.

How stricken my face must have been. The happy dotage, the holding hands, all of it crumbled back into dream-dust. And from their wreckage came a whimper: did this mean we'd never do that thing again?

Perhaps we might, you said with a smile.

But you wouldn't come to the post?

You wouldn't. And besides, you'd soon have to make a journey.

A journey. Where? Why?

The first snow had come.

And what did that mean?

It meant that you'd have to begin looking.

And here, unfortunately, entered the Other Arthur. Looking for McLeod?

This had not an adjectival thing to do with McLeod.

The Other Arthur would doubtless have had some obnoxious addition, but luckily there was now a surprising interruption. 'Ah, it's you, Arthur,' came Herse's voice from the edge of the clearing. 'You'll ruin your trousers in that snow.'

I was informing you, Esther, of the presence of the Sioux, I said, getting stiffly to my feet.

'Indeed,' said Herse. There was a stain on the collar of his jacket, a slight darkness about his chin. I could've sworn he hadn't shaved.

And what about them? I exclaimed. Shouldn't we make arrangements for our mutual defence?

They rarely killed traders, he said.

Why did everyone keep telling me that?

He didn't mean to be rude, but you and he had some business to discuss. Perhaps I might give you some privacy.

I took a few steps towards the edge of the clearing.

'Perhaps an island's worth of it, Arthur.'

The narrow strait to the mainland had become a Gulf. Returning to the post, I felt I might have better entrusted my heart to that bear, or the Sioux.

I didn't see you depart, but tried very hard to see you return. Rising early in the mornings to go sit by the lake and mope in sight of the flat rock where you'd usually have been, washing the night out of your hair. The first snow lay on the ground for several days, and the cooling lake water sent forth its vapours. But I no longer took any pleasure in the sight. This fantastical mist was only the coming Winter, sucking the last warmth out of the world.

The discovery of the sticks was like a chorus of owls. We began to imagine signs of the Sioux everywhere. It made our post a prison: we barely dared venture a pipe from it. At the same time, our supplies of food dwindled further, just as the Saulteaux were gathering theirs.

For by then the maple leaves were mostly fallen, and even the cedars – which had once held that miraculous green before the sun dipped – were rusted. It was the season when the deer, stupefied by desire, became most stupid. Here and there and everywhere they were being plucked from the groaning agonies and brief delights of their wooing to be transmuted into blankets and moccasins and smoked meat; for like those swains and maids of yesteryear, they were most vulnerable to metamorphosis when in love.

Or like the beaver itself. The prime snare and snickle of a beaver trap is castoreum: the musk and love juice of the beaver – the batted eyelid, the eager smile, the breathless whisper, all in one. In beaver world off they would go, a-beaver-wooing, and return a hat. But who am I to shake my head at the foibles of Castor.

I'd arranged a meeting with Herse, and, as he stirred the kettle for our tea, noted his pinched expression and stooped shoulders. I mentioned how Narcisse had recently discovered some mysterious footprints, and he continued to stare distractedly into the kettle, as though he'd not heard a word.

There'd been a peculiar proliferation of owls, I added.

Herse passed me my tea, gazing somewhere off above my head, as if to scrutinise some invisible cloud. There were patches of grease and soot on his trousers, his neckerchief was crooked.

I explained how our supplies of food were almost exhausted.

At this he took notice. But this was the very season to trade for them, he said. Which was quite true. We were sat hungrily in the middle of a harvest. In the country around, rice was being gathered, animals were being shot, fish were being pulled from weirs and nets, the last berries plucked from bushes. For those mooning Englishmen with their waterfalls have a monocle sort of view, calling wildernesses what those who live there would reckon a Sussex parish, with its farms and orchards and fields of ripening corn. And in all of this we could barely scrump a single apple.

The men were afraid to go out of sight of our hovel, I said, and the Saulteaux wouldn't trade with us. They'd been told we mixed our high wine with our own water, and befouled our trading blankets with our own procreative matter, and were beggars and thieves who slept with our sisters back in our own cow country.

It was all opposition, said Herse, shaking his head. And how heartily sick and tired of it he was. All he wanted was one tiny corner where this world would leave him alone.

Then, perhaps in our mutual predicament vis-à-vis the Sioux, we might put opposition to one side.

And what would McLeod think of this?

I told him I'd no clue where McLeod was even, only that he'd gone somewhere West, up Yellow River.

McLeod was a fool and so was his errand. He should've stayed put and made sure his men had enough to eat.

This brought me to another predicament, guided by the Other Arthur. I stared at my tea and perused the same invisible cloud as Herse. He sipped his own tea impatiently. 'She's not gone to meet him, Arthur,' he said at last, 'if that's what you're worried about.'

But why else would you go?

To find your father, of course! Did I understand nothing? Had my little sips of Passion made me blind to everything else? What in the name of God in his Heaven did I think had brought Esther here. Brought both you and he here.

I'd never seen this cross and crabbit version of Herse. My reply was a croaky, faltering thing. I confessed McLeod's theory of Herse's own motives. That he'd wanted to find his friend Copperhead (and here Herse forcibly reminded me to use his proper name, Ross) in order to convince him – and perhaps Long Arm too – to join Herse in the NWC. How in doing so he'd not only get hold of the Missouri furs for that Company but something more valuable still – the knowledge of their source. And this was why he and his Company were assisting you in finding your father, Esther, by giving you passage to the New Fort, and then here to Yellow Lake.

Herse's face turned a peculiar red-grey. That was what McLeod thought! That was his blockheaded notion! His windmills in the head! Then the anger began to ebb into a deep weariness. It couldn't have been more wrong, even for McLeod. After a lengthy exhalation of breath, he said, so be it. If he told me certain things, would I promise – for now at least – not to share them with McLeod?

I said there were already quite a number of things it might be better for me to avoid telling McLeod.

As it turned out, the first part of our little argosy had all along been in quest of a Chimera's fleece. According to Herse, those Missouri furs had never been intended for either the XY or the NWC. When Ross and Long Arm had been asked to explore the Missouri country, the two of them (in league with Herse) had hatched a scheme: to keep the furs they found there for themselves. Instead of delivering them to the XY fort at the Kaministiquia, Ross and Long Arm would find somewhere to hide them – their own Secret Post (just as McLeod had surmised). Meanwhile, Herse would spend the Winter in Montreal, to arrange their sale to some American traders, outside the sight and dominion of either Company. Herse had also arranged with Long Arm that he would transport you, Esther, back to the North West countries, if you chose not to stay in Montreal. If so, then both Herse and you would come join Ross and Long Arm at this post, wherever it was they had decided to locate it. All Herse must do was maintain his ruse to the NWC that he was undertaking this in their interest, using his daughter to draw out Long Arm so the Company might get their hands both on the Missouri furs and their source.

This was where Labrie had been involved. As Long Arm's old clerk with the XY, he'd been happy (for a small price) to help them. They'd made this arrangement with him: that Ross and Long Arm would meet with him during the winter, near the Rainy River fort, so they could inform him where they'd established their Secret Post. Labrie would then return to the Kaministiquia with this information and pass it on to Herse when he arrived there in the Spring.

The rest of the scheme was simple enough. Herse, Ross, Long Arm and you (if you chose to return, and knowing all about the scheme) would all rendezvous at this post, abscond their Companies, and sell the furs to the Americans. With the profits, they'd be free either to trade independently, or leave the trade entirely.

My head clinked with the sound of pennies dropping. And when had he heard about Labrie's death?

Not until they got to the New Fort, Herse told me. They hadn't seen his body at Lachine, and only knew what we did: that with his final breath he'd mentioned the Folle Avoine and Yellow Lake. Since then, Herse had had to wait here the same as us, playing the trader for the NWC men, waiting for Ross and Long Arm to arrive.

Of this, he'd been hopeful to begin with. The Two Birds had confirmed the pair had been in this country in the Spring. And there were rumours more recently amongst the Saulteaux of a trader having been seen in the country. Herse was almost certain this must either be Ross or Long Arm. And as they'd surely hear news of there being two new posts at Yellow Lake, you and he had decided that it'd be foolish to go chasing after needles in a haystack, especially a haystack that was potentially full of Sioux hornets. You'd both determined to wait here instead of trying to find the Secret Post, at least until the first snow fell. After that, you'd go looking.

But why hadn't Herse gone looking with you?

It was a matter of practicalities. If Ross or Long Arm was in the country, you, Esther, were the more likely to find them: you knew it better and would have the help of your uncle. And if they arrived at Yellow Lake when you were gone, then Herse would be here.

But why not tell McLeod about this? If he was already searching for Long Arm? Surely, it'd be better to find him any which way?

Because neither you nor Herse trusted McLeod. He'd previously shown that he might well choose his career above his affections.

I could have told Herse right then and there that wasn't true, and how I'd bet my bottom beaver McLeod gave not a flying Fig about his position in the XY, but rather everything about his affections. And I would have told him this too, if the Other Arthur had allowed me.

He was meant to wait, said Herse, but he'd begun to get a bad feeling, and every day it got worse. If there had been these sightings of a trader, then why hadn't he arrived here yet? If it was Ross, why hadn't he come to him?

The next day, Herse was gone.

The NWC brutes hadn't a clue to where, and in our hovel, the men wondered if perhaps the Sioux had taken him. Or else the bear. I kept my bone-box shut and hid what he'd told me from them — all of it.

A week passed and those rutting deer and besotted beavers began to seem like Aristotle compared to me. I became a squint-eyed jealous wretch, who sat about staring at a blanket and saw you and McLeod in it, coupling; who made every leafless tree a gentle bower, under which you kissed. The Other Arthur was a cruel alchemist: he turned castoreum into nightshade; he turned gold green.

The second snow of the year fell, and then the third, and then we stopped counting. We got hungrier and hungrier. When Spey saw that bear a second time, once again watching us from the treeline, we pursued its tracks as though they were steaming porkchops. They led us around the ponds and over the ridge to the bank of the river, where they vanished. The beast must have swum across, we reckoned, and nobody fancied tracking him across that Rubicon. It was the last thing we needed, said Hyacinthe. A clever bear. But I'd say Bruno was a clever one too, for he soon after went off to find a Winter den.

The passing hunters continued to avoid our trade, but brought us more rumours of the Sioux, who they said were everywhere this season. And holed up by fear in our living hovel we began to dream dreams as strange and prophetic as those of the Saulteaux. Hyacinthe and Narcisse squabbled. Spey moaned in his nightmares. Only Crebassa seemed at peace. It appeared he'd at last been successful in his wooing and had begun sharing the Widow's wigwam. Every morning he went promenading with her, in a cloud of happy pipe smoke, his living ear bent to her conversation.

And perhaps longing and jealousy, as well as an empty belly, gives you courage of a sort, because eventually I began to patrol my fowling Kingdom again, hunting in earnest now – as even the mocking grin of the silver fox on the stock of my gun had become pinched and grim – but alas to much the same effect. The fowls were mostly departed. The rest of the animals, knowing a hungry man, kept their distance. It was with a heavy heart I now related my tales of near misses and retreating behinds to the men. 'Perhaps it would be better, Mr Arthur,' said Narcisse one day, 'if you might hit one of those arses, as well as see them.'

8

The third time we saw that bear, it was carrying off Spey.

One afternoon, Narcisse and I heard Hyacinthe calling from the roof. Tumbling out the door, we discovered him in the performance of a peculiar jig, leaping from foot to foot and pointing violently towards the treeline. Following his stabbing finger, we glimpsed a dark shape slipping between the poplar trunks, and a patch of lighter straw which, with a mutual gulp, we realised must be Spey's hair. We were too stunned to move at first, but eventually Narcisse let out a high-pitched cry and rushed towards the trees in pursuit. Hyacinthe and I followed.

Once more, its trail led to the river, the tracks ending abruptly on its bank. But there was no halt this time. Narcisse was swimming before anybody had a chance to speak. We could hear him hollering and crashing through the trees on the other bank. Hyacinthe, reluctantly, waded after him.

I could not follow.

When next I saw them, Hyacinthe was dragging Narcisse back across the river. They were trembling with cold too much to speak. And it wasn't until we were back in the hovel that they were able to explain. There'd been no tracks on the other side. Not one.

The only explanation was the bear had swum downriver, carrying Spey with him. Narcisse, as soon as he'd thawed out enough to move, said he'd go follow. But by this time, it was getting dark. Narcisse said he'd go search, whether anyone came with him or not. Hyacinthe moved to block the door. I said we'd go with a canoe as soon as we had light in the morning. Hyacinthe said it was already too late, and we'd be looking for bones at best. Narcisse began to weep. Perhaps it'd be best if none of us spoke until the morning, I said.

Leaving Crebassa to look after the post, we set out at first light, heading up the river, carrying our last bag of wild rice, two kegs of rum to trade for supplies if we were fortunate enough to meet with some Saulteaux, and the fug of bad dreams in our heads.

For several pipes the snow on the banks of the river revealed nothing, except that ice was beginning to form there and we'd not have the use of the rivers and lakes for much longer. The first place we stopped to search for tracks, Narcisse, in his grief, managed to lose our rice. It was all I could do to stop Hyacinthe beating out his brains with a paddle. At the next place, I found some acorns beneath the snow and we ate them and lay moaning on the ground, holding our bellies.

'You have poisoned us, Mr Arthur,' said Narcisse.

'It is you who has starved us, you idiot,' said Hyacinthe to Narcisse.

I told them we'd stop a while here for me to hunt, as I was sure I'd seen the tracks of some partridges.

'Oh,' said Hyacinthe bleakly.

'Ah,' groaned Narcisse, and began to eat what was left of the acorns. Both sounded as if they'd starved already.

But sometimes, whatever the Good Book says, salvation

can be as simple as a stupid deer. And the one I discovered, no more than two hundred yards away, was wondrously so. Perhaps deranged by an influx of deer castoreum, and thinking me a fine and handsome buck, it waited patiently while I fumbled with my shot bag and powder horn and took a trembling aim. It might as well have fallen at my feet like an Autumn pear. I went to fetch Narcisse and Hyacinthe, who stared at that dead deer as though it were a basket of bread and sausages delivered by the Good Lady herself.

We had its hide already pulled down over its shoulders when the deer returned leaping to its feet, leaving its innards in a pile on the ground. It was a frightful sight: Death in Life, or Life in Death, or whichever way around you wish. The flesh and fat on its neck and shoulders gleamed horridly. When it snorted, a gout of blood gushed steaming from its nostrils.

Hyacinthe and Narcisse turned as white as its tail, crossing themselves. My own knees wobbled. The deer gazed directly at us, the pupils of its eyes as big and dark as ripened plums, took two steps, faltered, and then fell. I put another ball in its head, but Hyacinthe and Narcisse wouldn't even look at it. When I went to continue the butchering, they turned their backs, refusing to approach its body.

'But it's completely dead, now,' I said.

'We can't touch it,' Hyacinthe said.

'But why?'

'You don't understand.'

'Understand what?'

'It is the Devil.'

'That thing is a deer,' I said. 'A completely dead deer. And we are starving.'

But Narcisse and Hyacinthe would have none of it. We left a feast there in the forest. 'Better to starve than to eat a piece of the Devil,' Hyacinthe muttered once we were back in the canoe.

Less than a pipe further on, we came upon a set of bear tracks, though whether they were from Spey's murderer or not, who knew. We hid the canoe and kegs in some alder and began following them. We'd not gone half a mile before the snow began to fall.

Hyacinthe exclaimed he'd gone far enough in search of bones.

Narcisse said he'd travelled ten thousand miles to avenge a masticated nose.

There was a great deal more of this, and there would have been fisticuffs soon enough if we hadn't then arrived at the shore of a small lake. In a clearing by its shore, we discovered the bear tracks were now accompanied, or pursued, or overlaid, by a set of human ones. We debated the proper interpretation of these (Narcisse: they were Spey's, who was still alive; Hyacinthe: they were Saulteaux tracks) for so long that the falling snow began to erase them. And this erasure, I realised with alarm, included our own tracks – our sole guide back to the canoe.

We must return immediately, I announced.

At that moment, a small dog emerged from the woods. It eyed us warily, but eventually came close enough for Narcisse to scratch its ears. We decided it must be a Saulteaux dog, which made what happened next more alarming still. It began frantically sniffing and scratching where the tracks had almost vanished and set up a terrific barking – all of which were actions performed by Saulteaux dogs when their enemies were near, which enemies were predominantly Sioux dogs. There was no more debating, then. These tracks were a judge in a Black Cap reading out our names.

We ran, following what we thought was the direction of the river, but the snow had become a blizzard and our tracks had vanished completely. At last, losing our breath, we came to a halt on a long, low point jutting into a river we didn't recognise. The sun had begun to set.

I suppose Hell, like the Devil, can appear in many guises: for this point was one of the most delightful spots I was to see in all the North West countries. It was spread with tall pines and basswoods, growing asunder as if they'd been planted for a gentleman's park. Hummocks of stone and alder bushes made themselves grottoes in Sylvan shades. What a taunting spectacle to us, who inside were all shrieking wildwoods and howling plains! We scraped the snow from the ground beneath a giant elm, whose bark hung down in strips from its lower branches, offering some cover from those eyes we feared might be watching us already. We could risk making only the smallest, most miserable fire.

The snow clouds cleared and out came the moon, a disc of ice, and the air grew cold enough to crack branches. What an awful, star-bright clarity that night had, to stage horrid semblances and Phantasms. Every tree trunk played a man. Each falling leaf was a Sioux whisper. We fancied we smelt the smoke of their pipes and the meat on their breath. We shared not a word until Hyacinthe spoke, saying this was the work of that devil-deer. Some might have called this superstition, but why, I thought, under that cold moon, in that mockery of a park, should not all beliefs be as sound as others. The tommy-haw in our skulls wouldn't worry about what was housed there.

It was then we began to feel a growing heat, as Hell put on its more accustomed guise.

The bark of the elm had caught on the sparks of the fire. In seconds, the whole tree was ablaze and we were standing at the edge of a great circle of light, a beacon for our imagined murderers. There couldn't have been a pair of eyes within fifty statute miles that didn't see it. There was nothing else to do but flee again.

Soon afterwards, the moon vanished and down came the snow once more, the gods turning roughly in their beds and tearing up their pillows. In front of me was Narcisse's back, below me his footprints, and on every side a swirling, icy tumult. It had the momentum of a journey in a dream: one foot after another but somehow not moving at all. And then at some point the snow was dwindling and a butter-milky light was coming through the trees. Blinking, I realised Narcisse's back was something blurrily recalled – a dream not quite escaped – but in this waking world was absent. The snow in front of me was as pristine as a nun's habit.

For the next few hours, I would refer you to the earlier account of my journey with McLeod near the mouth of Brule River – the circles, the panic, etc – except substitute the *danse macabre* of desperate men in books with my fear of the Sioux, and that late-Summer morning with the pulverising, bone-cracking cold of Winter.

A red capot, a pair of leggings, moccasins in the snow. A man at the edge of a river, iced over along its banks. A hole in the ice and something writhing beside it in the snow. From Sioux to Saulteaux to the Two Birds turns the man, and now we are standing with that pike between us. We have our conversation, as related in the first pages, vis-à-vis furs and the Cow Country, etc, and agree on the terms of trade for the pike, etc, and then move to that part of our conversation I didn't elaborate earlier.

To make a nutshell of it. I asked the Two Birds if he knew the whereabouts of Narcisse and Hyacinthe. He did. They'd been discovered bickering in the woods earlier in the morning and would be staying at his camp a day or two to recover. I told him about the bear and Spey, and asked if he'd heard anything about McLeod. Not recently. And your whereabouts, Esther? He said it was a curious thing I should be interested in your whereabouts.

I apologised for our first encounter and the one keg. I was new in this country and had known no better.

Looking over my tattered clothes and frozen face, he said he realised this well enough. As for the kegs, that was the fault of McLeod, who should have known better. But who knew what went on in the Tall Tree's head these days? Not trade, to be sure. It seemed the only thing he did now was chase about looking for your father.

I was hopping from one freezing foot to the other and the Two Birds, grinning in his not-moving-his-lips way, asked if this was how we danced in Cow Country. It was a great mystery to him what his niece saw in us two fellows: who couldn't dance, who dressed so badly, who could barely hunt for their own food.

Two fellows! Then your niece sees something in me, I said

(*and McLeod still*, whispered the Other Arthur, whom I was surprised to find eager to make his appearance even here).

The Two Birds considered this a moment. Well, if his niece was inclined to have such poor and ridiculous affections, he said, of the two of us at least I'd not eaten a gull and all its eggs, and shown myself a stingy, treacherous sort of fellow.

I thanked him.

Of course, he continued, attaching herself to either of us would be the most foolish thing imaginable, like marrying a baby or a dotard or an idiot, but if she was determined to carry on along this execrable road then perhaps I might be the better side of it, like being hit by lightning could be considered better than drowning, or eating the innards of a duck better than eating the innards of a goose. His niece had been here at his camp, he said, but had returned recently to her island place.

And had Esther found what she was looking for? (*He will probably answer yes, you had found McLeod*, whispered the Other Arthur. *They are probably walking back there now, holding hands.*)

She hadn't found her father. Or Copperhead, either. McLeod was looking for them in one direction, she in another. And now it appeared Herse was looking as well. He'd tell me what he'd told his niece: that it would be wiser this time of year to be looking for deer. But she'd always been headstrong in this matter of finding her father.

You one way, McLeod the opposite. Out sprang the sun. Within and without. I thanked him again and was about to turn on my heels before realising I had no idea what direction to take.

And how might I get back most safely? I asked, preparing to memorise his Indian road directions.

'You follow this river.'
'And?'
'And you will reach your post.'

9

It was night when I arrived back at the trading post, having eaten my pike raw. The moon was bright enough for there to be shadows, and during my journey, my emotions had made more circumnavigations than Captain Cook. I was sad about Spey, and then elated you'd thought of me as one of those fellows. How coldly love skips around death sometimes. And then a plunge. *Fellows*, whispered the Other Arthur. The dreaded plural. *She has tender feelings for McLeod yet.* The world was a desolate and hopeless place. But the Two Birds said he would prefer me. I was walking on air, I was dancing. And then whisper, whisper and more desolation. But eventually these emotions settled to match the night. There was that glistening stillness to it, that glitter-studding of rime upon the bare, dark boughs, which made you feel this was another world entirely, one you should tread carefully upon lest you damage or disturb it.

Our living hovel was a dark rectangle against a screen of tiny diamonds, a plume of smoke slipping mysteriously from its chimney. How could this be? Hyacinthe and Narcisse were at the camp of the Two Birds. Crebassa would surely be with the Widow.

I opened the door.

'Arthur,' you said. 'I was hoping it'd be you.'

The circumnavigation had ended, and I'd found the

Northwest Passage and Terra Australis Incognita and El Dorado. My tongue felt like a flock of ducks taking flight. Somewhere in the confusion of sounds was a version of 'Why are you here?'

You would like to ask me one favour.

Any favour at all, stuttered Arthur the Knight of Chivalry. Some parlous quest, a combat to the death.

Could I not ask you any questions. That was the favour. What you wished for most in the world was one night where you didn't have to think or worry about anything. Because tomorrow, you would have to face these things.

Was this something to do with…

One favour, you said, holding up a finger. And nothing about what I was speaking about on my one knee at our last meeting. In fact, nothing at all would be excellent for a while.

And so let us sit silently in the hovel for a pipe or two, which time it takes me to realise what's different about the hovel. It smells better. It's been an awful long time since I've been away from the stench of men. All apart from my own.

We sit there for another pipe before you motion me towards the hearth, where a large kettle is warming on the fire.

'Take off your clothes,' you say.

'Why,' I begin, though dearly, desperately hoping we'll do what we did before.

'Because you stink.'

So off come my moccasins and capot. Off comes my shirt. The light from the fire exposes a mole on my hip, a purple birthmark beneath my ribs, which I see as though through different eyes and hope are not repulsive. My trousers are more difficult. There is a tentpole sticking out of me. The low, throaty hum of your laughter rises over the crackle of the logs.

'You can turn around, Arthur. I've felt you, so I'd like to see you too.'

I turn around.

'You're okay,' you say with a smile.

Then off come your clothes, too.

And there you are in the warm shimmer of the firelight. The first woman I have seen naked, your little belly curving into the roundness of your hips and thighs. But this time I won't play Narcisse and his whittling with words: it would be a feeble sort of sculpture. You are you, and you are very beautiful.

We cover the ground near my cot with furs and there they lie, beavers, fishers, otters, minks, as though their living parts have slipped away for modesty's sake and left behind their skins. Skins beneath us, skins around us, skins everywhere and exquisitely soft.

After a small chaos of elbows and knees, you lead me down towards your lower hair. Imagine, you say, I'm eating honey from a comb, or pollen from a flower. I must lick it with my tongue, soft at first like a hummingbird – and then a bit harder.

'No, no,' you say, 'not there.'

Except I don't know where here or there is. It's dusky and hot among the furs, and very confusing beneath my tongue.

'Here?'

'Up from there.'

'Here?'

'That's my stomach, Arthur.'

'So further down but not so far?'

'Yes.'

I try a little bit everywhere.

Good lord, you say, do I need a compass?

I'm in the middle of telling you I've never done this, when your hands take hold of my head and move it firmly down.

'There,' you say.

I try to be like a hummingbird, and then a bit harder.

The next day, we lay on the furs long into the morning, in acts delightful, and then sleeping, and then more acts delightful. What light there was oozed through the thin parchment of the window. It fell on the dull metal of the plates and cups, the teeth of the beaver traps, some furs that hung on hooks from the walls, my trousers on the floor. It fell on my index finger, which was lazily twirling a few strands of your lower hair. My cheek lay against your belly. Your own fingers were playing with the less lustrous hair on my head.

'It's like a small nest,' I said.

'What is?'

'This,' I said, continuing to twirl my finger.

I was saying your Monosyllable was like a bird's nest.

'Like a small and delicate bird's nest.'

'Everything is like this and like that with you, isn't it, Arthur?'

I twirled my fingers some more. All this was wonderful, and I didn't want it to be like anything else.

During the night, you'd whispered in my ear and ascribed me some qualities: I was shy and thoughtful and had no malice in me. I wasn't sure all of these were qualities I did possess, or possessed entirely – though, if you liked them, I hoped I did. Except then the Other Arthur (who most definitely had none of them) had begun to wonder if these were not qualities

McLeod lacked, and so he must have others you admired that I lacked. And then I'd begun to picture McLeod toppling from the crest of a waterfall, being swirled far, far away by a rapid. This didn't appear proof of an absence of malice. My hand upon your private parts didn't feel shy, either. How odd it seemed, that being close to another could make oneself appear multiplied.

'Arthur,' you said after a while, reaching with your hand to push my fingers a little lower, 'let's be less thoughtful for a while now.'

After we'd finished, it was you who was multiplied. This Esther was stern and sad and anxious. 'I must go and find Herse', you said.

I told you then that Herse had told me about the Scheme.

You said it was true, all of it, but now everything seemed to be going adjectivally awry. You'd expected to find Herse waiting here but discovered him gone. He must have become desperate to find Copperhead.

But why?

You said there were things it wasn't for you to tell me.

But in that moment my own desperation overtook me. Where would you be going? When would I next see you? Etc and regrettably etc.

Arthur. Do not do it. Please. Do not do the whole One Knee thing again. Don't take a pleasant night and turn it into an Englishman's marriage. You would refer me to our conversation vis-à-vis lovely things and liking me and not being a spinster aunt and such. Right now, you needed to find Herse. That was what you had to adverbially do.

Or maybe someone else… McLeod perhaps?

You spoke very eloquently then, with your feet. The tracks you left were bruises in the snow.

And how happy I'd have been to pause this several paragraphs ago, put down my pen, step back in time to push the Other Arthur out of my head, and then let the trick of ink and paper make this interlude a whole Winter and never rise from those furs. Like Bruno, who had gone to sleep in a cave in the woods to dream away the Winter.

10

Outside the living hovel, the ponds and lakes and rivers are freezing over and the country, thick with snow and scrawled with footprints, has become a book of quotations. This is how an Ideal Eagle might have read them from above: you're striding along a bank of the Yellow river, towards your uncle's camp; Hyacinthe and Narcisse are trudging back along its other bank; several of the NWC brutes are staring aghast at whisps of smoke still rising from a smouldering elm; a gaunt and tattered man is dragging himself through the woods.

Hyacinthe and Narcisse arrive in the afternoon, frost-nibbled and stinking, the living hovel returning immediately to its customary scent. Narcisse, in his misery, won't speak. Hyacinthe says he's so hungry he could eat bark. In our desperation we go to the Widow to beg her for the remains of any hares she's trapped. But the hares have turned white to match the snow, and are scarce, and there are only bones.

That evening, one of the NWC brutes comes to our hovel. His shoulders fill our doorway while he tells us that since Herse is gone, leaving no explanation for his absence, they are considering deserting their post. In the face of the Sioux, we should put aside all notions of opposition and he has come to invite us to join them. He's only waiting on the return of two of his companions from their trading.

I thank him but say we must wait for McLeod to return.

He wishes us good luck.

Hyacinthe says he's sorry for trying to punch him.

The next arrival at our door is McLeod.

He walks in bellowing. None of it makes much sense. The Forest of Adjectival Perplexity – this. The River of Adjectival Meanders – that. His face is like tree bark. His clothes are the grandchildren of the rags he departed in.

He waits for the ice to melt from his new beard before pouring himself a cup of rum, drawing his shoulders back into the pose of a Minister in a Parliament, and announcing in triumph that those weeks spent crawling through every adjectival swale and swamp in this adjectival country have at last ended in success. Or nearly so. Less than a week ago, he'd met a band of Saulteaux hunters to the South of Yellow River. Those hunters swore they'd recently seen a trader, travelling East in the direction of Yellow Lake. And more. McLeod had then himself picked up this trader's tracks, following them several miles before the snow erased them. But their general direction had appeared clear, and he was now almost sure they led to an area some miles to the south of us. And more still. One of the hunters had said this trader's right arm might well have been longer than the left! He has found him. Long Arm. Or all but.

But what of the furs, says Hyacinthe. He could not give a Cardinal's foreskin about Long Arm or any other trader: if McLeod wants to get himself and his member back into the good graces of his fiancé, that is McLeod's own business. Hyacinthe himself needs his wages from those furs.

Yes, says McLeod, but don't we see? Where Long Arm goes, the furs must be. The Secret Post is almost in our grasp.

At this, even Narcisse looks up from his despond. Hyacinthe speaks for them all: perhaps he might have found it sooner if he hadn't been following his member.

McLeod puffs out his diminished chest for another oration, saying he is going to find it directly, as soon as he's visited the island to let you know his happy news. He turns, takes two steps, and promptly faints upon the ground.

While fetching water to rouse him, I meet the two other NWC men returning. They tell me about the smouldering elm. This has an awful meaning, they say. It is surely a final warning from the Sioux.

Two hours later, the NWC men desert their post. Hyacinthe and I watch them from the hovel door, making their way towards the edge of the clearing in their snowshoes, and then disappearing into the trees.

That should be us, he says. That should have been us at Sault Saint Marie.

The water has no effect on McLeod. He lies on his cot, babbling, as we begin to fear the cold might have done for him, or else provoked a fever to finish its work. And I begin to regret most bitterly my daydream of him falling from the waterfall. Be careful what pictures you conjure in your mind, for who knows what they can do? Dreams have greater power and sway in the North West countries. The waking world follows after them like a servant.

The men now discussed going out to find the Secret Post themselves. Hyacinthe argued that once we had the Missouri furs, we could leave the Debated Lands immediately. But, said Narcisse and Crebassa both, that post could be ten miles from us and take months to find. If McLeod had a better inkling, why not wait for him to recover. But what if he didn't? Back and forth they went. But there is, eventually, one sure master and tyrant of all other thoughts and schemes. Hunger sits upon the big Throne, and eventually thoughts of food and eating devoured all else. Socrates might have walked into our hovel and our sole discourse would have been on beef and parsnips. There are Saulteaux beings who they say embody (if that is the word) starvation. They are a kind of skeleton men, the spirits of those who perish of hunger, and the Widow said they were a host of sour, ill-tempered, foul-mouthed, malevolent fellows. And who could blame them. Hunger is what hunger does. None of us were in the best demeanour.

We'd tried to hunt, but it seemed the only things in the woods around us now were sticks. The animals and fish had hidden from us. Hyacinthe made a soup of things that grow on rocks, which he called tripe-de-roche, but every drop of it was foul and left our bellies as empty as they'd begun. In our extremity, we went to ask Crebassa to beg the Widow to conjure for us, to help us find game. The Saulteaux called this a medicine hunt. She refused at first but, after much beseeching, agreed, fetching a small drum and a rattle from her effects. That night we listened to the beating of the drum and snatches of song coming from her wigwam, while the branches of the trees cracked in the cold and McLeod tossed and turned and whimpered.

In the morning, she said her dream had told her where to find a bear. She described its sleeping place. Somewhere at the edge of a beaver pond, beneath some pines, where a large boulder stuck up from the earth. We each interpreted this location in our own way and ranged out in search of it, thinking perhaps this might be Spey's abductor and we could have revenge and supper in one stroke. By noon, Hyacinthe had returned with a slab of bear flesh on his back. I went with him to collect the rest.

I cannot describe the brief joys of that feast (though before we made it, the Widow gave us instructions for the distribution and treatment of the bones, there being a strict etiquette for the devouring of bears) or how swiftly they turned to ashes. After devouring great hunks of meat, we sat back from the fire to smoke, and Hyacinthe delivered an encomium on the flesh of bears.

While he did, a light ignited in Narcisse's eye, though like the rest of us he was stupefied by the meat, our bellies in astonishment after being empty so long. Where had he found it? he asked Hyacinthe.

In a place exactly like the one the Widow had described, he said, picking his teeth with the rib of a pike. Close to a boulder, by a beaver pond, near a grove of pines.

But where was this?

A mile or so down the river.

Had I seen this boulder and beaver pond when collecting the meat? Narcisse asked me. But in truth, I'd not been looking closely at the scenery and couldn't recollect a boulder, or a beaver pond for that matter. There were most definitely trees, I said. Probably pines.

And was there a cave?

Oh yes, that I recollected. A small cave, and a large dead cedar near its mouth.

Narcisse began to retch. 'That was Bruno,' he cried out. 'You have fed us Bruno!'

'A bear is a bear,' said Hyacinthe with a shrug.

Narcisse threw himself upon him. And if Hyacinthe had still had a nose, it would've been devoured a second time. Crebassa shook his head and smoked his pipe. I jumped up to attempt to extricate them.

At precisely this moment, McLeod emerged from the hovel. His steps were weak, but his eyes were clear and steady. 'Good God, Arthur, I leave you in charge a while and it has come to this.'

'A while,' cried I, removing Narcisse's finger from Hyacinthe's eye. 'It has been a mighty long while.'

He came over to help me remove Hyacinthe's hand from Narcisse's neck.

'And where is Spey?'

'We have lost Spey.'

'Lost? How lost?'

'To a bear.'

'This bear you've been eating?'

'No. This is Bruno.'

'Bruno! Good frigging God, what has happened here?'

Once we'd separated the others, I began to tell him almost everything – how we'd not been able to trade for food, how Spey had been taken, how we'd gone to look for him, how we'd found the sticks in the snow.

Why hadn't I told him all this earlier?

How? He'd been in a faint and then a fever.

A faint! A fever! For how long?

Almost two days.

'For the love of Christ,' he said, scarpering towards the lake and your island.

11

He discovered that island to be deserted soon enough, but figured he nigh on had the pearl of his seeking in his hand. It would be a simple matter of finding the Secret Post, convincing Long Arm of the truth of what had happened on his disastrous expedition, and why he'd ended up in Montreal rather than your nuptial bed, and then presenting your father to you like a wedding ring.

Meanwhile, we split into our own islands. Hyacinthe and Narcisse refused to be within two hundred yards of each other: Narcisse going to sleep in our trading hovel, Hyacinthe moving into the abandoned NWC post. Which left McLeod and muggins in the living hovel, my green ears forced to suffer his prating about how he'd proved his affections, etc, etc. For a trader in charge of famished men and no furs at all, this was an insufferably Dawn McLeod, full of hope for his prospects with you. What torments the Other Arthur now found for me. What nasty little snares and snickles.

Why not close my eyes a while and reminisce about happier times, I'd think, during the long nights. When it was you in this hovel with me. Why not try to dwell on the things delightful? What matter the love-sotted chorus of McLeod's snoring. *But hello there*, the Other Arthur would then whisper in his weaselly, sidling way. *Do you see those things delightful, luxuriating in your mind's eye – the limbs here and there and everywhere, the dark warm nooks and shadows of the furs? Look closer. Is that not McLeod's face rather than yours? It is a Scotsman's buttock, Arthur, surely. And a fine one too. No mole on that hip. Like a hummingbird? That Scottish tongue is like a flock of them, Arthur. And see what a flock can do! Those cries, those gasps, where you barely coaxed a whimper. Or perhaps it was a sigh? And now let us peek a little below that fox hide. But my God, it must be a buffalo hide, Arthur, for look at the size of...* and so on and so forth. McLeod sleeping happily in anticipation, while I made myself a cuckold in retrospect and prospect, creating two imaginary horns out of an imagined past and an imagined future, like the stupidest braying Ass of them all.

After four days of this, jealousy and misery making me fearless, I fled to my fowling Kingdom and moped on the ridge, making a desultory survey of the land around, hoping to spot a second stupid deer. Below, Narcisse was fishing through the ice of the first pond, it being firm enough to stand on by this time, with Hyacinthe two hundred yards over from him, doing the same. Meanwhile, Crebassa and the Widow were making their way around the second pond, checking her snares.

And then the Pillars and Posts all began to converge.

At the far edge of the scene, coming from the West, two figures emerged from the woods, their footsteps dragging in their snowshoes like the gait of a hamstrung deer. A hat made of beaver. A hat made of hare. You and Herse. I was about to call out from my eyrie but held back a second.

For as you approached the first pond, another figure emerged near the creek and its stepping-stones. McLeod. He began to make his way across the ice of the pond, towards where the others were fishing, I supposed.

But why should you suppose this? whispered the Other Arthur. *What have we here? A coincidence? McLeod sauntering out at this very moment. He is there to greet Esther, you fool! He's known all along when she'd return. They've probably reconciled already. They probably met, and who knows what else, while McLeod was off searching the woods before.* And would have continued to administer his poison thus, most certainly, had I not then glimpsed another shape moving through the alders on the opposite shore.

The day was bright and clear. The shape was sleek and black. The naked branches of the alders shivered as it passed between them. And then it was gone. I wondered how no one else had seen it, and loaded my gun.

When the shape next appeared, a few moments later – standing on the shore of the first pond, near a boulder half-hidden by some cedars – it was a bear. Further on from the boulder, you and Herse had emerged onto the ice of the pond. McLeod was walking across it towards you, waving.

I called out a warning and everything stopped. McLeod's foot halted on the ice, his hand still raised. Narcisse and Hyacinthe remained beside the small dark eyes of their fishing holes.

I called out a second time. And now everyone was looking at me.

I made a frantic calculation: the bear was about a hundred yards from you, standing as still as everything else in the scene had become. I took a shaky aim.

My finger ached against the cold metal of the trigger. I

paused a second to look askance at where Hyacinthe and Narcisse stared up from their fishing holes, at where McLeod was standing on the ice, at where you stood with Herse. How did none of you see the beast? Why were you all looking at me? Why did your head begin to turn from me and my gun to McLeod? I took a deep breath, exhaled, and fired.

By some weird effect of the northern air, or a trick of the Saulteaux spirits, or who knew what, the sound and sight of my shot seemed to come from the bear itself, as if me and my gun were merely an echo or mirror. The powder flared in front of *its* face, the barrel flamed in front of *its* snout, a thin pall of powder smoke hung around *its* head. I witnessed this in an instant, and in the next, the bear had vanished, the alder branches were still, and McLeod was lying on the ice, a pool of red spreading around him as though he were wearing a crimson dress and had fainted, mid-twirl, at a Montreal ball.

And then everybody was turning their heads from me to McLeod and back again. I heard Hyacinthe call out. Narcisse dropped his fishing line. I saw you running towards McLeod.

12

The light came through the door, falling on packs of trading goods stacked like giant eggs. And furs. Some lying in piles, some hanging from the ceiling, some whitened by frost. There was such a brightness to this Winter light, its glinting and glistering, the way it shattered to diamond dust on the rime and snow. But stare too long and it would burn your eyeballs. Cold light could act like flames. Effects could dress up the opposite from their causes. I had shot at the bear to protect them, and now they considered me a murderer.

Or guilty, at least, of the attempt. McLeod had a bullet through his thigh. And I had been placed in Herse's NWC warehouse, which he'd allowed use of as my gaol. 'You know,' he said, closing the door behind him and taking a seat on a keg of rum, 'it might look better for you, Arthur, if you'd hit this supposed bear.'

It was not supposed, I replied miserably, sipping the tea he'd brought for me, brewed from some bitter leaf.

Then – and pardon him for mentioning it – I must be a far worse shot than he'd even imagined. For if this not-supposed bear was where I'd claimed, then McLeod would've been two hundred yards from it.

I didn't understand, I told him. It made no sense to me.

Herse said it was indeed difficult to understand, though he could see what sense others might make of it – the shot, my cries of jealous fury (as my warnings had now become)! A magistrate, for instance. There'd been days in the past when he'd been rather tempted to shoot McLeod himself. Not out of jealousy, of course, like me, but for a myriad of other reasons. However, even opposition must draw its lines somewhere, or else we'd all be dead.

But now his NWC men were gone, I said, he seemed quite happy for there to be no opposition at all. Which was true. Since returning, Herse had been as much a part of our Company as any of us, and had saved us from our hunger by sharing a hidden cache of supplies the NWC men had left behind. His tempers were brighter, too. Like McLeod and the others, he considered the Secret Post almost in his palm, and with it, knowledge of Copperhead and Long Arm's whereabouts. Each day he searched the surrounding woods. He remarked that he and McLeod's interests were now a great deal more mutual than McLeod and my interests, judging by what I'd apparently done.

It wasn't so, I cried, explaining once again the bewildering phenomenon of my shot appearing to come from the bear itself. Herse said he didn't think 'the bear shot him' would prove much of a defence. And here History had also played a cruel trick on me. Until recently, there'd been no law for the traders in the North West countries. I'd heard stories enough from Crebassa of the trade's glorious past, the various bludgeonings and murders which counted as the Good Old Days. Up here, such rosy reminiscences might describe, scales only weighed packs of furs and tobacco, and left men alone. But last year, as Herse informed me, the Crown and Parliament had passed an Act to extend their jurisdiction here.

The law was a crafty and determined stowaway, and arrived soon enough everywhere us traders went.

But seeing as we were in hypothetical United States country, and actual Saulteaux and Sioux country, and in practice the Companies' countries, how would this even apply? Who could decide on jurisdiction?

Herse gave me a meaningful look. Why wait and discover? Seeing as McLeod was only winged not dead – the bear seemingly, and by remarkable coincidence, being as poor a shot as me – why not take my lumps, freeze in here a few days, and then who knew? I might find the door wide open and the United States proper all below and to the east of me, where the laws of the British Crown were a bad memory and held no sway.

Which was excellent advice, except for two impediments: I was in love with you; and this country was a better gaol than anything built in Montreal – with the Sioux as its lock, the distance as its walls, and ten million trees as bars.

I'd consider it.

'I'd recommend you do, Arthur.'

He left the door quite open when he left.

But as it was, I discovered myself in the very worst cage. For I'd become a pariah. It was only Herse who spoke to me. The rest kept their distance.

And none as bad as that you kept. From the door of the warehouse, I could see the tracks across the snow, well-trodden enough to be a trail, leading directly from your island to the living hovel, where McLeod was recovering from his wound. *Well, well,* the Other Arthur would remark, *look who is nursing McLeod*. But it's you who has accomplished this, I told the wretch. You who has reconciled them. *Oh, Arthur*, he laughed, *but what did you expect? I am what I am — but listening to me is your choice. Do you remember her face when she saw him shot? Not clearly? Let me conjure it for you. Can you see it clearly now?* I can, I replied miserably. Each stricken line of it. Affection revealed in distress being as pellucid as glass and as definite as stone. *Now, can you see her face when she turned to where you were standing with your gun?* I tried not to see that face.

It was during this time that I began to dream of Young Godin and the bear.

In the first of these dreams, I found myself in a long tunnel, with the roots of trees and bushes hanging down all around me. The sound of voices came from above, and the scratching of sticks on the tunnel's ceiling. A faint light illuminated the scene – emanating from where, it was impossible to say – and I could see a figure walking in front of me. For every step I took, it also took one. A familiar cowlick crept up from the crown of its head.

'Godin,' I called. But the figure didn't reply. 'Godin,' I called again. But it wouldn't turn around.

The next night there I was again, in the underground place. It seemed to me the roots were longer, as though the trees above had grown, and I could no longer hear the scratching of the sticks. The figure was there, and again wouldn't turn around to face me. But I now considered the cowlick quite definite and so followed Godin further along the tunnel until we arrived at the entrance to an enormous cavern, which might almost be thought outside, except for the roots that hung down from what would have been the sky. In the pale illumination of that inexplicable light, which had followed me from the tunnel, was a spectral version of the Debated Lands – our post replicated, and Yellow Lake as well, with its islands and points covered in snow, and the white line of the river going through the dark, dreamed trees. The figure that was Godin pointed along it.

The following night, I found myself already in the giant cavern, following Godin's ghostly back along the banks of the underground Yellow River, doubled in every detail, though caught in that eerie light. I was reciting my woes to him, everything that had happened since French River, but he made no reply, only stopping now and again to point out some feature of the landscape – a tall pine here, a boulder there beside it, topped with snow. Eventually, we reached a tributary, with the water still not frozen. We followed this a distance – Godin pointing out a beaver dam, the roots of a fallen tree, a firepit ringed with sticks – until at last we came to a small clearing, and in its centre, a log dwelling and a sort of heap or pyre fashioned from spruce boughs. Godin ran his hand over his cowlick, before pulling back several of these boughs.

Sitting there inside was a bear. A frosty plume of breath came out from its snout.

Godin pointed at it. 'The sea,' he said, 'the sea.'

'But it is a bear, Godin,' I said.

The next night I did not dream at all.

During the days, I did little else than look at how the trail from the island to the living hovel was becoming more worn, and bicker with the Other Arthur, and peruse the pictures he brought to me of you stroking McLeod's fevered brow, and wonder how everything had turned out this way.

It was a freezing day in December when the Two Birds arrived at the door of my unlocked gaol. I invited him in, but he sniffed the air, looked at my unshaven face and filthy clothes, and remained outside the doorway. He said he'd come to visit his niece and bring some dried fish to trade, as it appeared my idiot colleagues had had little fortune with their fishing and hunting and did nothing but range nervously through the woods in search of some Secret Post. But at least the rest of them had managed not to shoot anybody.

I'd not shot anybody, I replied sullenly.

He said his niece was under the impression I'd shot McLeod in a jealous rage.

That wasn't what had happened.

Ah yes, said the Two Birds, there was the bear with the gun. Herse had told him. He'd have to tell his hunters to be more careful when next abroad, if the bears had begun to shoot back. He again glanced about the warehouse, sniffing the air, and said how was it we could live like this, worse than dogs. But it was a shame, he continued, for of the two of us woeful, hopeless fellows, he would have preferred me to have won the bewildering affection of his niece, and by shooting McLeod, I'd only succeeded in restoring her tender instincts towards him, and making her listen to his wretched excuses.

The despond must have shown clearly on my face, for the Two Birds offered me a puff on his pipe. He couldn't understand it: if I'd had a jealous rage, why hadn't I at least shot McLeod dead. What a feeble sort of jealousy was it anyway, if it left my rival alive and myself a blubbering wreck? If I had tender feelings for his niece, why not express them better?

I wasn't blubbering, I insisted, though there was a rime of ice at the corners of my eyes. I hadn't slept properly for several nights, having been beset by strange dreams.

Dreams. What kind of dreams?

There'd been a lost companion in them. And a bear.

A bear, he said. Perhaps I might describe these dreams to him.

I did, saying it must be some nonsense conjured out of my distress.

At this he rolled his eyes and sighed. We Englishmen couldn't even interpret a dream, though it be so clear a child might decipher it, or a squirrel. His dogs had a better knowledge of the spiritual world than me. He shook his head some more, much like my father. 'You could not even read this dream?'

I admitted I could find no special meaning in it.

Meaning, thundered the Two Birds. Meaning! What kind of dullard etc, etc, was I? These were very clearly a set of directions, and I should thank whatever Spirit had been so generous as to offer them to me, pearls before swine, etc. For they would lead me to this bear.

But why would I wish to find it?

Why was I living in this wretched hovel, reviled by my companions, thought a murderer – and a failure even at that – by his niece? It would surely be better for me if I found this bear. To prove my story and clear my name. And if that wasn't possible, I could at least eat it.

But wasn't it dangerous, to go out looking alone? With the Sioux rumoured to be here and there and everywhere. We'd found more sticks, I told him, to the West and South of us.

The Two Birds puffed on his pipe awhile. The smoke dallied in the doorway, as reluctant to come inside as the Two Birds himself. If the Sioux wanted me dead, he said, then I'd be dead already. If they wanted him dead, they would have considerably more difficulty.

I thanked him for his advice and, having finished his pipe, he lifted the hood of his capot over his head and prepared to leave, remarking with his unsmiling smile that he was only helping me because of his niece's baffling tastes. That at least I was a different kind of idiot to the other idiot.

13

And so on the coldest morning of the year, somewhere close to the shortest day, I set out to find that bear. Outside, my own water froze yellow on the snow and each breath turned instantly into a silvery cascade. In the frigid half-light, the stationary islands were dark coniferous shadows against the emerging white of the snow. Heat and warmth seemed like fables told by ancient men, the only thing resembling them being the churning furnace in my belly ignited by the wisps of smoke coming from the chimney of the living hovel, where I pictured your long fingers stroking McLeod's forehead. I was prepared to follow any errand now – be it a fool's one or not – if it would just get me away from this infernal post. I was fortunate, however, to find the door to our old warehouse unlocked, which allowed me to take a gun for my protection.

I wore a cloak made of a moose and a hat stitched together from a bundle of hares, and thus wrapped in its slaughtered denizens, entered the forest alone, following the snowy banks of Yellow River in search of a boulder, a tall pine tree, a beaver dam. In those shadowy minutes before dawn, the landscape much resembled the cavern, and I almost expected to find Godin there in silhouette, waiting for me.

Perhaps he was. For later in the day, after the light had begun to glitter so brightly on the snow that my eyeballs ached, I came upon a boulder heaped with a white hat, and a pine so tall it seemed to wave to me from the surrounding forest. The very features Godin had pointed out. And I see myself there in retrospect, wrapped in those dead beasts, and wonder again whose foot was on the treadle of what loom?

At last, as the sun approached halfway across one of its shortest journeys, the tributary appeared. In my dream, its waters had been mysteriously open and flowing, but here it was frozen hard with ice, which I walked along, carefully loading my gun: for by now I was beginning to consider my dream more accurate than any map, and at the end of it there would be a bear. It would have been wise to have trusted it wholly, and consider it more accurate than the apparent world.

I'd not walked a mile before – approaching the very beaver dam Godin had pointed to, and the pronged spider's mouth of a fallen tree's roots – my foot vanished through the ice.

After a shocked pause, I hurled myself onto the snow heaped along the tributary's bank, fully aware of my dire predicament. My soaking moccasin had already begun to whiten with frost. Within a few minutes, I was wearing an elephant's boot of ice.

It was necessary to make a fire, quickly, and – with this my sole thought – staggered club-footed towards some birches, discovering they formed a neat circle around a clearing. The sticks in the snow there also made a neat circle: ten of them, the ashes of a fire in their centre. So be it, I thought, resigned to whatever lay ahead. If my foot was to be flayed/devoured along with the rest of me, it might as well be dry and warm first. Gathering some birchbark and twigs, I sparked my flint and made a bonfire of the sticks, watching the smoke from it rise high into the sky. Let it be a beacon. But at least let my skin be warm a few moments, while it was yet attached to my body.

Yet nobody came for me. And emboldened by this Stoic acceptance of my fate, with my foot and moccasin dry, I set out to face my encounter with the bear.

The clearing and the trading post were exactly as they'd been in my dream. No smoke appeared to be coming from its chimney, and there weren't any other signs of habitation, so I went first to examine the pyre of spruce boughs, nervously double-checking my powder and flint, my Stoical side ebbing as quickly as the day.

For if my previous scant knowledge of dreams had told me anything, it was this: that apart from those of an amorous nature, you didn't want to go beyond the point of them at which you mercifully awoke. And if you did, would most probably find yourself hitting the bottom of a cliff, or taking your third or fourth inhalations of water from the weed-clogged depths of the village pond. Everything that happened now would be beyond where I'd arrived with Godin. The sky was turning a deeper blue. The sun was closer to the treetops. The worst things awaited me, even it were only the simple matter of waiting too long and being caught in the dark, where my gun would be useless. I approached the pyre.

Ho! I cried. Ha! But nothing moved in that squat green toadstool of boughs, not a needle quivered. Ha, hup, huzza! Nothing. My voice was a tiny ant in this frozen dragon world. How would it wake the beast within, who was meant to be sleeping until the Spring?

There was nothing else for it. Approaching closer, my breath held inward, moving on the tips of my toes, I took hold of a branch, flung it sideways, then leapt back and raised my gun.

There it lay.

Ho! Ha! Hup! Huzza! I cried again.

And continued to lay. Not a hair of it moved.

This bear was identical to the one Godin had shown me: its grizzled snout rimed with ice, its black fur intermixed here and there with faint patches of brown and grey. It was a thinnish sort of bear, as though the Autumn had not been generous to it; and a smallish sort, too, as though Nature herself had been niggardly with her gifts; and perhaps slightly worn and withered, as well, time and age having perhaps thrown in their own cruel portion. It looked rather like an old man fallen asleep beside his fishing pole on the bank of a stream.

An unexpected delicacy of feeling and sense of fair play began to rise in me. This was no gigantic and slavering foe. I didn't want to shoot it while it slept, and so decided to at least wake the poor creature first. Perhaps he might hobble away. God knows he wouldn't have to get far to avoid my bullets.

I threw a ball of snow at him. Not a flinch. Then a small rock. Not a murmur. Several pinecones, three sticks, and two more snowballs later, I went to prod it on the forehead with the barrel of the gun.

Off slipped its head.

A man's face peered back at me.

It was an unremarkable sort of face: the flesh tinged blue and powdered with frost like some dandy French prince; a raggedy black beard; brown hair; eyes of some colour once but turned now to icy white marbles. Thawed out, you wouldn't have been surprised to see it peering mildly at you over a desk in Ogilvy's office, as its owner penned inventories of kettles and blankets. But out here, in the fading light and silence, attached to the body of a beast, it was a white-blue horror and the shock of it had me half-fainting upon the snow.

How long this faint lasted, I cannot say, but eventually forcing myself to look again, the nature of this ghastly Composite became apparent. Stitches were visible through the bear's fur, running from its belly to its neck, and along the arms and legs. One had to admire the meticulousness of the skinning, the ingenuity of the disguise: the fore and hind-paws had been left perfectly intact, as had the muzzle, and there were slits beneath the claw pads to allow hands to hold a gun. The gun, I was now sure, that had been used to shoot McLeod.

A morbid curiosity overtook me, and I began searching the bear's fur for a sign that perhaps my own shot had been true. I unstitched it, uncovering the upper torso of the man within, dressed in a woollen shirt. A purple-red flower, spreading over his shoulder, told me it had been close to true, or at least close enough to have led to this.

Several sets of clothes had been strewn amongst the branches – as though the man had hastily undressed before putting on the bear – including a thick woollen capot, a flannel shirt, and two sets of undergarments mercifully encrusted in snow. Being half-frozen myself, I picked up the capot and went to seek shelter in the trading post, as the sun dropped below the tops of the trees.

Inside were more packs of furs than I'd seen since the warehouses at Lachine, so thickly stacked only the narrowest gap led in from the doorway. On entering, I'd made out the letters MR carved upon the door, and my first thought had been 'Mr who?', before it had come to me: MacDowell and Ross. My next thought was Good Lord, there are furs enough in here to buy a mansion in Montreal, and then to fill it again with furs.

The gap through the packs led into a cramped and dismal inner chamber, opening out from a crude stone fireplace. A tin cup sat on its hearth, some ancient traps with iron grins hung from the chimney, and two filthy heaps of unpacked skins lay on the ground. The fetor of grease and uncured pelts overpowered the faint scent of woodsmoke coming from a fire so pitiful I'd not noticed its smoke emerging from the chimney.

And now my earlier shock and horror were repeated. A pale smooth oval face was staring up at me from one of the fur heaps, appearing to have no human body either but belonging instead to the wolf and fox pelts surrounding it, a Chimaera with multiple tails. The difference was that this face was alive and a mirror of my own horror, for my own rough costume must have made me appear a similarly outlandish creature.

We continued to stare at each other before at last I cried, 'Spey!'

He nodded and rose, shivering, from the furs. 'It is you, Mr Arthur,' he said.

He would've been better off remaining in those furs. His own clothes were criss-crossed with rips and tears; a patch of skinny thigh was visible through his trousers, bluing and goose-pimpling instantly in the frigid air. The curve of his stomach, more rounded than his gaunt cheeks, pushed through a hole in his shirt. 'Take this,' I said, offering him the Bear

Man's capot. He refused vehemently. He would not touch that man's effing clothes. He'd prefer to freeze to death first. What an awful thing, that a man like that should have such a name!

The penny dropped. The penny clattered. Good God, I said. Was that man called Sugar? The man who McLeod was supposed to have abandoned?

He'd not had a chance to burn him yet, Spey continued. Though he'd gathered the branches for the fire and added in the wretch's clothes.

And it was Sugar who'd abducted him? In that same disguise?

It was. And had kept him captive here, inquiring constantly about McLeod's movements and intentions and whereabouts.

What a horror, I said. What a strange horror.

Feeding what sticks there were to the ever-feeble flames, I sat down with Spey and listened to his account of the last weeks. During this captivity, Sugar had given him a description of the twists and turns that had led him here to the Debated Lands. How Sugar had survived an accursed journey North with a damned adjectival Monosyllable named McLeod, and returning, had discovered himself rumoured dead, and possibly murdered, and perhaps devoured. And how, having no wish to let McLeod off whatever hook he might be squirming on for this, and seeing certain advantages in being thought deceased, he'd bided his time incog, disguising himself as an independent trader and travelling from fort to fort.

And then last Winter he'd been at the Rainy Lake fort, sitting in a dingy shack that passed as a tavern, when he'd happened to overhear a whispered conversation between three men sitting behind him, thinking him gone in his cups. One of them was called Labrie, and one of the words he kept whispering was Missouri, and Sugar had remembered something the Monosyllable – McLeod – had told him up North about a beaver El Dorado. He'd then glimpsed the eldest of the men hand Labrie a piece of paper, with what looked like a map drawn upon it. Putting this together with what the Monosyllable had said, Sugar had thought, 'Here is a plump bird that has just fallen into my lap'. All he needed was to get his hands on that map, which he was sure would lead him to a great bundle of furs.

So, when the men departed and made their farewells, Sugar had followed Labrie, shadowing him as far as the falls at Kakabeka before taking the opportunity to help a stout branch onto the back of his head and get a closer look at his pockets. And his hat. For it was in its crown he'd discovered the map, and with it this house of fur.

As for McLeod, that had been another piece of happy chance. Sugar had spotted him during the Autumn, paddling up Yellow River, and thought how Fortune had now contrived to deliver a second plump bird into his lap – his revenge. It was no great effort to discover the post at Yellow Lake and fashion his bear disguise to reconnoitre in, and it was then only a matter of awaiting his opportunity to get close enough to McLeod to shoot him dead. His only difficulty had been McLeod's constant toing and froing, and not knowing when he'd be at the post. Spey's kidnap had been to help him gather information about this.

But one day Sugar had set out in his infernal suit only to return injured. Spey had barricaded the door against him. Out came his blandishments. That Spey might have half of the furs.

That he might be a wealthy man. But he'd kept the door shut, and eventually the blandishments turned to curses, then to groans, and then at last to silence. By the time Spey opened the door, Sugar was curled up in the snow in his bear, quite dead.

And why hadn't Spey returned after this?

Spey said the reason was simple enough: he had no effing clue where he was. It was the forest and the cold that had acted as his gaol. By God, I said. I knew exactly what he meant.

But how was it I'd found him? And why had I come alone?

A dream had directed me, I told him. The rest was rather complicated.

Spey looked at me. A dream?

A dream and an old friend, I said.

What a dreary night we spent in front of that pitiful fire, which however many sticks were added would not warm us, though we were surrounded by enough beaver fur to keep a thousand heads snug. At some point, we must have fallen into sleep, for I remember waking to find the morning light struggling through a tiny parchment window. Across from me, Spey had already risen from his heap of furs and begun to remove his woollen undershirt, with its rips and tears, and I assumed he must have some more decent one to replace it with. But no. Instead of another shirt, he began to carefully wrap a strip of thick cotton around his chest. Unheeded, I observed. I observed more closely than I should have. I stared. And then, involuntarily, as one only lately acquainted with such things in the flesh, blurted out, 'My God. Those are breasts!'

Spey turned hastily away and remained for a long while in silence, with her back to me.

When she next turned to face me, she was weeping. And in that wretched dwelling, with its feeble fire and walls rimed with ice, began to offer me an account of how she'd come to these countries. There was hunger in it, and disguise, and a long voyage at sea. There were great hardships, and deceptions, and things she wouldn't speak of to me. When she was finished, we were sitting face to face on the cold earth floor and it was I who was weeping.

'But how had I not known this whole time?' I said.

'*You*'d thought that Sugar was a bear,' said Spey.

And what should I call her now?

She said I might call her Spey, as that was her name.

When, at last, we prepared to depart for the trading post, I asked if she'd like to set light to the pyre first.

Why bother now, she said, turning away toward the trees. Why not let him be food for the other beasts.

Agreeing heartily, and not wishing a thread of the scoundrel's cloth upon me, I went to toss his capot on the pyre. It was then I felt some paper, nestled in a hidden pocket at its side. Taking it out carefully, I gave it the briefest of glimpses, turned it over, and then, without a word, slipped it into my own pocket.

14

What did I expect on my return to the post? A little Triumph perhaps. Slaps on the back all around. An I-never-doubted-you and a Huzza. Arthur the innocent! Arthur the rescuer of Spey! Arthur the discoverer of the Secret Post and the Missouri furs!

We first met Herse, pacing along the lakeshore where once he would have strolled, wearing the same pinched, anxious looks as when the snows had arrived. I told him about Sugar and the disguise of the bear. Well, that was a new one, he said, and offered me an apology. I then informed him about Spey, who on our journey back had said she no longer intended to maintain her disguise, as what purpose did it serve here, anyway? Herse appeared less surprised by this than by the bear. 'Hello, Miss Spey,' he announced with a slight bow. He clearly wished to question us further but at this moment Narcisse came rushing our way.

There followed a touching reunion, with sobs and embraces, though again less surprise about Spey's new condition than might have been expected. Hyacinthe arrived next, and I described Sugar's disguise to him, pointing out that my shot had indeed hit its mark.

'I suppose you must have hit his arse,' he said.

And so, a very little Triumph was what I got. No one needed to remind me I was mortal.

And a fleeting Triumph, too. Because now, accompanied by Herse, I must enter the living hovel with my news, where even as you read you may see me in memory, coming through the door with frost on my lashes and trepidatious eyes, which have barely been closed for a day and a night and are dreading what they are about to see, which is this: you sitting beside McLeod's cot, and McLeod sitting up in that cot, looking far less pale and sickly than I'd hoped. In fact, looking more broad-shouldered and cheerful and rosy-cheeked than I've ever seen him.

'Well, well,' he says. 'Look who it is. Come to finish me off, have you?'

Since several cats have run off with my tongue, Herse kindly intervenes to recite my tale. Meanwhile, the whole scene is Manna to the Other Arthur. *Look how close she sits? You know what lies right there above McLeod's bandages, don't you? How often are the bandages changed? Who changes them?*

From some impossibly remote distance, the Moon perhaps, I see your face alter. At first, I'm resurrected from the dead in it, as the news of Sugar and his disguise absolves me of shooting McLeod. But – it slowly dawns upon me – there is another absolution in the news about Sugar. Him being recently alive, and murderous, and a kidnapper and scoundrel and thief, clears McLeod of the seagull and its eggs and everything else. It makes true what I'm sure he's been telling you these last days. And this is the second alteration: from forgiveness and relief to a sort of joy in you. But the third is the worst of all. Oh, poor Arthur, says this look. You see how things are different now. Lord help me from that look.

McLeod is saying things, perhaps sorry for suspecting me

of his attempted murder. It's hard to hear from the Moon. McLeod is asking things, perhaps about furs. McLeod is speaking to Herse, and then to me again. McLeod and Herse are both speaking to me. All of you are speaking to me. Who knows what about? I'm looking at your freckles and thinking, I will never again get closer to them than this. I'm looking at the gap between your teeth and thinking it might as well be the space between planets. I'm thinking, oh dear, how has my belly fallen out of the bottom of the world?

But eventually, as though they're rising from a well, a few words reach me. They seem to come from Herse and McLeod and you, all at once. They are asking, did I find anything else in that place? Any clue about your father or Ross? Some indication of where they might be?

Would you believe me if I said that before entering the living hovel, before I reached the post – indeed even as I'd placed it in my pocket – I'd planned to give that piece of paper to you? Would you believe me if I said that the Arthur you liked, who was thoughtful and kind and had no malice in him, had made that decision? But in that moment the Other Arthur had as firm a hold of my tongue as Perseus ever did Proteus.

No, I say.

I'm sure?

I am.

And the Other Arthur grasps my vision just as surely. For here is what is clearly before my eyes: that you and McLeod have reconciled. And here is what the Other Arthur has persuaded me to see: that perhaps I have the slenderest of chances yet; that if I keep hidden what's in my pocket maybe there might be a way to use it to win you back. Or at least to keep you here a little longer.

What can I say but sorry? That hovel is my Siberia. The memory of that moment is my Siberia. The ink that describes it is my Siberia. And some part of me is destined to inhabit it always, wailing in there like Bruno once did, staring down at his singed feet.

15

We had a fortune in our hands. We'd accomplished what our Company had taxed us with. And one third of us were as disappointed as a famished mouse falling into an empty barrel. There was no sign of Long Arm or Copperhead. And if the rumoured white trader had been Sugar all along, then there'd been no sign of them for a long, long while.

The men rigged several crude sleds, and there followed a general exodus to collect the Missouri furs, and for you and Herse to search the Secret Post for what was hidden in my pocket. Only McLeod, the Widow and I remained at Yellow Lake, where I retired to the NWC warehouse, realising I'd made it a gaol for a second occasion with that universal lock and fetter – a Lie.

Within, I confirmed what my glimpse before had revealed – that the paper was a map. Though crudely drawn, many parts of it were now recognisable to me. The western shore of Lake Superior, the Debated Lands, Yellow River, Yellow Lake. And South of that lake a small circle marked with MR, where the Secret Post had been. A story sadly done with and told.

My great surprise had come on turning the paper over and finding a second map there. This showed a large lake with two islands drawn in it, one of which had been marked with the letters HR. Below the lake were several squiggled lines, and in smudged ink what appeared to be the word 'Mire'. But in that moment I couldn't bring myself to properly examine the thing – despite knowing it might be an important clue as to your father and Ross' whereabouts – for it seemed mostly like a piece of Pilgrim geography writ large: Arthur's Deception. I concealed it between some NWC packs, as though my conscience wouldn't find it there.

Which was just as well, for right then came a knocking at the door, and to my surprise I found McLeod outside, leaning on a stick. His bandaged leg apart, he looked as though he'd strolled down from Olympus for a visit. The curls were back in his hair, his shoulders were ten feet wide, his complexion radiated good health and spirits.

He said he owed me an apology. But who was to know, it being such a curious occurrence with the apparent bear and such.

I shrugged and said everything in this country was confusing and confounding to me.

He hobbled in and manoeuvred himself onto a pack. Why wasn't I going with the others to collect the furs?

I'd found them, wasn't that enough? It was more than most of us had achieved!

Well, well, it seemed someone had grown a few sharp adjectival edges.

Being thought a murderer and made a Pariah would do that.

Being shot was hardly an amble at a country fair either, said McLeod. Not to mention other matters. And I thought, what *other matters?* What does he know? About you and me in the lake? The night in the hovel?

And what would happen now? I asked hollowly.

It would be wise for us to be away from here as quickly as

adjectivally possible, McLeod said. What with the alarming proliferation of sticks.

And after that?

McLeod unveiled your plans. You, McLeod and Herse would take a small portion of the furs and continue to search for Long Arm and Copperhead. Herse had told McLeod everything about what had been planned before, the whole scheme to sell the Missouri furs to the American traders and be independent of the Companies. The rest of the furs would be left with me and the men, to take to the XY fort at the Grand Portage. These would secure both my position in the Company and the wages and rewards promised to the men. I could claim to have no knowledge of the whereabouts of McLeod or Herse, and so would be the perceived victim and hero of the whole affair. For I would've been apparently abandoned, and yet still have managed to recover the Missouri furs.

How very neatly they'd arranged everything, I said, unable to conceal the bitterness in my voice. How smoothly matters had been resolved.

McLeod said 'matters' were not resolved at all. And wouldn't be until Long Arm and Copperhead were found.

I said I meant previous matters, everything that had happened before. It seemed they were mended.

McLeod looked at me for a long time. Having become relatively fluent in the translation of his face, I'd say his features said something like this: I know very adjectivally well about the lake and the night in the hovel and am trying extremely adjectivally hard not to punch you in the face; I am trying very, very hard to hold out a hand to you instead of a fist; I am trying excessively adjectivally hard to stay up on this Higher Ground.

While this is what he said with his mouth. He was making a great adjectival effort to think like the Americans regarding *those matters*, viz the past was mostly a mistake and ruled by fools and tyrants and traitors. Far better to dwell in the future. That sort of thing.

How utterly dismaying it was. And just like my damnable luck in this doubling country: that the Other Arthur should turn out a Devil and a Wretch, while this Other McLeod should be revealed as an Adonis and a Saint.

After McLeod left, I went out to wander through my fowling Kingdom, thinking enviously of how all the fowls were in some warm sea somewhere, snickering merrily to each other with nothing to consider but the fact of being fowls. Around and around I wandered, under the bleak Winter sky, until eventually my thoughts found another compass point to follow. My jealousy was one thing, my heartbreak another, but what did they amount to, in the end? I had no hold on you and, if my affections had been true, I'd swallow this bitter pill and see you happy with another. Herse was my friend. Damn it all, McLeod was also my friend. My concealment of the maps was abominable, and I was disgusted with myself and what I'd become.

Coming upon some sticks beside the second pond, I pondered lying down beside them and accepting my flaying/murdering/braining, whatever it might be. I most probably deserved it. And why not admit there was also a horrid part within me – where the Other Arthur sat on a throne with all his Devils – that saw the solution to my own misery in some general annihilation. Like some gloomy old fanatic, looking to salve my own private condition in the end of the world.

Meanwhile, back at the post, the men had returned and were making preparations for a celebration. For them it was all so simple: the furs had been recovered; they'd have their wages and rewards; they knew our time here was nearing an end. A column of smoke rose from a bonfire by the lakeshore. Approaching closer, I saw most of them had dressed in costumes for the approaching revels. Old Crebassa was wearing Sugar's bear. Narcisse had made a dress from blankets. The Widow was adorned in Crebassa's finest shirt and sash. Spey was dressed in Narcisse's trousers and capot. Even McLeod had made an effort and was wearing a clean shirt. Only Herse sat apart, dressed in his usual outfit, though this had become so grubby and neglected it too appeared as though it were a costume – a mirthless parody of Herse. I couldn't bring myself to look at what you wore.

As evening fell, they began to cavort around the fire, combining every dance they knew, or had seen – jigs, waltzes, reels, approximations of the Saulteaux steps they'd borrowed from the Widow. How dreadful it was to be outside the warm bright circle of this fire's light. 'You see,' I suddenly exclaimed aloud to the Other Arthur. 'This is the only position you are capable of relating to the world: observing it from the darkness, looking in.'

Do you think she is holding his hand, Arthur? he replied.

He was utterly beyond reform.

It was then I resolved to take back the rudder of my own

wits and put an end to this. I set out towards the NWC warehouse, entirely decided. I would deliver the map to you and let everything take its proper course. I'd put the Other Arthur in chains and fetters. I'd allow the Ages to follow their destined succession, giving thanks for what had been allowed me in this one, and accepting those that would follow.

16

It was as dark as a whale's belly inside the warehouse. The Missouri furs had been stored in it, making it difficult to figure which packs the map was hidden between, and so I went to fetch a candle from the living hovel.

How different the sky was from the night of the first party! Clouds pushed the dark down upon us like the lid of a cauldron, and instead of utter stillness a breeze was blowing in, tumbling the sparks of the fire across the frozen lake. But no, I wasn't to think of that other night. It was an Age elapsed and gone. The breeze strengthened, forcing me to guard the flame of the candle like a vestal on my return to the warehouse, while the others danced in silhouette around the blaze, taking on strange shapes and forms. It seemed the cry of some bird came to me as it flew by unseen, but this must surely be the whoops and hollers of the party I thought, for the high wine had made their tongues as various and outlandish as their dress. Inside the warehouse, it was as silent as the thousand beaver graves it housed, with only the whistling of the rising wind outside. A few of its exhalations came through the walls, swaying the candle's flame, and with the aid of its flickering light I found the map and was about to put it in my pocket when I heard that sound again – the calling bird. This time I made it an owl.

Its call turned into footsteps, padding around outside so

loudly it appeared the Sioux were no longer even taking measures to conceal themselves. I'd like to say my next action was to rush out the door and go warn the others, but the truth is my legs no longer worked and my voice appeared to have sunk into my bowels, which in turn were dropping towards the ground, which itself had decided to open beneath my stationary feet. I felt such a sensation of falling it seemed a horrid sort of miracle to look down and see myself still standing helpless before the door, and that door beginning to slowly open, and standing there – the candlelight flickering across his painted face, his deerskin leggings, his scarlet shirt and glittering brooches – the agent of my End. My God, I thought, what a hot fury there is in his eyes. The candle dropped from my hand and I waited, eyes closed, to be brained in the darkness.

But nothing arrived apart from light.

At first in globes and oblongs of orange on the backs of my eyelids, as when you close them against the sun, but then a more sustained sort of brightness. A bead of moisture dropped from my brow, the breath fled from my lungs, and at last opening my eyes I discovered the door closed and the whole room aglow. Fire was leaping up the bark of the walls.

I scarcely managed to hurl myself, gasping and coughing, onto the snow outside. There was no sign of any Sioux. No owls were calling. And then there was a moment – like closing your fingers over a cut thumb, or when you break a porcelain bowl in your father's study and sit there hoping he won't notice, that he will in fact forget entirely and forever he even owned such a bowl – when I thought, well, maybe nobody will notice this fire and it will fizzle out quickly enough, only singeing a fur or two. A moment followed, seconds later, by a roaring, crackling exhalation of flame as the shingles on the roof took light. Those flames rose amazingly high. It was as though we'd stored dragon's tongues in that warehouse. And still my mind could only contemplate the littlest of consequences, such as, 'They will surely see it now', and not, 'I have burnt a house full of money'. And then the wind began to carry the sparks and pieces of flaming bark, like the tiny flapping progeny of a Phoenix, across the short gap between the warehouse and the NWC post. It was aflame before I even reached it, and while I tried hopelessly to put it out, a third beacon lit up. Our living hovel. And next, our trading hovel. It was as though I were in a forest of masts alive with St Elmo's fire.

By now everyone had rushed over from the lake. McLeod was speechless. Herse was speechless. I was speechless. Everyone was speechless. At first, nobody noticed Hyacinthe rise stumblingly from where he'd fallen drunk in the snow, his face painted blue and red, his hair decorated with silver brooches, his deerskin leggings laced with frost. He took one bleary look at the conflagration, another at me, and then turned to the others. 'I saw it,' he slurred over the tumult and crackling of the fires. 'I saw him light it. The White Frog has done this.'

The stink of burnt hides lingered in the air and the embers of the fires were still glowing as the sun rose the next morning. Everyone remained in their costumes, as I had burnt their clothes. I'd also burnt Narcisse's wooden harem and Crebassa's ear. I'd burnt everything.

I won't attempt to describe my feelings, as they weren't entirely attached to my wits. And who knew what my wits were attached to. All through the night, as the flames had lit up the edge of the forest and the ash blackened the snow, I'd only been able to think of that map, as though the conflagration were too large a subject to contemplate, and I must cling instead to the last thing to concern me before it began. I now picked my way through the smouldering remains in search of it, as if by this hopeless quest it were possible to pretend the rest wasn't really happening.

I was more than half a madman. The others thought me completely so, taking my behaviour as the answer to their questions, which – posed variously and forcefully, and in several languages, and with many different adverbs and adjectives – came down to this: what have you done and why have you done it? I replied by prodding the ashes and embers with a stick, mumbling, 'It's somewhere here. I know it's somewhere here.' Hyacinthe had to be restrained from inquiring more closely with his fists. 'I saw him in there with a torch,' he kept repeating. 'I saw him.'

At some point, Herse approached me. It was somewhere here, I babbled.

What was? The furs were gone, everything was gone.

The map, I said.

The map?

Herse's face began to change. Did I mean to say there'd been a map at the Secret Post?

It's somewhere here.

Somewhere here, he said, looking across the flaming ruins, which were a figure for his altered face. Did I mean to say there had been, and I had had it?

Since finding Spey, I told him.

But he didn't understand? They'd asked me if I'd found anything. He was looking at me as though I was someone else. There was no ironical anything in his manner.

What was in it? Where did it show? he asked, in a voice much colder than any day that Winter. I must realise it was worth more than all those adjectival furs. It was the first, and last, time I ever heard him curse.

On one side it showed the Secret Post. On the other it showed somewhere else. Perhaps a great lake. An island. I couldn't properly recall. Which in that moment was the truth. It was as though the fire had swept through my memory and burnt it there as well.

Another side? Somewhere else? A *second* map?

Yes.

And I couldn't remember it?

No.

I had burnt and forgotten the only clue left of Ross' whereabouts, Herse said, before his lips closed very tightly and he turned away from me in shuddering disgust, as if to prevent himself inflicting the violence Hyacinthe had already promised me. And there was something in that turning away that flipped me somewise back into my senses. I dropped my stick to the ground and attempted to explain how it had been an accident, how I'd mistaken Hyacinthe for the Sioux, how I'd been about to hand over the map. But Herse wouldn't look at me. His back trembled.

And where was McLeod in this? Through the course of the night he'd been an amazed bystander, not entirely certain of what he was seeing. He'd helped to restrain Hyacinthe, but in a head-shaking sort of way. He must have been thinking, 'Why have I become such a collector of disasters?' Yet it seemed his reconciliation with you had made him constantly Dawn, and there'd been an unexpected gentleness to his questions: 'Why have you done this, Arthur' rather than 'What have you adverbially done?' I'd robbed him of a small fortune. I'd fallen in love with the woman he loved. And in exchange, he'd offered me bewilderment and pity, a bargain hardly deserved.

But this changed soon enough when he overheard my exchange with Herse. Herse had no sooner turned away than McLeod was there snarling before me.

What was this about a map? About maps plural?

I began to explain how when I'd found Spey.... He'd heard all adjectival that. Why in God's name hadn't I given.... etc. But damn all that, it didn't matter now. There had been a second map, of somewhere different from the Secret Post. That was what I'd said. A second map. What was in it?

I didn't properly remember.

I had better start adverbially remembering, then. He picked up my scrabbling stick and thrust it back into my hand.

'Draw it,' he demanded.

'Draw what?'

'Draw the other fucking map, Arthur.'

'Where?'

'In the fucking ash. In the fucking snow. I don't care. Just draw it.'

I scrawled the vague shape of a lake in the snow, a few squiggles below it, the tentative shape of an island... but it was hopeless. My head was full of ashes.

'This is fucking useless,' said McLeod. 'Unless these squiggles are... unless this lake here is....'

And now we arrive at the part of this picture I least want to draw: the part where you enter it. There you are, standing at my shoulder, watching as I try to draw a country I don't know with a stick. You asked, quietly and simply, 'Why did you hide it, Arthur?' I would have given ten thousand prime beaver pelts then for McLeod's snarling and rough language. The quietness of your voice might as well have been an anvil dropped upon my head. How I wished for an adverbial, how I yearned for a well this and well that. But there was less fire in your voice than there was left in the embers. I knew it then, as surely as the shushing fall of a guillotine's blade: the afternoon on the island, the time in the lake, the things delightful in the furs, they were over, they were done with. I sat down in the snow and began to weep.

And am still sitting, and still weeping, surrounded by the others as they stand in the ruins of the post, hating me, with the stink of a Montreal mansion's worth of burnt beaver pelts in their nostrils, dressed as bears and women and men and Sioux and Saulteaux, when Narcisse calls, 'What is that?'

On the far shore of the lake a black dot has emerged on the snow, growing slowly larger and larger. It's a beast with many legs. It's a beast with many voices. It is a sleigh pulled by dogs.

In silence, we watch it approach across the ice. It skirts the edge of the second island, disappears a moment, and then re-emerges, larger again. There are three men visible on the sleigh. One of them stands to the front, controlling the dogs, and his voice comes hup-hupping to us along with the barks and yelps of the hounds. A second stands at the back, holding it steady, occasionally leaping off to help it over some hummock of snow or patch of sticky ice. A third stands between them, and does nothing at all.

It disappears behind the first island and, when it reappears, it seems the man in the middle has grown wider and continues to do so with each swishing yard. The dogs are heaving and panting.

'It is the Sail,' proclaims Narcisse.

'What's the Sail doing here?' says McLeod, who can't even muster an adjectival.

Herse says nothing. He has yet to speak since turning away from me.

Fifty yards from us, the driver calls out, the man at the stern digs his heels into the snow, and the dogs skitter to a halt. The Sail steps off and looks at us, and then beyond, to where the buildings are still smouldering. 'Good God,' he says.

'Good God,' he says again, still speaking in general, but gradually directing his speech to Herse. 'What's happened here?' The two NWC sleigh-men are filling pipes and staring at us. One of them pushes back the hood of his capot and scratches his head. 'In Christ's name, what's happened here?' repeats the Sail. 'And why is that man dressed as a bear?' One of the NWC men blows a kiss to Narcisse, who is shivering in his dress. Nobody replies. The Sail says, 'You have been attacked by the Sioux? They've destroyed your post?'

'Not the Sioux,' Herse says at last. 'The XY man, Stanton, has destroyed our post.'

'Both of our posts,' adds McLeod.

'By Christ. And everything with them?'

'Everything,' says Herse.

'Everything,' says McLeod.

'Is this true?' the Sail asks me. 'Stand up there, man!'

'An accident,' I stammer.

'An accident,' bellows the Sail, purpling in the face. 'An accident. Two NWC posts and all their furs. Burnt. Destroyed.'

'One NWC post,' says McLeod. 'The other, XY.'

'Two NWC posts, Mr McLeod. And you would call me sir if you were wise.' At this, the Sail draws a letter from his coat, the delivery of which has been the purpose of his Winter journey. He reads it out aloud. There are many legal phrases, the ornately bland language of trade and charter. But the gist is clear enough. It is a proclamation stating that the Companies have been merged, combined, conjoined. There is no longer XY and NWC. There is only NWC, and everything here belongs to the Company, singular. Everything that is presently ashes on the snow. Herse and the Sail are now the sole authority here, on this borrowed, stolen, ground.

'What shall we do here, Mr Herse?' asks the Sail.

Herse turns to me. 'I would put this scoundrel in irons, Mr Mackenzie. If we had them.'

PART FOUR

The Gaol

1

My Lord above but it was cold in that cavern of wood.

In the darkness, my breath sheened the walls with ice. The stove in the corridor outside gave out barely enough warmth to keep my flesh soft. If I didn't drink my water and eat my broth within an hour they froze as hard as stone. Day and night didn't exist. The doctor, Munro, told me afterwards that my captivity in there lasted four days, but it felt like forty. He said he was sorry for the necessity of even those four. My colleagues had been adamant about keeping me incarcerated until they departed. They must have disliked me a great deal, he'd added.

My eventual deliverer was an angel. 'Mr Arthur,' had come a voice from the piney gloom. 'Doctor Munro wants to see you.'

'Seraphin,' I'd cried. 'Is that you?'

'It is, Mr Arthur.' He unlocked the door and told me to shade my eyes.

An excellent piece of advice, as even the faint light in the corridor overwhelmed them. Outside, the glister and brightness of the day would have seared them like eggs in a pan.

But once they were accustomed, I had a view of the New Fort in a different season, a new guise. For a start, it was almost empty. The thronged streets had been denuded of their

Peacocks. The shops and stores – that had had the whole world in them – were closed up; the workshops, with their carpenters and blacksmiths, silent. All the din and hustle-bustle were gone. You might've heard a mouse's footsteps upon the snow, which covered everything. Even the Giant, who, in the distance, lay deep in hibernation, wrapped in his white blanket.

God knows how long it'd taken us to make our way back here – through the snow, across the ice, following the Sail and those unlucky dogs. We'd been fortunate to get the use of some dogs and sleighs ourselves, but I won't dwell on that journey, it being the most miserable one I hope ever to make. My first days in the trade were made of molasses in comparison. Nobody spoke to me. They could hardly look at me. Hyacinthe couldn't even bring himself to menace me.

Seraphin's features seemed to have gentled since I'd last seen him, at the New Fort. He was more pigeon than hawk. I asked how he'd fared in our absence. He was content enough, he replied rather curtly. He'd hardly been gabby before, but I supposed he'd spoken to the others and heard of my infamy. I asked him where they were? Not at the fort, he said. And how had his squashes done? At this, he brightened. They had done extremely well. So well he'd been invited to assist with the garden at the fort here.

By now we'd arrived at a building near the front gate. He ushered me in and told me to wait. Inside was a long room with three beds on each side, a crucifix and rosary beads hanging on the wall above each of them. I made my way towards a smaller room adjoining it, from which emanated the smell of woodsmoke and a little heat. Sure enough, a fire had been lit there and the flames played about the bottles in a large glass cabinet – camphor, potassium nitrate, calomel. Another cabinet housed various frightful looking instruments, fit for an Inquisition. I was staring at these when a voice interrupted me. 'In the end, I mostly give them cinnamon. Or Rush's Pills. Seldom a need for those, except the lance. There was a plethora of boils this Autumn.'

The voice belonged to a stout, brandy-faced man, who was standing with a thumb tucked into his waistcoat. 'Munro,' he said, holding out his other hand. He might have been a country practitioner in Sorel. Only his hair, a prophet's mane, spoke of this wild place. He gestured to one of two chairs beside the fire. I was quickly drunk with its heat, and then a bit more from the glass of brandy he offered. Now the others were gone he'd be happy enough to give me the freedom of the place. There was a private room for me here if I didn't mind sleeping in an infirmary. He then fixed me with a steady, inquiring look, the wrinkles gathering at the corners of his eyes. I didn't intend to burn down this fort as well, did I?

I had never intended… it had been a terrible accident… that was….

He held up a hand. There was no need, he said. I'd have plenty of time to arrange my explanations. As for himself, he was satisfied that I was in my wits, as nobody in possession of said wits would have purposely burnt down their dwelling during a Winter in this country. We could speak of it later, but for now he'd let me recover from my journey and incarceration. 'Help yourself to some cinnamon,' he said, indicating the cabinet. 'It will certainly improve your breath.'

I asked if he knew where the others had gone.

He said there'd be time enough to discuss that.

My hard bed and rough blankets were like clouds in a picture of Heaven that night. My last thought before sleep was that if these were to be my gaol and gaoler, then I'd had my first piece of good fortune in a long while.

2

The next morning I was to breakfast with Munro, and while he tended to a man with a dislocated shoulder I took the time to look about the fort. The square in front of the Great Hall was covered in snow, and several children were playing there, under the eyes of their Saulteaux mothers. Some men were hauling a sled heaped with logs towards the kitchen. A milch cow was lowing somewhere outside the palisades, and I thought how this at least could not be counterfeit, as surely the Sioux wouldn't deign to speak cow. And I realised then how my nerves must have been drawn as taut as fiddle strings since the moment we'd arrived at Yellow Lake.

Munro's house was near the infirmary, its front room an apothecary. I passed by shelves of coloured bottles, and bowls of roots and powders, to find him in an adjoining room, lifting a steaming whitefish from a bowl. 'Our breakfast, Arthur. And our dinner too, unless one of our hunters gets a moose.'

Over our whitefish, he described some of the arrangements at the fort during the Winter months. There were several Saulteaux families who hunted for him and assisted at the fort, as well as ten voyageurs. He oversaw the trade in the surrounding area, as well as making preparations for the Great Rendezvous in the Summer. His doctoring was only part of his duties, for even doctors here must also be involved in the procurement of furs. Saving skins had a double meaning in this country, he joked.

All the while he spoke, I felt an unwinding, a loosening. When he asked if I might like to offer an account of what had happened – as the Sail would offer his to the NWC Big Wigs, and so perhaps it might be best if I added my own version – out it came. About Sugar, McLeod, Herse, Spey, the Sioux, Bruno. All of it. I didn't even conceal the pitiful spectacle of Arthur in love – though I skipped and softened several of the Other Arthur's infamies, which was more than the rascal deserved.

'I see,' said Munro. And he might even have somewise understood, for later I'd hear something of his own story from several of the men at the fort. That he'd once been a student of some promise in Montreal, but there'd been an affair with a woman who was also subject to the affections of an English officer. There'd been words. There might have been a duel. There'd certainly been something that necessitated a swift journey to the North West countries. It seemed Munro had suffered his own Triangle. I could barely picture this mild and gentle fellow brandishing pistols at dawn, but neither had I known what the Other Arthur could make me.

I asked him what they'd do to me. The NWC. The Company I now belonged to, though had never joined. Such were the shifting sands of this world.

Munro said they'd doubtless be furious with me for a few months. And then in the rush of things, and the confusion of the conjoining of the Companies, most likely forget me. I'd probably be sent down to Montreal without my wages paid.

I asked again if he knew what had become of my companions.

He said Herse had gone on to the Rainy River fort, while the nose-less man – he was not sure of all the names – had gone with the Orkney woman and the young Frenchman to an outpost somewhere not far to the West of us. The Sail – he was sorry, Mr Mackenzie – had sent them there.

And the ear-less man?

With a flicker of a smile, he remarked it often seemed the North West countries performed more surgeries than him. He didn't know for certain, only that he'd travelled somewhere with his Saulteaux wife.

And the other two? I asked, and waited his reply as though he were poised, lance in hand, above some huge and tender boil.

He was afraid he wasn't sure where they'd gone either.

But they'd left together?

Yes.

Down came the lance.

And here Munro added something, which he said he didn't know for certain was connected to those fellows we'd been looking for down at Yellow Lake but might well be. During the Autumn, he'd spoken to a trader who, early in the Summer, had made a journey to the New Fort from Red River. He'd taken an unusual route, going South of Lake of the Woods, through the Great Mire. To his surprise, for he'd not expected to meet anyone there, he'd come across two traders – or at least he assumed them so – paddling north towards the lake. It was a curious encounter. Neither had wished to speak with him and had barely slowed their canoe as they passed by. They hadn't given their names or Companies, or any indication where they were going. All he could say of them was that the younger one had red hair and had wounded his leg, which was dreadfully swollen and had begun to stink.

Did he think this was Long Arm and Copperhead?

He knew nothing for certain, only that no one could have been expected to be in that mire. Except, perhaps, if you were travelling to Lake of the Woods from the Debated Lands.

3

A few days later, one of the hunters got a moose, and while we tucked into steaks the size of thighs, Munro discussed the miraculous hearing of these beasts, and a Saulteaux tale he'd heard of them being able to exist under water, and the way the Saulteaux hunters would outlast them with snowshoes in the Winter when the snow was deep. At last, he poured us a glass of brandy, cleared his throat, and said, 'What shall we do with you then, Arthur? If you're to be here until the thaw.'

I told him I'd assist in whatever way possible, though I remained rather green in the trade and it appeared my apprenticeship would likely perish in its cradle. Then an idea came to me. Might I assist him with his doctoring work? Though lacking experience, I might do something in the way of holding things, or making bandages, or whatever one did.

Munro was pleased by the suggestion, saying he'd be delighted with the assistance. Perhaps he might show me some things this very evening. He began with the apothecary, where he went from bottle to bottle, giving me the names of the substances and their properties. And much to my surprise, I discovered this was a type of Latin I liked.

I was a slow learner, I said. And hoped this wouldn't tax his patience.

Munro smiled. 'The Winters here are very long, Arthur.'

And so began my career as a doctor's assistant, to which, after several detours, I've lately returned, being far better at it than I ever was at trading.

I was fortunate with my teacher. Munro was a genial, practical, patient fellow. At the fort, I witnessed many of the ways the body can be afflicted. I saw burns and breaks and strains; agues and dropsies and fevers; Cupid's Measles, the King's Evil. I stood beside Munro as he bled men and made bandages and set bones and mixed purgatives and emetics and tonics. And in that infirmary, surrounded by the bodily woes of others, I found a kind of answer to my father's gloomy philosophy. For it was not all passing Ages and declines in there, nor some grand progress either. It was one man or woman maybe feeling a bit better. A leg mending. A cut healed. A fever passed. Not always, not completely. But sometimes. And as Munro said, understanding the human body had not reached its zenith in old Athens.

I would have been happy to spend the rest of the Winter there, if it hadn't been for two events. One took place in the waking world, the other came to me in my sleep.

4

It was Godin who brought the map back to me.

I'd been at the fort several months when the dream arrived. Having spent the afternoon assisting Munro in removing three of a Frenchman's frostbitten toes, and the evening reading a description of the various benefits of Turlington's Balsam in the treatment of cuts and bruises, I'd fallen into a deep slumber.

I was once again looking at Godin's cowlick. However, we were no longer in the underground place but instead on an island. From what I could see, it was thickly wooded with birch and basswood and poplar. We were standing in a clearing, which had been planted with corn and squash. Godin beckoned and I followed him along a narrow trail until we reached a small beach of gritty sand. To one side the lake spread as far as I could see, on the other was another island, obscured in a mist.

Why are we here? I asked. As before, only his back was visible, no matter what angle I stood at. His face was never revealed.

As if in reply, Godin took up a stick and began to draw in the sand. He drew a large lake; he wrote Mire beneath it; he drew one island, and then a second, which he marked with the letters HR. And once he was done, I realised it was the burnt map, restored. Or at least the side of it that showed the second place. He made one addition too, writing Lake of the Woods above it.

He said I must make him a promise.

Anything, I said.

I must promise never to put this map on paper.

I promised, and thanked him, and we sat down together on the sand for a time (or what counted for time in the dream).

'What was it like?' I asked him at last. 'The sea?'

'It wasn't how I expected it to be,' he said.

'And where did it –'

And there I was, back in my bed, with the groans of the Frenchman coming from the infirmary. But the map was as clear in my mind as the morning was in my eyes. This was the last time Godin would meet me.

It was Hyacinthe who brought the others back.

'We have a new patient in the infirmary,' Munro announced one day after lunch, some weeks after my dream. 'You might want to see him.'

Hyacinthe was sitting on one of the beds, holding his wrist. 'I have sprained it,' he said coldly. 'I didn't know this place was also the gaol,' he added, more coldly still.

I told him how heartily sorry I was for what had happened. I'd been abroad in my wits when he'd given me the fright with his costume, and I'd dropped my candle. It'd been an accident.

Sorry would not pay his wages, he said.

Well, perhaps everything was not lost on that front, I said.

No, not lost. Burnt.

I asked him what they'd been about these past months, and eventually – grudgingly, still frigidly – he answered. It turned out the Sail had exiled McLeod, together with him, Narcisse and Spey, to some Godforsaken post around a hundred miles or so to the West of the New Fort. It was a dismal place. Worse even than our old XY posts. Not like this one, he added, glowering at the infirmary. It had taken them three days by dog and sled to reach here.

There was a little kick in the shin from the Other Arthur. And Esther was also there, with McLeod?

Yes, she had been.

Had been? My heart lifted.

They'd departed the woebegone post some weeks ago.

They. A downward lurch, a plunge. And where were they now?

Who knew? There'd been nothing about McLeod's leaving in the Sail's orders. But McLeod had spoken of Lake of the Woods, so maybe they'd gone there. Hyacinthe would himself leave, if only he had the means, he continued, his temper darkening. If only those means had not become some blackened snow at Yellow Lake.

Them, I said. It had taken *them* three days to reach here?

Oh, yes. Narcisse had come with him. He couldn't handle the dogs with one hand. Though, he grumbled, he'd say his one hand was better than Narcisse's two hands, which had made a terrible zigzag of the journey. He was outside.

'He doesn't want to see me?'

'Nobody wants to see you, Mr Arthur.' Hyacinthe now told me how Narcisse and Spey had been planning to use their wages to go to America and buy an apple tree. But what could they buy with blackened snow?

Spey had travelled with them here as well?

Spey had remained at the woebegone post, he said, falling into a lament about how it'd been better when Narcisse had been in love with his wooden women, seeing as now he had to suffer the noise of their –

Well, yes, indeed, I said. Perhaps there was no need for the full details of this happy development.

A very comfortable gaol, Hyacinthe repeated, looking about him. How was it that my treachery and destruction had earned me such an easy –

Seeing the direction of Hyacinthe's thoughts, I moved quickly to intercept them. I had something he and Narcisse both might want to see, I announced, and was very glad for it.

5

I'd been at the fort some weeks when Seraphin had approached me one afternoon in the infirmary. He'd shuffled from foot to foot and looked over several bottles of Rush's Pills, before saying he had something to show me on the other side of the river.

How odd it had felt to return there, to the first of my North West country dwellings. Much had altered. Was this even an XY fort anymore, seeing as the XY no longer existed? But in other respects, nothing had altered. It remained the same rickety, slanting hovel. Perhaps somebody would find a mouldering board fifty years from now and think the whole Company nothing but a Roman numeral. The spiders and mice were at least asleep for the Winter.

However, entering the warehouse I discovered one significant change. It wasn't empty. There in the corner was a tarpaulin and, lifting it, Seraphin revealed some fifteen packs of furs, saying he'd discovered them buried in a cache when harvesting his squashes. He figured they were most probably a portion of the Missouri furs, being Labrie's share for helping Long Arm and Copperhead.

And he hadn't told Munro about them?

Seraphin said that when he'd discovered them, there was still such a thing as the XY Company, and thus reckoned they belonged to McLeod and the rest of us. As for himself, he had no interest in them. 'I am done with peltries, Mr Arthur.'

This is where I now led Hyacinthe and Narcisse (whose greeting had been as frosty as Hyacinthe's), pulling back the tarpaulin like a magician unveiling an enormous rabbit – or its fur, anyway. And though it cannot be said this was followed immediately by forgiving slaps on the back, there was a decided thawing in their humours concerning me. It wasn't a mansion's worth, but enough at least to cover their wages and more. Would it be possible for me to accompany them and these furs back West to their woebegone post, I asked? A shrug seemed a fair recompense.

I was sorry to leave the New Fort, and couldn't bring myself to abscond without a word. It being imprudent to tell Munro my plans outright, for speaking of them would implicate him, I approached the matter obliquely. If a hypothetical man were in a hypothetical gaol for a hypothetical offence and were to hypothetically... and so on.

Munro said he'd be sorry to see me hypothetically go, but he'd not stop me. And, in all truth, by the time the hurly-burly of the Rendezvous arrived in summertime, probably no one would remember my existence. But he did feel obliged to ask: after everything that had befallen me, was venturing into new country wise?

Me and what was wise for me hadn't been on nodding terms for a considerable while, I said. But having been given something I thought lost irrevocably – a map of some significance – it was my duty to return it to those it had been meant for. There were also several other items I owed my companions from my prior Company.

So be it, he said, and we shook hands. But before I turned to leave, he added that I should keep up my medical studies. I might not be so bad at it, he thought, if I was to persist, which gave me a strange and unaccustomed jolt of gladness. It felt like I'd been waiting for a 'not bad' my whole life. 'Not bad' warmed my footsteps as I headed out into the slowly melting snow.

PART FIVE

The Island

1

From Hyacinthe's description, I'd expected to find their post some barren, dismal rock, and the three of them reduced to boiling their parchment windows for broth. Instead, I found Spey sitting inside a cabin that was as snug as a country cottage compared to our hovel at Yellow Lake, stewing what appeared to be a whole school of trout in a copper kettle. The cabin was nestled in a stand of fine red pines, on the shore of a long, winding lake. She greeted me rather coolly at first, and then more warmly as the others brought in the packs from the sled.

If this was the Sail's idea of exile, perhaps he was a more generous fellow than I'd supposed. But in truth there was hardly a fur to be had within fifty miles of this post, which in the eyes of the Company made it a Desert and a Purgatory. A signature in Montreal might have made Hyacinthe and Narcisse NWC men on paper, but the Sail would have them sent down to Montreal soon enough. McLeod had only jumped the gun.

We sat before the steaming kettle and, as the others wolfed their fish, I gave them a fuller account of my intentions. To begin with, I wished to locate Old Crebassa and offer him his share of the furs. Afterwards, I'd visit Herse. And, lastly, would find you and McLeod. I had amends to make.

Narcisse told me finding the first two should be easy enough. Crebassa had set up house with the Widow not too far away, and Herse had gone to the Rainy River fort. As for you and McLeod, he could only repeat Hyacinthe's suggestion about Lake of the Woods.

Hyacinthe spat out a bone. Crebassa would be happy enough with the furs. But I'd be about as welcome as a dose of Cupid's Measles to the others.

So be it, I said. But hoped I had something a little better to offer them.

After a bellyful of trout, I announced my intention to set out the very next day to visit Crebassa.

Once he'd wiped the tears of mirth from his face, Narcisse said did I remember my attempt to carry one pack at the Long Sault? How would I transport Crebassa's share of the furs?

Perhaps I might borrow a sled and snowshoes then, and a couple of dogs.

A sled, managed Hyacinthe between guffaws and thigh-slappings. And dogs. And snowshoes. Would I like some directions too? Or would I be like the great navigator, Mr Thompson, and find my way through the country by reading the stars? Did I remember my night in the forest by the mouth of Brule River?

Spey remarked I'd only recently had some difficulty locating the Necessary Place.

Well, it seemed to me it'd been dug a mighty long way back in the woods. But roast me as they wished, I proclaimed indignantly, I was determined on this journey.

Once their laughter had abated, they explained that even were it possible to overcome my deficiencies in navigation and transport, we were now approaching that amphibious time of year when the preponderant element of the North West countries was going through its metamorphosis. The snow would be slush in days. The ice might turn to water any time. However, Hyacinthe suggested that after a week or two they could probably help me deliver Crebassa's share. But why the need to see Herse? And was it necessary to go chasing after you, seeing as in that race it was clear McLeod was wearing the Laurel and the Bay.

I told them my intention was simply to deliver the map.

The map I'd burnt?

I'd not burnt it on purpose.... But none of that mattered now. I'd recovered a copy.

And where was it? Might they see?

I'd not recovered it in a material form.

Not in a material form?

The map was in my head, I explained. In some measure, I was the map.

I was a map?

It was a complicated business. Dreams and what not. All three of them looked at me, and then at each other. Narcisse whispered something to Spey and then asked if I might step out a moment while they conversed.

By the time Narcisse beckoned me back in, it had been decided. They'd take me as far as the Rainy River fort as soon as the ice broke. They'd only been waiting here in any case, for the Sail to return and apply the final rites.

But where would they go?

Spey said she and Narcisse would go to America – the more America sort of America rather than the Yellow Lake sort of America. Somewhere with an orchard.

And what would he do? I asked Hyacinthe.

He said he supposed he'd go with them. The Americans had fur men too.

2

It took two weeks. The snow started to melt. The ice on the lake began to groan and creak and candle. And at last, one night a wind came up and it tinkled a symphony of tiny bells, and when we woke there was clear water everywhere. Two days later we were in a canoe and on our way.

How oddly comforting it was to have Hyacinthe's back before me again. Though this time Narcisse had the stern, and I had a paddle in my hand and some clue as to how to use it. We took a route through a small river, swelled by the ice melt, crossed several lakes and short portages, before arriving at a lake with wonderfully clear and glittering water. I counted six islands scattered across it, and eventually we came to a secluded bay, guarded by two bare rocks. On one an eagle was eating a fish. On the other a gull was watching him, hoping to steal a morsel.

What a fine spot Old Crebassa and the Widow had chosen. Their wigwam sat near a shelf of smooth rock, lapped by the clear water. The jutting rock made a cosy harbour, with enough room for two canoes. There were fish drying on poles. Smoke drifted out to us as we approached, some from the fire, some from Crebassa's pipe.

It was a happy reunion. We ate boiled trout and listened to the last fragments of wind-driven ice tinkling along the shore. We shared some shrub, and I caught the taste of those warm climes I'd missed in it before, and then we recounted stories of our time together and toasted Young Godin. I told Crebassa I was sorry for his ear. That I'd destroyed it in the fire. Oh, I shouldn't think of it, he said. The truth was he'd spent far too long talking to that ear. He preferred speaking to his wife, who had two perfect – and perfectly alive – ears. I asked him if he'd given this place a name? He told me it already had one. The Saulteaux called it Sitting Down, and that was what he intended to do here.

The next morning we took our leave.

I can't recall the names of all the lakes and rivers we passed through. There was somewhere called Crooked Lake and we stopped there at the base of a cliff, where it was rumoured you might see, embedded in a cleft above, the shafts of some Sioux arrows fired long ago in the Old French Time. A sign much like the sticks, to say: 'We have been here, and were not afraid to be here.' But we couldn't make anything out clearly, only a few twigs that might have been either their remnants or the beginnings of an eagle's nest. While Narcisse and Hyacinthe hotly debated this, I reflected how in many ways this is what the Sioux had always been for me: a rumour in the shape of my own fears; an ignis fatuus to run from, while I set the real fire.

There was a river called Malice, a lake named for a cross. And then Rainy Lake and its maze of islands, before – at last – we reached the most beautiful of rivers, which was called the Rainy, too. But here we're approaching the fort, and two sad events must intervene and slow my progress. To begin with, I must say goodbye to Hyacinthe, Narcisse and Spey.

We landed a mile or so before the fort, on the Northern bank, and sat down for a pipe. I knew this was as far as they'd planned to come in this direction and stood up, prepared to embark on a speech thanking them for bringing me and more generally for being my companions, etc, puffing out my chest to begin.

'You will be able to get a canoe from the fort,' Hyacinthe said, forestalling my oration. Then he glanced across the river and remarked, 'The other bank is America.'

'It looks a lot like this bank,' said Narcisse.

Perhaps in the eyes of an idiot it might, Hyacinthe said. But to him it was obvious. The trees were a little bigger. The pine needles rather greener. He'd once met an American fellow who'd read a book by the President, in which it was said that the plants and animals in America were even bigger than in Old France.

But how could the trees be bigger on one side of a river than on the other? said Narcisse. And until a few years ago it hadn't even been decided that that bank was America. Had the trees become taller when they'd decided it was? Were they taller at Yellow Lake? And besides, he'd once heard a French Professor say that the plants and animals – by some general law of Nature – were smaller in America than in Old France.

Well perhaps they should measure them when they arrived. Perhaps –

'There will be trees for an orchard,' said Spey. 'That's all that matters.'

'Probably taller –'

'Enough,' said Spey.

Since I was already standing for my speech, I said I hoped

there were trees enough for many orchards. And added that if they planted one, it might easily outlast a Nation and grow apples that would just be apples and the size that apples were.

And with that our pipes were done. I walked with them down to the bank and watched as they climbed into the canoe and embarked. Narcisse and Hyacinthe continued to debate the natural productions of America, the packs of furs nestled between them, but then stopped midstream, turned broadside to me, and lifted their paddles in farewell.

3

When beginning this, I didn't truly know what parts of it, in addition to poor Godin, would be the darkest for me – the fire, the reconciliation of you and McLeod, the Other Arthur. But I see now that the following must be added to that bleak list.

Herse wasn't living in the fort, I discovered, but in a shack a mile or so further down the river. Lord knows I'd had experience enough of hovels these past months, but that shack was drearier than any of them. It wasn't that it was rickety, or cold and unwelcoming (though it was), but rather its general atmosphere of squalor, which lingered over everything like a miasma or murk. And then there was the Herse I found in there.

How to describe the man who opened the door? Perhaps best to make a list of words the very opposite of the Herse I'd once known. Filthy, unkempt, slovenly. He shuffled out from the shadows of his pit, his eyes blank and expressionless, their wryness flattened out like a piece of tin under a blacksmith's doleful hammer. His clothes were smeared in grease and as smoked as a Winter whitefish, his shirt a rag, and his hat would have run my former one close.

'Herse,' I cried in astonishment. The whole way from the fort, I'd worried he'd refuse to hear me out and send me off. His fury had been utter and unbending that dreadful morning, remaining unabated the entire way back to the New Fort. My last glimpse of him was as we'd come through its front gate, and I hadn't needed a telescope to see he would have been happy for me to sit in that gaol until the mosquitoes returned in the Spring and bled what remained of me.

But this Herse was a ghost. He stood in the doorway, blinking at the light as though it were the soap he'd clearly long avoided, and said, 'Oh, it is you.' The voice was so bloodless and hollow I wished he'd shouted 'Go to the Devil', and beaten me with a stick instead. This shack was the worst sort of Siberia.

I won't record the whole of our interview: there'd not be dialogue enough. Herse had barely any language left in him. I brought out my treasure – the announcement of the map in my head and description of what it portrayed, the Lake of the Woods and the islands, and the letters HR written on one, which I said I couldn't yet figure, but thought could be like the MR on the map for the Secret Post, except perhaps this H was a mackled M, or else the letter for some other name for MacDowell, apart from Long Arm. But Herse only looked more distant and despondent still, saying that it didn't matter, none of it did. That it hadn't mattered before, either, on the night of the fire. If he'd known then what he knew now, he would have burnt the map himself.

He told me the same story Munro had, about the trader's encounter in the Great Mire, having heard it from the head of the Rainy River fort. He said those men must have been Ross and MacDowell. And that swollen, stinking leg must have been Ross' leg. And that meant....

I said I'd also heard this story, admitting – for Godin's fate augured badly – it didn't sound good. But there was no absolute certainty the man was Ross. Nothing was written for sure until it reached the Final Book. And then I announced my intention of finding McLeod and you, and going to the place marked on the map. He must come with me. What could he lose?

'Ross had my books,' he said, as if he hadn't properly heard me. 'He said he'd make a place for them. All I had to do was get there. That was all. And I didn't.' With this he staggered back and fell onto a chair draped with a filthy buffalo robe. A piece of log spluttered in his fire.

I told him I'd go find them, whatever the case.

'Do as you wish,' he said. 'But leave me be.'

The next day I traipsed back and found Herse still sitting on his buffalo robe. The fire was out, and his thin bony face was almost blue. He uttered not a word to me this time. I built up his fire and heated some of the indefinite gruel one of the men had given me at the fort.

He must eat this, at least. Though it wasn't duck, I feared. And I had no tea.

Herse said nothing.

And continued to say nothing until the sun began to set and I had to return to the fort.

The day afterwards was clear and sunny. It was warm enough to melt the small patches of remnant snow in the shadows, and all around was a sense of Nature sucking in its breath and readying itself for the great race of the northern Summer. There was such a lightness in the air, and such a brightness to the light, it was as if the world had thrown off a cloying blanket in the night and got up to rinse its face. But of course, I suddenly thought. But of course. And went immediately to find the man who ran the Company shop and begged him for some soap and a brush.

On my return to the shack this time, I was armed.

'For Christ's sake leave me be,' muttered Herse from his pit.

'Opposition, Herse,' I chirped, and began to drag his coat off his shoulders.

'By God, man,' he cried. 'I told you to leave me be.' This was better, already.

I had a kettle on the fire in a wink, and was soon enough outside with the coat, in a flurry of suds, scrubbing like a sailor. I returned for his waistcoat and trousers and, when done, a breeze-bodied version of Herse was dancing a jig from the branch of a birch tree. While this dried, I took the brush and attempted a resurrection of the beaver hat. And if it didn't gleam like Castor in the heavens, it was at least more like the beast it had been before.

And so it was with Herse, as I returned the clean clothes to his body. Item by item they appeared to revive him slightly, as though one could perform a kind of Vitalism with trousers and a shirt. 'Arthur,' he said, as I slipped his coat on him, 'what on earth are you about?'

'One moment,' I replied, reaching for his hat.

Once it was on his head, he looked about him like a man waking from a dream and announced, 'This place is a pigsty, Arthur.'

Perhaps we'd do well to be away from it then, I told him. I'd procured a canoe and supplies enough for a few weeks. Would he come with me?

4

I saw no better river than the Rainy in all those countries. It ran for ten pipes with hardly a rapid or obstacle, through wild meadows, under oaks and elms and basswoods, serenaded by a gentle chorus of frogs trying out their wooing songs. My father would have looked at this place and imagined an infant Thames, with Brutus lately arrived from Troy standing on its banks. Or perhaps Arcadia. Or Thessaly. Or some place where people lived side by side with gods and lived on milk and honey. But it was no echo of an Ancient Time. It was not like then or like there. This was the North West country, in this time, in this Age, being itself entire.

Herse and I paddled down it. I hoped it did him some good. It did me plenty.

At the end of those ten pipes, we entered Lake of the Woods. And here was a predicament. On the map in my head there were two islands. On Lake of the Woods there appeared to be ten thousand.

Setting out, I'd somehow imagined – ignoring my lesson about Miraculous Solutions – that my map and journey would achieve everything I desired, or at least almost everything (I wasn't sure any map or journey would stop you loving McLeod). That Herse and my friendship would be restored. That you and McLeod would for certain be on this lake and finding you a relatively simple matter. That I would be forgiven. Caught up in the larger sentiment and resolution of making my amends, a few smaller practicalities had been neglected, such as the relation of my map to the Actual world.

To begin with, Herse wasn't much use in our search, familiar though he was with the shores of this lake, mostly sunk as he yet was in the Slough of his Despond, and perhaps assailed by the memories of the time he had once spent in the Lake of the Woods district. Having no clearer direction, we paddled West, along the southern shore, which was fringed by sand beaches, and behind them sandy hills. The lake here was pleasingly shallow, studded here and there with boulders and tiny islets which we stopped along the way to examine, though what exactly we were meant to find, or how we were meant to identify the islands in my head, was another small practicality I'd overlooked. From rock to islet to boulder we went, until I began to wonder if we were destined to paddle along this shoreline perpetually, like some ghost hulk out at sea, or at least until we encountered you and McLeod doing the same. Herse barely spoke a word, as if this hopeless wandering brought a return to his pigsty. After three days, we came to a low wooded point, and I determined to stop there to attempt to rouse Herse from his low spirits and consider some more sensible course of action.

Whether it was through the intervening hand of the Fates or Godin or who knows, it was at this spot we met a Saulteaux hunter. He was alone and had been camped there several weeks, stopping on his way from the west, where he'd been hunting beaver, to join his family near the Grande Portage. Because I had no Saulteaux, Herse was now forced to become more garrulous. From the hunter, he discovered you and McLeod had stopped at this same point a week before. He said you were journeying very slowly, obviously following my own poor strategy: paddling along and stopping at each island you came to.

This hunter had a curious history. He was named after a bird of prey – the Falcon – and told Herse he'd once been a white man – or a white boy, at least: a farmer's son from the Ohio valley. He'd been kidnapped as a child by the Shawnee and come to live with the Ottawa, and then later with the Saulteaux. His conversation with Herse was all in that language, for he'd lost his English entirely. He'd lived and hunted with his family across much of this country, from Lake Superior to Rainy Lake, and had recently been trying his luck around Red River. He was a striking-looking man, with stern eyes and high cheekbones.

This conversation with the Falcon seemed to unlock something in Herse. Afterwards, he beckoned me over and, when he spoke, was almost like the Herse of old.

'We are after another needle, I suppose,' he said.

'Another what?'

'Needle, Arthur. In a haystack. That's what we started with, wasn't it?'

I admitted there were a lot of islands.

He said we might bob about in this canoe until Winter came again, if we were to explore a third of them. But on my map – since I only had to close my eyes to consult it – were there any other words or letters or markings? Any at all, apart from Lake of the Woods and Mire and HR?

I closed my eyes and as always it was as though Godin had

written there in ink on the backs of my eyelids. Every detail as clear as day. But there was no additional mark or symbol I could discern.

Nothing on the shoreline? Herse asked.

Nothing.

Herse tapped his pipe against a stone, and spoke again to the Falcon, conveying to him, I assumed, the nature of my map and its limitations. The Falcon nodded and uttered a few words in reply.

Their shape, said Herse. Did either of the islands have a particular shape?

Only a sort of general island shape, I said.

Lord, but there was no such thing as a general island shape, Herse cried. Was Rhodes the same as Skye? Was Ithaca identical to Ireland? I must look again.

I looked again and did begin to discern a particular shape for the first of the islands. A serration. Or two triangles conjoined. Perhaps an 'M', I said.

An 'M'?

But now I'd seen it, that 'M' was clear as day, and I felt foolish for not discerning it before. The three of us smoked our pipes some more. When I attempted to speak, Herse held up his hand and said he must think. He finished his pipe, packed another. And then announced he thought he had it, what the 'M' signified. It was Massacre.

Massacre?

Massacre Island, he said. Which was indeed somewhere on this lake. He'd heard of it during his time here.

Oh wonderful, I thought. Just my luck. Not Mango or Milk or Mutton Island. Herse turned to the Falcon and they conversed a while before Herse nodded, shook his hand, and stood up. We took our leave of him then and returned to the canoe.

Why Massacre? I asked as we embarked.

Herse said he'd tell me the story as we went.

It was not a happy story, I assumed.

No, said Herse.

And did he know how to get to this lovely-sounding place?

Roughly. Though the Falcon had given him more exact directions, Herse said. Followed by a remark on navigation to the effect that it was all very well going about with a compass and sextant and having the skill of Mr Thompson, but in the end, travelling in these countries mostly came down to making sure to learn the words for 'What is over there?' and 'Where do we find…?' in as many languages as possible. A cynic might suggest the Knight had been made a Sir mainly because he was good at asking for directions, so he drily said.

It was good to have Herse more like himself, I thought.

5

It is customary in the Travels of those mooning Englishmen to pause here and there for some topography; to say – on rounding this or that promontory, or ascending this or that hill – how 'the land revealed itself', like Nature was some troubling man who displays his unmentionable self at night outside a tavern. But since you'd been on this road before us, and Herse and I were more engaged in paddling than mooning, I'll confine myself to the main aspect: Lake of the Woods was very large. We paddled on it for another three days, until a plume of smoke did indeed reveal itself, rising up from an island to the North of us, which I expected Herse to inform me was named Murder or Devil or some such thing. But, as we approached, it revealed something else entirely.

McLeod was standing on an outcrop of grey rock, streaked here and there with red and white quartz or marble. As we approached closer, he turned towards some lichen-streaked boulders and called out, 'You won't believe this. It is fucking Arthur. And Herse with him.' And out you stepped.

Pillars and Posts, I wrote somewhere far back in this heap of paper, with the addition of some blushing musings about goddesses and foam, etc. Well, if that occasion was a Pillar, then this most certainly felt like a Post – a post which that slumbering Giant, awakened, had pulled out of the ground and used to club me in the stomach. How extremely rational I'd been in Munro's infirmary. It had become a Palace of Reason, wherein I'd seen my behaviour for what it was – deplorable – and what a gentleman must do – make amends. In there, my situation had appeared as logical as a piece of mathematics: there was no Triangle; your affections were with another; and I had the strongest obligations as a friend. And now here you both were, in the flesh, and it was like the Palace was going up in flames and Professor Newton was running naked and raving across the grounds. My God how the bedlam in our blood persists!

As we landed, I opened my mouth to say 'Esther', and found not a word in there. A moth might have flown out of it. You didn't say a word either and I couldn't read your face. Your freckles were like little cannonballs, punching holes in my heart. McLeod and Herse were speaking but it was as if I were overhearing them in another room.

'Why have you brought *him* here?' said McLeod.

'You're mistaken, William. He brought me. I think he has something for you.'

'Apologies will do us no frigging good.'

'A bit more useful than that, I hope. He says he has the map.'

'The map! How's that possible?'

'He says it's in his head.'

'In his head, you say!' For a disturbing moment it looked as though McLeod might split it open with his large, rough hands and see what he could find in there.

And then, at last, you spoke. 'Let him explain.'

It was fortunate for me that you believed in the efficacy of dreams.

When at last I found my tongue, I explained about Godin coming to me with the map, and how I could conjure it when I closed my eyes. You nodded, first to me and then to McLeod. He passed me a stick and told me to draw it in the dirt. I told you what Godin had said — that I wasn't to write it down.

McLeod harrumphed. McLeod glowered. 'So, we'll have to lug him with us the whole frigging way?'

It was better than searching every adjectival island on the lake, you told him.

Since we knew the location of the first of the islands, and could hopefully find the second using my map, it was decided we'd depart together the next day. This gave me the whole afternoon to attempt to make my amends, to learn a new way to know you, to try to assuage the bedlam inside me, to do all manner of things.

I chose instead to sulk.

Perhaps it was some miserable cousin or offspring of the Other Arthur — a wounded sense of how my grand gesture had been so coolly received, a frustration about the cruel persistence of desire — but whatever its origin, this Sulk spoiled everything. You said you'd like to talk with me a while, as Herse had gone to sit by the shore and McLeod was away elsewhere, trying to catch some fish for supper. I'd wanted nothing more for months (knowing I couldn't have the rest). It was what I'd hoped and yearned for.

I'd prefer to take a solitary walk, I huffed.

As large sulks do, it made me small. The island was bigger than it seemed, and clambering over its boulder-strewn shores I considered it moodily as a Pilgrim land — the Island of Woe-Is-I. Why did my sinking stomach make a continuing mock of me? Why did it keep falling off cliffs? Why did it stomp on my better thoughts and inclinations and make me an idiot? And stumbling through this fraught terrain, I barely even noticed McLeod.

There was his canoe, floating beside a half-submerged boulder about twenty feet out from the shore. McLeod was standing in it, holding a fishing pole. Several of his first words returned to me, about staying on my arse in canoes – the North West countries having taught me something, at least. Meanwhile, the Sulk reflected on the cruel unfairness of the world. How McLeod had metamorphosed from that wreck, that staved galleon lying in the street in Lachine, into this figure who wouldn't have been out of place throwing a discus on an urn. It was as though he'd passed his lovesickness on to me, and now I must appear what I felt: shrunken, contemptable, foolish. And, of course, this gap in the door of my thoughts was all the Other Arthur needed to barge in. *Well, well, Arthur. Look at McLeod there. The cat with all the cream, and now getting some fishes too.*

I won't listen, I said. Meanwhile, out on the lake, McLeod's rod began to bend.

Just imagine. In a few years he'll turn to her in their much-used bed and laugh and say, do you remember that little Arthur fellow? The White Frog. And on and on he went, sketching that terrible vista of the future in which a person becomes an amusing story for their once beloved.

It must have been a mighty fish because, as the Other Arthur poured his poison into my ear, McLeod began to wobble in the canoe. And then to sway. And then to topple. He fell sideways against the boulder, his head rebounding from it. Then he was lying in the water, as still as you like.

Ah, whispered the Other Arthur. *Do you see? If you wait only a few minutes, what might you have? A woman in her sorrow and mourning. A woman in need of comfort.*

My God, even at the point of disaster he was incorrigible and disgraceful.

McLeod had still not moved. A gull wheeled overhead. Somewhere a frog carried on its chirruping, though I'd not been aware of it before. I took a step towards the water's edge.

Nobody will see. Nobody will know. Five minutes and you'll have everything you want. Every morning will be full of things delightful. Every evening too.

Another step. The water went over my ankle.

You'll never have another chance. You'll never have –

Two more steps and it was over my knees. The thoughts of breathing in water began to wake. The drowned castles and towns unfurled their soaking pennants.

You'll never – And then I cried out. Maybe the weight and press of all the old fears forced it out of me, maybe the tumult of a freshly broken heart. But perhaps I merely wanted to drown out the scoundrel's voice. I howled. I bellowed. I caterwauled. The water touched my belly, and then my chest. And just as I was forced onto my tiptoes, my face upturned, the water dripping into my ear, my fingers touched McLeod's collar. Clasping hold of it, I began inching him back to the shore as if I were dragging a log – the Tall Tree felled – before flipping him over and hauling him the rest of the way. By the time my feet touched terra firma, Herse's hands were there beside mine, though I hadn't seen him arrive. You were running towards us.

You punched his chest once, twice, three times, and on the

fourth he began coughing up water. After a few minutes he was sitting up, still half-dazed, and his lips were moving. You and Herse were pointing at me. I think you were explaining what had happened, and I think McLeod was trying to thank me, but in truth I couldn't hear a word anyone was saying.

I was sitting on the shore, listening to the inside of my own head, and discovering a blissful silent nothing there.

The next morning we all four of us set off for Massacre Island, in two canoes.

6

Here is the story that Herse had given me about the island. Back in the Old French Time, some traders had been travelling from a fort on the western shore of this lake. They had a Jesuit priest with them. While camping on an island they'd been discovered and ambushed by a passing Sioux war band, who killed every one of them, leaving their severed heads sitting on their blankets. Herse said that during the attack, the Jesuit had tethered himself to some stone or tree, to stop himself running away when his time came, which inevitably it did. That was the story. Whether it was true or not, he couldn't say.

But since stories make places, as much as wind and rain and ice, when we arrived at the island it looked much like its name and that deed. The lake deepened, off its shores, and yet the waters were still around them, as if the waves had lain down, and the thin, motionless air seemed to make even our whispers loud. There were rocks all along its shoreline, sloping sharply into the water. They appeared somehow more grey than any we had seen, almost black, splattered here and there with patches of red-gold lichen. We kept our pipes in our pockets and passed by it with a shiver, filled with bleak thoughts and forebodings, wishing we'd had some better waypoint. Fortunately, the 'M' Island was not our destination.

To the [...] and [...] of Massacre Island, after making our way *a certain* number of pipes, we came to the other island.

It appeared abruptly. And without a word, our two canoes came together and we paddled in time towards the nearest shore. It shared the baffling properties of that shifting island of reeds and rushes on Yellow Lake: if you didn't keep your eyes constantly fixed on it, it seemed to wander this way and that. Anyone behind us would have thought us all doused in shrub and our course a drunken meander.

The nearer we approached, the less promising it looked – a close relative of Massacre. Boulders lay strewn along its shoreline, which in places merged to become small cliffs. There were several shrunken, windblown pines and birches topping these, a fringe as sparse as a few hairs brushed over a balding man's ear. My initial impressions were: this is a woebegone rock, nobody could be here, or have been here; I have dragged myself hundreds of miles to find this place and convinced the others to follow me. Followed by: Godin, what did I ever do to you to deserve this? Or was that even you?

At first, we couldn't find a place to land. The shore was like a porcupine with granite quills. I could read the book of McLeod's face well enough: it was opened on the chapter entitled 'Arthur's Adjectival Idiot Plan'. I was glad Herse's face was behind me. But just as it seemed there was no hope of even landing here, a narrow gap emerged between two boulders, wide enough to get our canoes through. It opened out into a tiny harbour.

Both canoes landed, and McLeod stood on the shore to survey the place. 'The Island of Desolation,' he announced.

Was I sure this was the place in my head? you asked. That

the map had located it to the […] and […]? McLeod was right, it did seem a bit adjectivally bleak.

Herse had already begun to walk sombrely ahead.

But those countries had one trick left for me. For while the island's shore offered one aspect, twenty paces inland it looked like something else entirely. Suddenly, we were walking among thick-trunked poplars and basswoods and wild cherries, on the point of greening, with some leaves already opening. You could feel the lushness of it, smell the rich and loamy soil. I can only suppose its interior was slightly concave, like a shallow bowl, and its barren edges concealed what it held. And though its size had seemed modest enough from our canoes – a few miles around at most – it now appeared far more extensive.

I was about to turn to McLeod – thinking perhaps he might acknowledge his too hasty judgement – when I spied the dwelling through the trees. Herse, a few strides ahead, must have already seen it but had said nothing. He'd not spoken since we'd landed. To reach it, we crossed through a meadow dotted with tree stumps and a few patches of black where the branches and undergrowth had been burnt. Little green buds were beginning to unfurl between the grass. Perhaps squashes. Maybe beans.

It was a garden.

'My God,' said McLeod.

But there was only me to hear his words. You'd already run ahead to knock on the door. Herse maintained his previous pace, the way someone does when they want simultaneously to arrive somewhere and not arrive there.

And now I hesitate, as I did then, and wait at the edge of that half-wild garden, as did McLeod and I both, with a shared instinct that what was inside – or who might answer the knocking – wasn't for us to discover. So let me pause, and let you and Herse go in, and see what you will see.

7

I never read either of those letters. I only know they were waiting on the table: one to you from your father, the other to Herse from Ross.

When, eventually, McLeod and I followed you inside, this is what we saw. Herse was sitting on the floor, cradling his letter on his knees. You were standing by the window, holding yours. There was a shelf, fashioned ingeniously from a piece of driftwood, with several books sitting tidily upon it, books of plants and flowers, Herbals – Gerard's, Culpeper's, Blackwell's. There was a bed built around the trunk of a birch tree, which rose up to support the roof. The floor was heaped with old spruce boughs, which were beginning to make the place fragrant – the sap in them rising yet, remembering the season. There was a small piece of glass (as rare and precious up here as sapphire) in the window. Along the far wall was what I knew must be the remainder of the Missouri furs, twenty or so packs of them, rising to the roof. And for all that it was more primitive and hastily assembled than even the worst of our hovels, I sensed this great difference: it was the first trader's dwelling I'd stood in that felt as though it had been built to be properly dwelt in. Not only for a season, not only for business, but as a place to live.

We stood there a moment or two before McLeod approached you, without a word, and taking your hand, led you outside. I was about to speak with Herse. But looking at him as he stared at that paper on his knees, I knew he was too far away to hear me – much farther away than I'd been on my Moon that awful day at Yellow Lake. And that my 'awful' had been a speck of dust, a mite, compared to this.

For though I couldn't read Greek, and could read Dreams only inadequately, I could read this on Herse's face: which was that I'd spent these past months believing I was living in my own love story, and then at the edge of yours and McLeod's, but this hadn't been the whole of it, not even the most of it. This was Herse's love story too, and I'd never known it. But I could see it now as clear as day. This dwelling had been built for them. Herse and Ross. This was the little corner where the world might let them be. This was the home the Missouri furs were meant to have built.

And so, without a word I backed out the door, leaving Herse with the words of Ross.

And went to join you and McLeod outside, sitting amongst the first shoots of the beans and squashes, where you related some of what your father had said to you in his letter.

With Ross gone and no one else arrived, he'd thought it best to be on his way. The Winter had been hard, but he'd survived it and now the sun was out, and the ice was off the lake. As for Ross, he'd nursed him as well as he could. But his leg had been cruelly injured and wouldn't heal. He'd left a letter for Herse, and if Herse was still a living man you should make sure it got to him.

How cruel it was, the way the world had of giving with one hand and snatching back with the other. At first, everything had gone as they'd arranged and hoped. Better. The beavers of the Missouri country must be the Lords and Ladies of beaverkind, so fine were their furs. And they'd got a heap of them.

They'd discovered this island on their journey out to the Missouri country. They'd been keeping an eye out for somewhere safe to cache whatever furs they got, until there was an opportunity to transport them further South, into the United States. At the same time, Ross had been searching for somewhere for himself and Herse, once Herse arrived and the furs were sold — somewhere nobody would find them if they didn't want finding. This island was perfect. Stepping past its grim perimeter was like finding a pearl in one of the first oysters you shucked.

Everything as hoped. The Fates — generous and grinning — throwing what they needed into their laps. By chance, Ross had spoken to an old trader at Rainy Lake who'd told him of a long-abandoned trading post down South, some miles from Yellow Lake. A place nobody would remember and was now in America. And so they'd put both these places — the island and the post — on their map, and delivered it to Labrie.

It was an odd thing for an old fur man to say, but perhaps when Fortune smiles too much, her lips can turn into a frown. And the beginning of that treacherous smile was that they'd been more successful than ever hoped and got too many furs. Two journeys had been needed to transport them all from this island to the abandoned post. They'd taken the first portion early in the Spring, before travelling back towards the island to collect the rest, thinking Herse (and you, if that's what you'd chosen) would be arriving soon at the New Fort, and (following the map they'd given to Labrie) would be travelling towards Yellow Lake. And if Herse missed them there for any reason, he would have the second map to lead him to this island.

Everything as arranged. And then one fleeting moment and everything was altered. Returning to collect the second portion of furs, they'd taken a route through the Great Mire, a route almost nobody took, and by which they'd hoped to avoid meeting with anybody from the Companies (as it was, they had met one, but had refused to give their names). They'd traversed most of it, when one evening – caked with its mud – Ross had decided to take a dip and wash himself. He'd been standing on a smooth boulder at the edge of a small brook when he slipped and fell and that was that. They weren't sure at first if his leg was bruised or broken, but its brokenness had become clear enough as they'd gone on. When they got back to the island your father had tended him there, hoping it would heal, thinking Herse would find them, eventually.

Your father didn't know why Herse hadn't come. The only thing that made any sense was that some accident or illness had also befallen him. Ross had lasted just over two months, his leg blackening and stinking. Poor Ross, who'd run a thousand rapids, faced all the dangers of this life, undone by a quiet brook. It seemed it was never the thing you watched for that did for you. He'd buried him on the West side of the meadow. And by then the only option was for him to winter on the island.

As for you, he reckoned you must have decided to stay in Montreal a season longer, having found something in that world to hold you there. And if so, he was glad. He sometimes feared he'd made a restless, lonely sort of life for you in this country, since your mother died, and had never wanted to make it a cage for you.

But if you were reading this, then he supposed you'd chosen to return. In which case, he'd only gone on ahead. This is where he was going (you didn't name it). It was a grand country, and full of beavers, and outside the grasp of the Companies – for now, at least. And if those Companies did catch you up, you could go further, and then further again. There was lots of country left before reaching the ocean.

He recalled, as though it were yesterday, the sight of you paddling along Rainy River in your uncle's canoe. You'd looked too small even to hold the paddle. He remembered standing on the bank, astonished, and then rushing out into the water toward you. He didn't know – and he was sorry to say it, for fathers should probably pretend to know – what changed within us and what stayed the same, but if you were reading this then part of you was still that girl, and if you paddled a little further you'd surely catch him up. As for himself, wherever he was, he'd be watching and waiting and always would be.

After a pause, I asked what you'd do.

You'd find him, you said.

And you? I asked McLeod.

What did I adverbially think?

And when would you go?

Right away, you replied. He couldn't be too far ahead.

While you and McLeod began your preparations, I waited outside the dwelling until at last Herse emerged. Appearing more composed, he came and sat with me amongst the squashes and beans. Wherever he'd travelled inside, to whatever cold and barren Comet of Grief, he'd now returned. Or half-returned, at least. For he gave the impression that some part of himself remained there yet and had left behind a costume of Herse, a speaking shell, to act as substitute – a player to make his motions back on this world.

He asked what the others planned. I told him they were going to follow your father together, somewhere westward.

And what would I do? I said I didn't know. But since the Company had decided my time in these countries was at an end and I was destined to be sent down to Montreal, then to Montreal I'd go.

In that case, he said, I need only paddle to the [...] for maybe two or three days before I came to a long peninsular called [...]. If I searched it, I'd find a portage trail. I should wait there for one of the Northern brigades of the NWC to travel by, as they would soon enough. They'd take me back as far as the New Fort.

But what about him?

He said he would live here. He would finish what Ross had begun. He had furs enough to trade with for anything he needed. He'd play Mr Crusoe and make the shack a home, filling it with plants and flowers. He'd make this clearing a garden. He would make this island the memory of Ross. As for the map in my head, that we'd used to find this Haven, he said, maybe it was best I kept it in my head.

I told him I would. I said I'd already made that promise. But that I hoped he made it a better island than Crusoe's, with a garden as wonderful as that of Babylon.

And with that I'll make my way toward the edge of the

meadow and, leaving McLeod to make the final preparations for your journey together, will take a stroll with you around the island. I won't relate it. I'm happy enough to have that stroll in my head. And though it's no lie to say I would've crawled over every boulder on every island in that lake for it to have been me making those preparations instead of McLeod, I treasured every step. At least it was me alone who walked with you, and not the Other Arthur. I hope you knew that, and remembered I wasn't so bad a fellow.

And now we four are all down at the little harbour and McLeod is shaking my hand and slapping me on the back.

'I'll say goodbye then, Arthur. I'll say good fucking luck.'

'Good fucking luck yourself,' I said.

What I said to you, you know.

And with that I stood beside Herse on the beach and watched you disappear between the rocks and out onto the open water. To where, I cannot say.

The truth is I have no idea where to send this. But if my father was right and Golden Ages must pass, or be taken from us, or fade or crumble or decline, then I would say this to him: it is memory that makes them, and decides whether they be Gold or Silver or Bronze or Fur. And what memory makes it can make again if it chooses, turning Posts into Pillars, allowing time and tide to run hither and thither and wheresoever they will.

I remember us looking at your bag of places, and hope that's what this heap of paper is: a little book or bundle filled with those places we were briefly in together. And I have one request to make: if this ever reaches you, can you put it in that bag with the rest. It's my way of saying I think of you. I think of you travelling across plains and mountains, through forests and glades. I think of you paddling along rivers and lakes, moving through countries unknown and yet to be decided. I think of you arriving at the edge of new and boundless waters and calling out 'The sea, the sea'.

ACKNOWLEDGEMENTS AND THANKS

This novel, not unlike its characters, has navigated many rivers, and crossed quite a few portages, along the way to reaching the final port of these covers. I'd like to say a huge thanks to Warren Cariou and everybody at the University of Manitoba's Centre for Creative Writing and Oral Culture – where I embarked on the first chapters – for their great kindness and hospitality during my time there. I'm also extremely grateful to everyone at Yaddo and Norton Island, where it began to take shape, and to all my colleagues at Cardiff in the Reclamation Yard workshop for their support and advice.

It would take too much space to thank all the excellent scholars and writers whose work helped open a window for me onto the world of the late eighteenth- and early nineteenth-century fur trade in Canada, though I would like to thank especially William Moreau, both for his pellucid and wide-ranging introductions to the journals of David Thompson and for generously taking the time to discuss this era with me. During the research and writing of the novel, I spent many fruitful hours – through the pages of their journals – in the company of nineteenth-century fur traders. However, I must single out one in particular, who, once I'd discovered his writing, became the primary inspiration for the novel's main character, Arthur. George Nelson's journals offer a wonderfully vulnerable, unfiltered, and intimate portrait of a young man struggling to navigate the new physical and cultural worlds he'd been thrown into. My novel draws mainly on the journals that record Nelson's first years in the fur trade, where despite (or perhaps because of) being beset constantly with travails, confusions and failures, he emerges as a marvellously vivid and sympathetic figure. Nelson would go on to become one of the most humane, open-minded, and acute observers of the Northwest and its peoples. If, as writers sometimes do, I imagine Arthur having a life beyond this book, and growing older, and possibly wiser, I can only hope he becomes more like him.

Along the way, this novel has taken on quite a few new cargoes, and jettisoned quite a few others. I owe a special debt of gratitude to its first readers. Veronique Baxter and Richard Davies, whose suggestions helped me see there were a lot of trees in front of the woods; Gwen Davies, who helped bring those woods into view; and Abigail Parry, whose sharp eye saved me from many an anachronism, solecism, and infelicity. They have all made this a better book. *Diolch o galon.*

PARTHIAN Fiction

Hummingbird
TRISTAN HUGHES
ISBN 978-1-91090-90-8
£10 • Paperback

Winner of the Edward Stanford Travel Writing Awards

'Lean, lyrical...beautifully nuanced and utterly touching'
– Claire Allfree, *Daily Mail*

Revenant
TRISTAN HUGHES
ISBN 978-1-912681-66-2
£8.99 • Paperback

'Superbly accomplished ... Hughes' prose is startling and luminous.'
– *Financial Times*

Shattercone
TRISTAN HUGHES
ISBN 978-1-912681-47-1
£8.99 • Paperback

'A book of such distances – spatial and geographical, but also temporal, emotional, relational and existential.'
– *Wales Arts Review*

Take Three Canadians

Gail Hughes
Tyler Keevil
Tristan Hughes

"Set in a landscape that is vast, lonely, and forbidding... Canadians know the geography of these stories"

CHRISTINA E KRAMER